Christmas Bonus, Strings Attached
by Susan Crosby

'There is one condition,' Nate said.

'There are strings attached?' Lyndsey asked him.

His gaze softened. 'Aren't there always?'

'No. Not from me, anyway.'

'Why doesn't that surprise me?' Nate cupped Lyndsey's face, brushed his thumb along her cheek. 'I was only going to say, enough with the thank-yous.'

The tender look in his eyes erased any uncertainty she had. 'How about this instead?' She twined her arms around his neck and pulled herself up on tiptoe, bringing her mouth to his.

'This is good,' he said, gathering her close.

'This is dangerous,' she said.

Cinderella's Christmas Affair
by Katherine Garbera

ᘒ ᘓ

'I want to take you to bed and break down all the barriers you put between us.'

'Tad, go away.'

'Why?'

'Because I'm not the girl you want.'

'Yes, you are.'

'Because I like the same Christmas tree you do.'

He gave her a half smile that took her breath away. 'No, because you're beautiful and sexy and you've haunted my dreams since the last time I saw you.'

She took the tray and left the living room. She couldn't think when he said things like that. When he made her believe that forever and happily ever after might still exist. It was as if everything her ex-lover and ex-boss had taught her disappeared. But she knew better.

'I'm not your dream woman, Tad. I'm no man's.'

Available in December 2004 from Silhouette Desire

Midnight Seduction
by Justine Davis
(Redstone, Incorporated)
and
Keeping Baby Secret
by Beverly Barton
(The Protectors)

ↄ ⚭ ͼ

The Heart of a Stranger
by Sheri WhiteFeather
(The Country Club)
and
Secrets, Lies…and Passion
by Linda Conrad

ↄ ⚭ ͼ

Christmas Bonus, Strings Attached
by Susan Crosby
(Behind Closed Doors)
and
Cinderella's Christmas Affair
by Katherine Garbera
(King of Hearts)

Christmas Bonus, Strings Attached
SUSAN CROSBY

Cinderella's Christmas Affair
KATHERINE GARBERA

*All the characters in this book have no existence outside the
imagination of the author, and have no relation whatsoever to anyone
bearing the same name or names. They are not even distantly inspired
by any individual known or unknown to the author, and all the
incidents are pure invention.*

*First published in Great Britain 2004
Silhouette Books, Eton House, 18-24 Paradise Road,
Richmond, Surrey TW9 1SR*

The publisher acknowledges the copyright holders of the
individual works as follows:

Christmas Bonus, Strings Attached © Susan Bora Crosby 2003
Cinderella's Christmas Affair © Katherine Garbera 2003

ISBN 0 373 60112 3

51-1204

*Printed and bound in Spain
by Litografía Rosés S.A., Barcelona*

CHRISTMAS BONUS, STRINGS ATTACHED
by
Susan Crosby

Behind Closed Doors
by Susan Crosby

Where red-hot passions just can't be controlled!

Christmas Bonus, Strings Attached
Private Indiscretions – March 2005
Hot Contact – June 2005

SUSAN CROSBY

believes in the value of setting goals, but also in the magic of making wishes. A longtime reader of romance novels, Susan earned a BA in English while raising her sons. She lives in the central valley of California, the land of wine grapes, asparagus and almonds. Her checkered past includes jobs as a synchronised-swimming instructor, personnel interviewer at a toy factory and trucking company manager, but her current occupation as a writer is her all-time favourite.

Susan enjoys writing about people who take a chance on love, sometimes against all odds. She loves warm, strong heroes, good-hearted, self-reliant heroines... and happy endings.

Readers are welcome to write to her at PO Box 1836, Lodi, CA 95241, USA.

To my believers, Georgia Bockoven,
Robin Burcell and Christine Rimmer.
You know what you mean to me.

To Melissa Jeglinski, editor, advocate and friend.

To Ken, one last time—for the good life,
for the great sons, forever.

"You know how I feel about divorce cases, Ar."

It *was* him. Nate Caldwell. Live and in person. He must have come into the building the back way. She didn't know what to do. No one had ever come into the office after midnight before.

"I would if I could, Nate. It's impossible." A female voice grew louder as it neared. "I'm working three cases of my own and I took two of yours already so that you—"

A door shut, silencing the conversation between Nate Caldwell and Arianna Alvarado—two of the three owners of the Los Angeles-based ARC Security & Investigations, and Lyndsey's bosses for the past three months. They must have gone into Nate's office, which was so close to Lyndsey's cubicle she could fly a paper airplane into it.

She had gotten used to the eerie silence of working alone late at night, and now, well, having someone in the building threw her off her routine. What should she do? Print up the case file she'd just typed—her last, fortunately—and sneak out before they saw her? Except…

She had to put all the reports on the various investigators' desks before she left. Including Nate Caldwell's.

She moved to her entryway and listened, able to discern voices but not words. He was definitely upset about something, a tone far different from what she usually heard in dictation, when his voice was smooth, the flow of words easy. Judging by the reports she transcribed, he was smart. Judging by the comments of her friend Julie, who'd recommended Lyndsey for the job, he was thirty-two, charming, quick to smile, attractive, polite and thoughtful. In other words, the perfect man.

Oh, God. Twenty-six years old and she had a crush on a man she'd never met, a fantasy she let herself escape to when her life got dull. She couldn't knock on his door and present him with his report—it wasn't good to tamper with fantasies.

The document finished printing. Do or die, she thought, then stalled by delivering all of the reports but his. Should she interrupt? Their voices were a soft jumble of sound now. Apparently he'd calmed down. She moved closer to his office.

Oh, why hadn't she worn something other than a black sweater and jeans? Why hadn't she taken the time to put on a little makeup?

Why couldn't she lose fifteen pounds in five seconds?

Better to take the coward's way out and leave his report on Arianna's desk along with a note.

Lyndsey tiptoed down the hall, easing past his office. She opened Arianna's door quietly, wrote a quick note then left, backing out of the room and shutting the door soundlessly.

She turned—

"Who are you?" He was right there, no more than a foot from her.

She pressed a hand to her thundering heart. "I'm... Lyndsey McCord."

He glanced at Arianna's door then back to Lyndsey. "What were you doing in there?"

"Working." She tried to act calm. "I...transcribe the investigators' reports." *You might notice that I put yours on your desk, error free, every night, Monday through Friday.*

He looked her over so blatantly that she didn't know whether to feel complimented or harassed, until he walked away without a word.

Well, of all the rude— Lyndsey leaned against the door, stunned. So much for the perfect man. Nate Caldwell might have fooled Julie, but not her—

Oh, come on, Lyndsey. Here you are, creeping around the office. Of course he would question it.

Disappointment settled over her as she made her way

back to her cubicle. Another fantasy bites the dust, which was really frustrating, since she'd learned that one good fantasy could sustain her through twenty harsh realities.

She unplugged the string of twinkling Christmas lights decorating her work area then signed her time sheet.

"What's your name again?"

She jolted around. Her heart went back into overdrive. The man had a penchant for invading a person's space. "Do you make a habit of sneaking up on people?" she asked before she could censure herself. He was her boss, after all. She should bite her tongue.

"I wasn't sneaking. I was following."

"Well, I didn't hear you."

"I only asked your name."

The story of her life. She was one of those people who faded into the background. This time it stung more than usual. He wasn't only her boss, in her fantasies he'd carried her away to some exotic location and read poetry to her. The reality was he couldn't remember her name for fifteen seconds. "Lyndsey McCord," she said at last, resigned.

"Can you cook?"

The question was so out of the blue that she didn't respond at first, barely managing to keep her expression clear. She wasn't about to lose her job because she got snippy with the boss. She needed the position for at least two more months. "Of course I can cook."

"How well?"

"I worked for a caterer for a couple of years."

"Come into my office."

And *she* was worried about being rude?

"Please," she heard Arianna call from within his office.

Nate stopped, turned and looked at her. "Please," he repeated.

"I've already clocked out," she said, trying not to notice how his eyes were deep blue and intent. Never mind that square jaw, the shallow cleft in his chin, and a 2:00 a.m. shadow that only added to his appeal, if you didn't count his personality. His streaky blond hair looked like he spent a lot of time at the beach.

"I have a proposition for you, Ms. McCord." With that, he entered his office, obviously expecting her to follow.

You need the job, she reminded herself, trailing him. You really need the job.

"Come sit down," Arianna said, smiling encouragingly and patting the seat beside her on Nate's sofa. Lyndsey perched there, her hands locked in her lap.

"I need you," he said, hovering over her.

She felt her cheeks heat. Her best fantasy flared back to life. "Excuse me?"

"I need a wife. You'll do."

You'll do?

"For the weekend," Arianna added calmly after shooting Nate a quelling look that Lyndsey appreciated. "You and Nate would pretend to be married domestics. It's a marital infidelity case. I know it's last minute, but we really do need you. I'm sure you've realized from the number of case files this week that we're completely booked over the holidays, particularly for security needs."

Lyndsey liked and admired Arianna, but any job involving Nate Caldwell was out of the question now that he'd so rudely destroyed the fantasy that had kept her entertained for months. It would be one thing had he remained the man of her dreams.

"I'm busy this weekend."

"Doing what?" Nate asked.

She crossed her arms. "I don't believe I'm required to share my personal life. And anyway I'm supposed to work Friday night. Tomorrow."

"My assistant can fill in," Arianna said, making it too hard for Lyndsey to say no.

"Why me?" she asked Nate, suspicious.

"You fit."

"I fit?" What was that supposed to mean?

"It pays three hundred dollars a day," he added, ignoring her question. "Is that incentive enough?"

She managed not to let her jaw drop at the amount. But the advantage was hers. He needed her. She pushed him, not wanting to be in the background anymore. *Pay attention to me.* "I make thirty dollars an hour."

"You make that much because you get a nighttime incentive."

"That's my rate. It calculates to seven hundred and twenty dollars a day, in case you're wondering."

"You expect to be paid to sleep?"

"Would I be on call twenty-four hours?"

"In theory."

"I rest my case."

"Five hundred," he muttered, crossing his arms as well. "That's equivalent to mine."

"You're taking a pay cut?" Arianna asked, shock in her voice.

He sent her a cool look.

Lyndsey contained her excitement. In one weekend she could make enough money to fly her sister home from college for what would have been their first Christmas apart. So what if she didn't like Nate Caldwell?

She adjusted her thinking. She didn't know him, and she had heard good things about him. Surely she could deal with him for a weekend if it meant she and Jess would be together for the holidays. "What would I have to do?" she asked.

"Cook and clean for a philandering husband and his mistress—"

"*Alleged* philandering husband," Arianna interrupted. "Observe and report. Whatever you're asked to do, within reason. We're not sure of all the details yet."

"It doesn't sound like a two-person job."

"You're right," Arianna said, then smiled sweetly at Nate. "If Mr. Caldwell could do more than reheat pizza, you wouldn't be necessary."

Lyndsey debated. She didn't understand why an investigator of Nate Caldwell's stature would take such a basic job. ARC's referral-only clients had one thing in common: they were high-profile, whether their background was in business, politics or entertainment. They demanded and got discretion. A divorce investigation seemed too mundane for the firm, or at least for the owners. She couldn't remember typing up a divorce case for Nate, Arianna *or* Sam Remington, the third partner.

"Well?" Impatience coated Nate's voice.

She was half tempted to say no, just to irritate him a little. She decided not to push her luck. "I'll do it."

"I'll pick you up at eight in the morning." Without another word he walked out the door.

"Yes, sir," Lyndsey said with a little salute to his back, then recalled where she was and who she was doing it to. "Sorry," she said to Arianna. "That was unprofessional."

"He was rude, which is unlike him." Arianna stood. "I won't apologize for him, but I will tell you he has good reasons for not wanting to take this job. I appreciate your agreeing to help out, Lyndsey. We really were in a jam."

"Was it your idea to ask me or his?"

Arianna eyed Lyndsey, her head cocked, her gaze steady. "Does it matter?"

Lyndsey waited.

"His," Arianna said at last. "Come into my office for a minute and choose a wedding band to wear."

"I know it's none of my business," Lyndsey said, "but why did you meet here tonight? It's so late."

"The office was midway for both of us. I couldn't talk sense to him over the phone, and we were both in our cars. In fact, my date is waiting in the parking lot." Arianna flashed a smile. "I do love a patient man." She opened a desk drawer and pulled out a small black case, which she opened to reveal an array of wedding and engagement rings. "Take your pick."

Five minutes later Lyndsey slid into her car. She wrote a mental to-do list: pack, sleep for a couple of hours, shower, tame her hair, go online to check on airfare for Jess from New York to L.A. Could she get a good price only two weeks before Christmas?

After her engine coughed to life, she let it idle. At least it wasn't raining. Wet roads and worn tires weren't a good combination. Maybe there would be enough money left after the plane ticket to get some work done on her car.

You fit, he'd said. Fit what? she wanted to know. She hadn't felt she fit much of anywhere for the past seven years, ever since she put her life and dreams on hold to raise her half sister. She hadn't counted on being mom as well as big sister, but then neither had her mother planned on dying at thirty-eight.

Lyndsey pulled out of the parking lot and headed for home, a fifteen-minute drive. *You fit.* He probably meant she looked like she'd be good at taking care of people. He'd be right, of course. She'd done little else for a long time.

She certainly didn't fit with him, but maybe she could still have fun. They were supposed to look married, after all. She imagined his reaction to her calling him honey. The thought made her laugh. Suddenly he quit being a fantasy and became a man. A person. Just another human being.

She stopped for a red light and glanced at her left hand. From a selection of wedding rings in Arianna's desk she'd chosen one that was two bands woven together, nothing flashy but not too plain, either. On her thumb was a man's matching ring.

She tried to picture how she would act, even though she knew little about what the actual job entailed. She wouldn't fawn over him—she imagined too many women did—but she could establish an intimacy that would look genuine to onlookers, like actors did for their roles.

Nate Caldwell wouldn't know what hit him.

Ms. Lyndsey McCord's little Spanish-style stucco house was nestled in a quiet, old West Los Angeles neighborhood that hadn't been touched by the many revitalization efforts making their way around the city. The lawns were well tended, for the most part, as were the homes. Even in the daylight, Christmas decorations were visible on most houses, although not Lyndsey's. The moment Nate pulled up, her front door opened and she came outside, garment bag and overnight case in hand.

He appreciated that she was ready. No last-minute primping. No adding something to an already bulging suitcase. No asking his opinion of the clothes she was wearing or taking. The novelty was refreshing. They exchanged greetings as he met her on the walkway and took her bags, which he stowed in the car as she locked her front door.

"No alarm?" he asked when she slid into the passenger seat.

"The best kind—good neighbors," she replied.

He watched her buckle her seat belt in the four-year-old sedan. The car was one of several the firm kept for certain undercover work. She looked rested, yet, like him, she'd had only a few hours' sleep, he thought as he eyed her.

Nate enjoyed women, and generally they liked him. It

seemed that Lyndsey did not. He saw it in the way she avoided eye contact and heard it in her short answers as he started to brief her on their assignment. They had to look like a couple, compatible and comfortable, if this operation were to succeed.

Time to undo the damage.

"I apologize for last night," he said. "Nothing was going right."

"Okay." She stared out the windshield. After several seconds of silence, she asked, "Where are we going?"

Did "okay" mean she'd accepted his apology? "To the client's house in Bel Air first, then down to San Diego for the assignment itself. Del Mar, actually."

"Expensive real estate."

"Yeah. Money's no object."

"Money is always an object," she said.

He smiled but she didn't seem to notice. He took a quick survey of her. She looked professional in her blue slacks and crisp white shirt. Her chin-length brown hair wasn't as wildly curly as last night but still got tangled in her trendy glasses with the forest-green frames that matched her eyes. Her curves were…curvy. Temptingly female. No starvation diets for her. She seemed comfortable in her own skin.

He noticed how still she sat, like last night. Her hands were folded neatly in her lap as if she went undercover every day.

"Arianna picked out the rings?" he asked, noticing them on her left hand, irritated and relieved that Arianna remembered. It wasn't like him to forget details. Damn Charlie for calling in his favor.

"I completely forgot." She pulled a band off her thumb and passed it to him. "I chose them, actually. I thought they suited us. The working us."

Ignoring the shards of memories that cut into him, he

shoved the ring on. He would've pocketed the damn thing except he had a job to do, a role to play.

"You started to tell me about the assignment," she said.

"It's fairly routine. Wife found out her big-time corporate husband plans to spend a few days at their weekend retreat in Del Mar with his assistant. Didn't tell her he was going. She's got a spy in the office, apparently."

"Classic."

"It gets better. The wife was previously the guy's assistant. The relationship broke up his first marriage. They've been married almost ten years. She's thirty-five, he's fifty-three. They've got a ten-year bailout clause in their prenup. He's been acting strange lately, and she figures he's about to dump her for the new assistant before he has to shell out millions more. She needs proof of infidelity to secure her financial position."

"There's that money thing."

"As you said. I'm not sure how the wife got to arrange the domestic help, but she worked it out with Charlie Black, the P.I. we're replacing. I wanted to meet the client personally before we started." He gave her a quick look. "Ever done anything like this before?"

She shook her head, sending her curls bouncing. He wondered if they were as soft as they looked.

"I did a little acting in high school. It's kind of the same."

He didn't correct her. There would be no script to follow. The job forced you to think fast on your feet. He'd enjoyed her quickness last night regarding her salary— once he got home and thought about it, that is. And she certainly had no trouble standing on her own feet. He half suspected that if Arianna hadn't been there, Ms. Lyndsey McCord would have given him a piece of her mind. He figured she'd handle her part okay. In a way she reminded him of Arianna before she'd become so sophisticated. One thing that had never changed about his partner was her straight talk. He sensed the same about Lyndsey.

They arrived at the client's Bel Air mansion and were shown into an ultrafeminine sitting room then were joined by the client a minute later. Nate wasn't often wrong about people—anticipating accurately made the difference between a good and a great P.I.—but his expectations of a trophy wife were shattered when she walked in the room. Instead of tall, blond and Botoxed, she was a short brunette with vulnerability in her eyes and wariness in her posture. She introduced herself as Mrs. Marbury.

"You're young," she said, looking from Nate to Lyndsey.

"We're competent," Nate replied.

She sat, then indicated they should, also. "I didn't mean to imply—" She stopped for a moment. "I just want to be sure I get the proof I need. You'll be discreet?" She looked at Lyndsey for an answer.

"Very," Lyndsey said.

"I'll need photographs."

"We'll take care of it," Nate said, drawing her attention back to him.

Mrs. Marbury pulled open a drawer in a side table and withdrew an envelope. She passed it to Nate. "I wrote down as much information as I thought you might need. Needless to say, Michael didn't hire our usual cook, so he won't expect you to know where everything is. He did request certain menus, which I've included. The recipes are in the drawer next to the stove. You'll need to buy groceries before he arrives."

"When will that be?"

"Around dinnertime."

"Does he think we're hired out by an agency?"

"No, his vice president of operations—my friend— raved about a domestic he'd used recently when he took his girlfriend to our place for a week. My friend's praise was part of a test, one my husband failed by asking for the man's phone number. Mr. Black, the other private investigator, took over from there.''

''Does your husband expect a man, then, instead of a couple?''

''No. Mr. Black took care of that.''

The woman had backbone yet still seemed fragile, Nate thought. Was it her husband or her comfortable life she was more upset about losing?

''You'll find cash for groceries in the envelope.'' She stood. ''I expect you to check in with me once a day.''

''All right.''

''I should warn you,'' she said to Lyndsey. ''He thinks women have their place, and it's not in jobs he would consider a man's domain, like private investigator. The more female and distracted you act, the more efficiently you'll be able to work and the less inclined he'll be to be suspicious of you.''

She sat back, looking weary. ''Can you see yourselves out?''

''Of course. Good day.''

Neither spoke until they'd driven out of the neighborhood.

''What's your take on Mrs. Marbury?'' he asked. He appreciated how she'd remained silent except to answer the client's direct question. Discretion went a long way in his business.

''Her heart is breaking,'' Lyndsey said.

Nate almost groaned. This was exactly why he'd wanted to work with Arianna on this case. She didn't sentimentalize anything. ''Don't tell me you're a hopeless romantic, Ms. McCord. This job requires objectivity.''

''I'm objective. And no one's ever accused me of being either hopeless or a romantic.''

Something in her tone made him pay attention. Defensiveness? Ego? Pride? "Why do you think she's so much in love with him?"

"Women in her position usually look perfect. It's part of their job. Yet I don't think she'd even brushed her hair. She's so upset, so depressed, she couldn't pull herself together."

"She's worried about losing the money."

Lyndsey looked at him. "You are so negative. Who burned you?"

Everyone who mattered. He stopped the words from slipping out. "I've seen it all before," he said instead.

"Do they have children?"

"Charlie didn't say." Nate felt unprepared for the job, which ticked him off. He always did his homework first. Being thrust into the assignment without complete background put him at a disadvantage. He didn't like being at a disadvantage. Plus he despised divorce cases. "Why don't you open the envelope and see what's in there."

Lyndsey pulled out the contents. "They eat well. Five hundred dollars for food."

"It's probably to include wine and champagne."

Lyndsey turned over the sheet. "There's no alcohol requested."

"Maybe there's plenty on hand. What else does she say?"

"He'll be using an alias—Michael Martin. He must be famous if he's using an alias, but I've never heard of him."

"CEO of Mar-Cal Industries. And on the board of several corporations and charitable foundations."

"I guess I don't travel in the same circles," she said, smiling at Nate.

It changed her whole face.

She continued. "Our Mr. Marbury/Martin is allergic to shellfish and strawberries," she continued. "He likes his coffee and newspaper brought to him in bed. He's a light sleeper who doesn't sleep through the night and doesn't like to fend for himself, so he'll wake up the help to fix him a snack in the middle of the night.'' Lyndsey looked up. ''See? Twenty-four-hour duty.''

He resisted smiling at her bulldog attitude. ''You're being fairly compensated, Ms. McCord. Anything else?''

''She drew up a floor plan. It's a big place but not that many rooms. A bedroom and an office, a living room with a deck to watch the sunset, she says. Kitchen's roomy but not huge and it backs up to the servants' quarters, which are…um.''

''Which are?'' he prompted after a minute.

She stuffed everything back into the envelope then tossed it onto the dashboard. ''I'm gonna need a bonus.''

He glanced over and saw the bulldog look again. ''Why's that?''

''According to the floor plan, Mr. Caldwell, we'll be sleeping together.''

Two

It was a double bed.

Nate paused, luggage in hand, after he stepped into the servants' quarters at the beach house. Not king-size, or even queen, but an impossible-to-sleep-in-without-touching double. He was six foot two. Lyndsey was about five-seven. He lifted weights. She wasn't petite.

He felt her come to a halt behind him and peek around his shoulder.

"Kind of small," she murmured.

"We'll figure out something," he said, although he couldn't imagine what. The rest of the motel-size room held only a dresser, a small glass-topped table and two serviceable chairs. The floor was hardwood, not carpeted. He hadn't slept on a floor since his army days and didn't intend to sleep on one now. Nor could he expect Lyndsey to.

In silence they put away their clothes. She was done

first and moved into the bathroom with her toiletries. When she emerged a minute later, she met his gaze.

"I'll leave you to come up with a plan," she said, her eyes sparkling. "I'm going to get dinner started."

She breezed past him, a subtle scent drifting in her wake. He breathed it in then carried his shaving kit into the bathroom and stopped short. A clear-glass stall shower dominated the space. He swore it was bigger than the bed. Easily big enough for two.

Her comment in the car about having to share a bed had jump-started his imagination. Reality revved its engine now.

He stowed his kit in the vanity then fingered Lyndsey's flowered travel bag next to his. Her wholesomeness appealed to him. Her buttoned-to-the-neck blouse should have camouflaged any hint of sex appeal but did the opposite. Usually he turned a one-eighty upon meeting a woman like her, one who waved the flag of independence yet also seemed destined for home and hearth. The marrying and mothering kind. Problem was, he couldn't turn his back on her for the next forty-eight hours, even with the other strike against her—she worked for him.

Still, his curiosity was aroused, a rare occurrence. He gravitated toward women who were emotionally undemanding and sexually experienced. He knew where he stood with them and was rarely surprised.

Not this time.

He checked his watch and estimated they had about two hours before Mr. Marbury/Martin arrived. Nate grabbed his digital camera and followed the clatter of pans to the kitchen, which had a common wall with the servants' room.

"Stop working for a few minutes and come check out the house with me," he said, the sight of her wearing a starched apron reinforcing his homey image of her. He tucked his camera into a handy corner of the kitchen, a compact room that could be shut off visually from the combination living/dining room by closing bifold shutter doors installed along a pass-through counter.

The living room furniture faced a glass wall with a view of the beach and the Pacific Ocean beyond the rooftop of the house in front. The master bedroom enjoyed the same panorama, the bed positioned to take in the ocean vista, as well. A sumptuous master bathroom adjoined the bedroom and contained a whirlpool tub and an etched glass shower stall. The bathroom connected on the far wall to a home office.

"Do you really expect to get pictures of them, you know, doing stuff?" Lyndsey asked when they stepped onto a deck that stretched across the front of the house and wrapped around the living room.

Doing stuff? He almost smiled at her phrasing. "Not in bed, if that's what you mean. My best opportunity will be from the kitchen into the living room and out onto this deck."

"You think they'll be messing around in front of us?"

The horror in her voice finally did draw a smile. "People accustomed to servants don't notice them. They won't ask us personal questions. In fact, they'll probably ignore us altogether except for giving specific instructions about food or other comforts. If they notice us beyond that, we haven't done a good job."

"You don't set up surveillance equipment? No video or microphones?"

"Not my style. It's bad enough having to photograph what I *can* see."

"You really hate divorce cases, don't you? You implied it to Arianna the other night."

"I stopped doing them years ago. The firm accepts them, but not me."

"Is there a particular reason?"

"I've seen enough. So, how's the kitchen?"

Silence hovered between them as she caught up with his quick change of subject. "Well equipped. But if I'm cooking, what job does that leave for you?"

"Whatever else needs doing, particularly anything where I can gather information on them. It'll almost be a vacation for you, Ms. McCord."

"A vacation," she repeated wistfully, as if the concept were foreign. She turned away and leaned against the railing. "I love the ocean," she said, lifting her face and inhaling. "My mom took my sister and me to the beach a lot. It was cheap entertainment. We always had so much fun."

Her hair had coiled tighter in the ocean air. He let his gaze drift down her appreciatively, lingering on the neatly tied apron bow and the strings that trailed down her rear.

"What about the sleeping arrangements?" she asked, facing him.

"You sleep under the sheet. I'll sleep on top."

"Are you a right-side or left-side sleeper?"

"Take whichever you want. I'll adjust."

She pushed away from the railing and ambled toward him, then tapped a finger to his chest. "Marriage is full of adjustments, isn't it, honey?" she said, fluttering her lashes before strolling away.

He considered the privileges of marriage…the big glass shower…the very small bed.

Then he reconsidered his need to keep the job a job while pretending to be married to her. He had a feeling she wasn't going to make it easy on him.

Her unspoken challenge made him laugh. *Bring it on, Ms. McCord. Bring it on.*

From the kitchen Lyndsey heard Nate greet Michael Marbury and his assistant, Tricia. Lyndsey pressed her hands to her stomach and blew out a breath. *You can do this. You can do this.* The words tumbled over and over. She looked at the floor, took another breath and left the kitchen, almost crashing into Mr. Marbury.

"And this is my wife, Lyndsey," Nate said. "I'll be right back with your luggage."

He strode off, leaving her alone with the couple, neither of whom looked at her. Mr. Marbury seemed to be admiring the view out the front window, and Tricia stood staring at Nate. Well, really. She had a man of her own—

Lyndsey put the brakes on her thoughts. Possessive? Over a man she hardly knew, except in her fantasies? She couldn't blame the woman, however. His broad shoulders filled out his sage-green polo shirt; his trim waist and long legs were emphasized by perfectly fitting khakis. He was a sight to behold—her sight. For this weekend, anyway.

She set aside her surge of jealousy to debate whether she should direct her words to the man or the woman. Who was in charge? The fifty-three-year-old trim, gray-haired man with the air of authority or the twenty-five-year-old auburn beauty with an even more authoritative look? Since the man never made eye contact, Lyndsey spoke to his assistant, hoping to draw her attention as she seemed to be waiting for Nate to return.

"May I get you something to drink?" Lyndsey asked.

Tricia blinked. Her expression cooled. "We'll unpack first." She urged Mr. Marbury toward the bedroom. He went like a puppet. "Is dinner almost ready?" she asked over her shoulder.

Lyndsey ran a mental list. The salad was done except for slicing the avocado, and a fruit and cheese plate was prepared for dessert. She needed only to steam the asparagus, heat the sourdough baguette and grill the salmon. "Twenty to thirty minutes, or longer if you'd prefer."

"No. The earlier the better," Tricia said. "On second thought, we'd like ice water now. In fact, I need an ice bucket kept full in the bedroom at all times, so please make sure ice is always made. I'll fill it myself when it's empty." She followed Mr. Marbury into the master bedroom and shut the door.

"Right away," Lyndsey said to an empty room. A minute later she heard Nate pass through with the luggage then a low murmur of voices from the bedroom as she fixed a tray with an ice bucket, goblets and bottled water.

He came into the kitchen. "I'll take that to them. Nervous?" he asked quietly.

"A little. They're so…unfriendly, even to each other. I expected them to be joined at the hip."

"Then the job would be too easy," he said with a wink. "One of the things I like and hate about this business is that my expectations are rarely met."

He left with the tray, but his departing grin relaxed her, and she got caught up in the spirit of the experience. They were playing parts in an improvisation. She should just enjoy the adventure and not worry about the outcome.

She double-checked the table, which she'd set earlier with exquisite linens and china she found in a hutch, then gave a vase of yellow tulips a slight turn and stepped back. Perfect.

Twenty-five minutes later she served up four plates. Nate knocked on the couple's bedroom door and announced that dinner was ready. Lyndsey closed the shutters between the kitchen and dining area, and she and Nate ate standing at the sink while the couple dined more leisurely.

Tricia came unannounced into the kitchen when they were almost finished with their meal. She held up a hand as they came to attention. Her expression was a little friendlier. "We don't need anything. I just wanted to thank you for the meal. It was perfect."

"You're welcome," Lyndsey said, pleased.

"What is that wonderful smell?"

Lyndsey glanced at the oven. "Chocolate chip cookies. They weren't on the meal plan but—"

"Say no more. They make a great midnight snack."

"Yes."

"Michael and I were surprised to hear a couple would be filling in for Mr. Black, who had come so highly recommended. The job hardly seems to need two people."

"We're newlyweds. We don't like to be apart," Lyndsey said, the words popping out. She turned toward Nate, who came up behind her, his eyes conveying a fascinating combination of tenderness and heat. She swallowed.

"Oh? How long have you been married?"

"Three months on Sunday," Nate answered. He rested a hand on Lyndsey's shoulder.

Tricia leaned against the doorjamb, her arms crossed, her gaze settling on Nate. "How did you meet?" she asked.

"On a blind date," he answered without hesitation.

"We hated each other," Lyndsey added, embellishing, feeling Nate's fingers press lightly into her flesh. In approval? Or as in, *Don't get carried away?*

"Really? Hated each other?"

She nodded. "I thought he was arrogant. He thought I was flaky, didn't you, honey?"

"Pretty much."

"So what happened?" Tricia asked.

"Can't ignore chemistry," Nate said.

Lyndsey patted his hand. He entwined her fingers with his. She took a quick breath, caught off guard by his warmth. Chemistry, indeed.

Tricia's friendly expression faded. "Mr. Martin requests

that you retire as soon as the kitchen is cleaned up. We won't need anything else, and we'd like privacy until morning.''

Lyndsey hid her surprise. What happened to his wife's assertion that he would wake up the help to fix him a snack during the night? ''Of course, ma'am. Would you like coffee brought to you before breakfast?''

She considered it. ''You can set up the coffeemaker tonight. I'll turn it on in the morning when I get up, probably around six-thirty. We'll breakfast around eight.''

''I'll leave you some cookies on a plate,'' Lyndsey said.

Tricia waved a goodbye.

Nate put a finger to his lips before Lyndsey could say anything. In silence they cleared and washed the dishes. The cookies were baked and moved to cooling racks then plates. She poured two glasses of milk and asked him to carry a plate into their bedroom.

Their bedroom…

It was eight o'clock, the beginning of a long night.

Nate turned on the television in their room, leaving the volume loud enough to cover their conversation. She plunked her fists on her hips. He wasn't surprised at the first words she spoke.

''You said they wouldn't ask personal questions.''

He was as surprised as she, although he shouldn't be. This case wasn't following predictable patterns. ''You improvised well,'' he said, and was rewarded after a moment with a smile that lit up her eyes, even behind her glasses.

''I did think you were arrogant, you know,'' she said, taking off her glasses and laying them on the table as she sat down.

''You don't now?'' He watched her shake out her curls with her fingers. She looked tired. Considering how little sleep they'd gotten the night before, it wasn't surprising.

She picked up a cookie and seemed to study it. "Maybe you just have excessive confidence. Did you think I was flaky?"

"Those were your words, not mine." He sat in the other chair. "I didn't know what to make of you. You were creeping around like you didn't belong there."

"I didn't want to interrupt, but surely you knew I worked there."

"I knew someone came in during the night to transcribe the reports. I'd even seen a car in the parking lot when I pulled in. But I was ticked off, so it didn't register. I apologize for not coming into the office since you were hired, and introducing myself, which I should have done. Arianna reminded me that I hadn't." He grabbed a cookie, took a bite then toasted her with it. He hadn't had a homemade chocolate chip cookie in a long time.

"I know your voice so well I felt like I'd already met you," she said.

"I imagine you know everyone's voice," he replied, curious at the faraway look in her eyes.

"What? Oh, of course I do. Voice *and* idiosyncrasies. For example, you rarely hesitate and almost never change your mind or insert something at the end. Sam and Arianna file good reports, too. You're all efficient."

"Have you met Sam?" Sam Remington was the third partner of ARC Security & Investigations. He, Arianna and Nate had met in the army, then opened their agency six years ago, after planning it for years.

"I've met him several times. He's the quiet one. He's got a way about him that makes you want to take a step back, you know? He's, I don't know the word exactly, fierce, maybe?"

"Intense."

"Yes. But once you get past that he's easy to talk to and really thoughtful."

"In what way?" Damn, these cookies are good, he thought, grabbing another.

She shifted in the chair, not answering him right away. "It'll probably sound silly."

Intrigued, Nate eyed her over the rim of his glass of milk. "I doubt it." *Sam* and *silly* weren't two words Nate would ever put together in a sentence.

"You know how analytical he is," she said. "Good with numbers."

"*Great* with numbers. And computers."

She nodded. "He has an old Rubik's Cube...."

"I've seen it in his office."

She cupped her glass between her hands, spinning it slowly. "Whenever he's in town he leaves it on my desk. I'm supposed to mix it up for five minutes then leave it on his desk. The next day he solves it and gives it back, along with a note saying how long he took to do it. His record is one minute and thirty-three seconds."

"How does that make him thoughtful?"

"It makes me feel like part of the office when I could easily feel invisible. When he's out of town I miss it."

"And Arianna? How would you categorize her?" he asked.

"Competent. Cool under fire yet warm. We connected on some level when she first interviewed me. I like her a lot. She's good about checking in with me a couple of times a week, either by phone or in person."

"I think I've just been criticized."

"Not at all. With you I was perfectly content just to fan—" She stopped, coughed, took a swallow of milk. "Excuse me. I was perfectly content to *tran*scribe the reports. I knew what the job entailed when I took it." She put her empty glass on the table and stood. "I'm going to get ready for bed."

He knew the situation was about to get awkward so he

focused on the television as she took sweatpants and a T-shirt out of the dresser and disappeared into the bathroom. He decided to take their empty glasses to the kitchen. Maybe he could hear or see something.

He eased open the door and moved quietly down the hall. Silence greeted him. No voices, no television, except from the servants' quarters. He waited a while. Nothing.

By the time he returned to the room, Lyndsey was in bed, the covers pulled over her shoulders, her back to him. He took his cell phone into the bathroom, called Charlie Black then Mrs. Marbury to give her a report, choosing his words carefully.

He joined Lyndsey a few minutes later. With the television and lights off, the room seemed even smaller. Like her, he wore sweats and a T-shirt. He smelled soap and toothpaste, different from his.

The only other woman he'd spent a celibate night in bed with was Arianna. Not that he hadn't been attracted to her, years ago, when they first met. Then they talked and he came to appreciate her intelligence—not to mention she could put a man in his place with just a look. She was no object. He was glad he'd caught on to that early in their acquaintance or he might have ruined what had become a solid friendship and a great business relationship. The sexual attraction was long gone.

This intimacy with Lyndsey was different. He felt naked.

Nate became increasingly aware of her, even though she didn't breathe audibly or move an inch. He wondered which one of them would give in first to exhaustion and fall asleep. Probably him, since he had a feeling she would stay awake all night if she needed to.

He slid his hands under his head and stared at the ceiling.

"Was that your girlfriend you were calling?" she asked into the quiet.

"The client."

"Oh. What did you tell her?"

"That they arrived, that they weren't talkative or demonstrative, and that they had retired for the night."

"How did she take it?"

"Without emotion. So, what do you think of your first undercover job?"

"I love it," came her instant response, then she rolled onto her back and turned her head toward him, tucking the covers under her chin. "It's fun."

"Fun?"

"Shouldn't it be? Nothing's going as predicted, which makes it kind of exciting."

He thought about it. While he loved what he did, he'd stopped acknowledging what made the job so appealing. "You seem to be a natural."

"I do, don't I?"

"Yeah. But don't get carried away with the role. It's easy to trip yourself up."

"You mean like those things I told Tricia?"

"Anything more would've been overkill."

"See, I knew that." The excitement was back in her voice. She turned on her side, facing him. "But she seemed to buy it all, didn't she?"

"I think so."

"She was jealous."

He had closed his eyes and was drifting a little, so her words didn't register for a few seconds. "Jealous?" he repeated.

"She checks you out all the time."

"She does not."

"Does so. She's hot for you."

He laughed.

"It's true."

"No, it isn't," he argued. "She's devoted to her boss. She's solicitous of his every move. I think she'd cut his meat for him if he'd let her."

"And what is it with him, anyway? He's supposed to be some big-shot executive, but he lets her make all the decisions. That man hasn't said two words in front of me."

"They stop talking in front of me, too. One box I carried from the car was paperwork, though."

"Maybe this trip is business, not pleasure. Maybe it's all a big misunderstanding."

"If that were the case, why wouldn't he tell his wife about it?"

She got quiet for a minute. "Oh. Right."

"I've learned to trust a spouse's intuition. Suspicions are usually justified."

"So Mrs. Marbury couldn't be overreacting?"

"It's unlikely."

"You said that nothing in this case is running to expectation."

She had a good mind, a logical mind. He appreciated it. "True."

"That doesn't lead you to think that Mrs. Marbury could be wrong, too?"

"Let's look at it from her point of view. She knows him like no one else does. He starts acting differently. She finds out he's going away for the weekend with his assistant, and not only does he not invite his wife along, he doesn't even tell her where he's going. Infidelity isn't new territory for him—a fact Mrs. Marbury knows, since she was his assistant before she became his second wife. She not only knows he's capable of cheating, she even knows how he does it. They probably had weekends away under the guise of business trips themselves."

He could almost hear her thinking. He closed his eyes, feeling his muscles relax and his body grow heavy.

"Why didn't they just have food delivered?" she asked suddenly. "We're potential witnesses."

Because they're used to being waited on, he thought but didn't say aloud. He needed sleep. So did she.

He made a sleepy sound as he rolled to his side, away from her. He heard her sigh.

"She does so have the hots for you," she whispered.

He grinned.

Three

─────

Seeking the source of the heat behind her, Lyndsey wriggled backward until she felt a wall of resistance. Much better, she thought sleepily. Warm. Three seconds hadn't passed before her eyes popped open and she realized exactly what she'd snuggled against—a hard male body.

How could that be? He was on top of the sheet, she was under—

No, she wasn't. She didn't feel cotton against her bare feet but the textured weave of the blanket. He hadn't violated her space; she'd violated his.

How? Then she remembered. She'd gotten up around three o'clock and slipped into the bathroom to take off the bra she'd worn to bed as if it were armor. It was cutting into her. She must have gotten under the blanket instead of the sheet when she climbed back into bed. She was surprised she'd gone back to sleep so easily.

Lyndsey eased away from him. His hand came down on

her hip, stopping her. A few seconds later his whole arm slipped over her, trapping her against him. If he moved his fingers two inches higher he would touch her breasts.

Her body went on alert. She couldn't draw a full breath. Her breasts swelled. Her nipples turned hard and achy.

She should move. Instead she relaxed against him, welcoming the comfort of his body and the desire that flared inside her without apology. She angled her arm a tiny bit to see her watch. Almost five-fifteen. How much longer could she enjoy him until he woke up? In all her fantasies, she hadn't imagined this reality, this chemistry. This sense of rightness.

She knew the moment he awakened. His breathing changed, his body tensed. His hand flattened against her stomach, his thumb pressed into her breast. She waited for him to move. It seemed like an hour passed before he eased himself away, but it was probably only a few seconds.

Her breath released on a long shaky exhale.

"Lyndsey?" His voice was soft yet questioning.

"I'm sorry," she said, scrambling away, rubbing her arms against the chill of the morning—or was it embarrassment? Or, more likely, disappointment? "I don't know how I ended up on top of the sheet. I didn't do it on purpose, I promise. I wouldn't—"

"Stop," he said, interrupting. "It's fine."

She sat on the edge of the bed, her back to him. "But I violated your space. I—"

He made a sound she couldn't interpret. She looked over her shoulder in time to see him sit up against the headboard. He combed his hair with his fingers. "It's no big deal."

Maybe not to you, she thought, irritated at his blasé attitude. He probably woke up next to someone at least once a week. She never had. Not that she was inexperienced, but she hadn't wanted to set a bad example for her sister by having a man sleep over. She'd had few relationships through the years. Guys gave up on her when they realized how little time and attention she could give them. Her independence probably made them think she didn't need anything. She did. She just didn't know how to ask for it.

For all she knew, Nate had a girlfriend.

The thought depressed her. Of course he had one. He had everything to offer.

"Hey," he said.

"What?" She didn't mean to sound belligerent, but she knew she did.

"Don't sweat it."

"Okay."

He got out of bed. "I'm going for a run. I'll pick up a newspaper on the way back."

She climbed back under the covers until he left the room. Taking advantage of his absence and the early hour, she took a leisurely shower, not bothering to do much with her hair since it would only turn into ringlets in the damp weather.

By the time she went into the kitchen she was in a better mood. She turned on the coffeemaker then took grapefruit out of the refrigerator to section. Blueberry pancakes and bacon would complete the menu, but there was no hurry. She could set the table while the coffee was brewing.

Lyndsey used the white everyday china instead of the fancy dinnerware of the previous night. She found green place mats and napkins to contrast nicely with the yellow tulips and was humming to herself when the bedroom door opened. Tricia stepped out, shutting the door quietly behind her. She carried the ice bucket.

"Good morning," Lyndsey said, surveying her. Tricia had already brushed her hair and wore a black silk peignoir over a matching lacy nightgown that peeped out at her ankles as she moved. "The coffee's ready. Shall I fix your tray?"

"Yes, thank you. Cream and sugar, too." Tricia followed her into the kitchen. She dumped the melted ice into the sink then moved to the refrigerator to refill the bucket. "This is a beautiful house, isn't it?"

"It's wonderful. I love the view."

Tricia scooped ice into the bucket then set it aside and leaned against the counter, waiting. "I hadn't been here before."

Lyndsey just smiled, not wanting to say something she shouldn't.

"How do you like being married?" Tricia asked.

"It's also wonderful," she said as she pulled mugs out of a cupboard.

"And the view's not bad, either," Tricia said.

Lyndsey laughed as if she enjoyed the joke, but she didn't. Not one bit. How dare this woman ogle her husb— Her pretend husband? "Nate went for a run and to get a newspaper," she said, pouring the coffee. "He should be back soon."

"Good. Michael likes his paper early. So, is this what you and your husband do for a living?"

"Not exclusively. We only take weekend jobs. I'm still in college. He's in construction. It's slow right now." That would account for his tan, his streaky blond hair and his muscles, she decided.

"How long did you date before you got married?"

"Long enough to know he was the one."

"How does anyone know that?"

The question almost seemed rhetorical. Was she expecting an answer? "I guess if it's right you know."

"Don't you think everyone feels like that when they get married?"

"I can't speak for everyone, only myself."

"Do you think he'll be faithful?"

What was going on? Lyndsey focused on fixing the tray—first the mugs, then sugar and cream in beautiful porcelain containers. Spoons. Napkins. Was she supposed to engage in this conversation? Would she glean something that could be used against Mr. Marbury? "I expect fidelity. Wouldn't you?"

"I would hope for it."

Ah. The difference between us, Lyndsey thought. I wouldn't marry a man I didn't expect to stay faithful, to love me until death. Her biggest fear was that she would fall in love with someone who wouldn't stay when the going got tough. She hoped she'd at least learned something from her mother's mistakes.

She heard the back door open. Soon Nate appeared.

"Just in time," Lyndsey said, relieved to have him back. "You can add the newspaper to the tray."

He slipped the paper along the edge of the tray after giving Lyndsey a curious look. Was her discomfort with the conversation visible? She hoped so. She wanted him to step in and change the subject.

"Good morning," he said to Tricia, coming to Lyndsey's rescue.

"Good morning," she said in return, looking him up and down.

Lyndsey said *See!* with her eyes. Nate's took on a mischievous sparkle.

"I'm going to take a shower," he said to Lyndsey. "Unless you need me for something."

Do I ever. I need you to kiss me. I don't care that you're sweaty and need a shave. You look like heaven.

"I'm fine," Lyndsey managed while recalling the feel of his body along hers and his thumb on her breast. He winked.

"You can carry the tray into the bedroom first," Tricia said to him, grabbing the ice bucket and preceding him to open the door.

When he came back, he stopped in the kitchen long enough to yank Lyndsey's apron ties undone. She smiled as she retied them and blessed whatever hand of fate had put her in the office later than usual the night before last.

Hours later Lyndsey stood in the kitchen while Nate cleared the lunch dishes in the dining room. Mr. Marbury finally spoke, and it was with the authority she expected from a man of his position.

"Your wife told Tricia that you work in construction," he said to Nate. "I have a job for you."

Lyndsey clamped a hand over her mouth as she listened, horrified. She'd tripped them up, even after he'd told her about the dangers of overkill. She shouldn't have made up the story in the first place, but she should have told Nate about it, at least.

"The wood rail along the top of the balcony needs to be replaced," Mr. Marbury continued. "The materials were delivered last week and are in the garage. I'll pay you extra, if you'll do the job today."

His tone of voice indicated he wasn't asking but telling, no matter what his words were. There was no "if" involved.

"Yes, sir," she heard Nate say.

A few seconds later he brought the dishes into the kitchen, gave her a direct but cool glance and started loading the dishwasher while she finished the marinade for the chicken they would have for dinner. Her heart thumped in her chest in rhythmic torture. A minute went by. Then another. Two more. He finally came up behind her, put a hand on the counter on each side of her and leaned close.

"Was there anything else you forgot to mention?" he whispered.

He was angry. She was distracted by how close he stood, how his breath gave her chills, how the muscles and tendons in his forearms made her long to run her hands down them. "I'm sorry."

"I don't suppose you know how to replace a railing?"

She shook her head.

"Face me, please."

She swallowed and turned. He didn't budge. They were inches apart.

"Any ideas about how to get us out of this?" he asked.

"I could fake an appendicitis attack."

His eyes were as blue as the sky at twilight, giving her a glimpse into a dangerous side of him she hadn't seen before, one that thrilled her in ways she never would've imagined. She couldn't stop staring at him, trying to see deeper, to understand who he was. Because she really liked him. A lot. A whole lot. She needed to find reasons not to, because she had a feeling he could break her heart into tiny, slow-healing fragments.

Then it occurred to her how to get them out of the jam she'd gotten them into.

"I know how to use an electric drill." She set her hands on his chest, excited. Out of sheer necessity she'd learned the basics of home repair. "I can drive a nail in straight, too. I could do it, Nate. You just need to look like you're the one in charge."

His mouth twitched. He smiled. Then he dropped his head and laughed.

"What?" she asked.

"You. You're so sincere." His smile hadn't faded, although he still seemed to be regrouping from his anger reluctantly. "I know a thing or two about construction."

"You were toying with me? You let me be scared for no reason?"

"Most women enjoy being toyed with now and then."

Her breath hitched at the innuendo. "I'm not most women." She was proud that she could form words. Amazed, actually.

"No, you're not. You're—"

The kitchen door swung open. Lyndsey jumped. Nate merely turned his head. They must look as if they'd been caught kissing.

"Excuse me," Tricia said.

He backed away but slid his arm around Lyndsey's waist. "Is there something else, ma'am?"

"Michael says you'll find tools in the cabinet next to the washer and dryer in the garage."

"Thanks." He dipped his thumb into Lyndsey's waistband.

She didn't breathe. Tricia didn't move.

"I'll get right to it," he added.

Tricia left without comment.

"If I'd known my cover was going to be that I worked in construction, I'd have brought my pickup," he said quietly to Lyndsey. It was clear he was still irritated with her but was trying not to show it.

He hadn't moved his hand. She wished she could just lean into him and enjoy it. She'd made an error in judgment. Was he going to trust her to do a good job from here on?

"You have a pickup?" she asked, putting distance between them before she started wiping down the already clean counters.

"I'm a country boy at heart." His tension still hummed.

"Sure you are."

"I am. What'd you figure I drove?"

"Something sporty and convertible. And red."

"Got one of those, too. A Corvette. Different cars for different purposes."

"Any others?"

"A Lexus. You need a four-seater now and then."

"Because you double-date a lot?"

He grinned. He wasn't bragging about the cars, she decided, but being honest. She wondered what it would be like to have a vehicle that started up the first time you turned the key. Or had a working heater. Or tires with treads. She only had to hold on another four years, until Jess graduated and got a job. Lyndsey would treat herself to her first brand-new car then.

"This job is turning out to be one surprise after another," he said cryptically. "Let's go see what kind of carpenters we make."

"I can't wait to see you in a tool belt, honey," she said, batting her lashes, hoping to wipe out whatever remained of his anger.

He raised his brows. "Are you toying with me?"

"If you're like most men, you like it."

"Well now, I think you just shimmed me between a rock and a hard place. I don't believe I'm like most men, but I do like you toying with me."

Lyndsey wondered how they were going to get through another night in a bedroom alone after all the flirting and touching. The anticipation made her feel more alive than she could remember feeling. More feminine. More desired.

If this was a one-time opportunity, should she deny or encourage? Tempt or wait to be tempted? Was it better to satisfy her needs and have regrets or not satisfy them…and have regrets? She'd thought a fantasy fulfilled wouldn't be a good thing, but maybe she was wrong.

She had all afternoon to think about it. He'd be the biggest heartbreak of her life, no doubt about it.

* * *

Her chance to make up for her rookie mistake came without much warning later that afternoon. The railing had been replaced and looked perfect, but they were sweaty from working in the sun, so Nate showered first, then Lyndsey got in. Fifteen seconds hadn't passed before she heard his voice.

"Are you a fan of irony? They want me to go rent *True Lies* from the video store," he said.

Startled, she crossed her arms over her body. Through the steamed glass, she saw he'd barely opened the door and was talking through a crack.

"Okay," she said. What else could she say?

Instead of the door closing it swung open. He walked toward her, his hand covering his eyes. She stood frozen as he fumbled for the latch and pushed the shower door open.

"Come here," he said, low.

Hot water beat against her shoulders, her back, then her rear as she stepped toward him.

"They're looking comfortable out on the balcony. Get into the kitchen as soon as you can. You might snag a few photos while I'm gone if they think you'll be in here a while."

"Okay." Even though he'd sort of blindfolded himself, the idea that she was naked in front of him sent tornadoes of awareness whirling through her, touching down every so often in a new erogenous zone, gathering strength.

"You remember how to use the camera?" he asked.

"Of course." He'd shown her the day before.

"Good. I'll be back as soon as I can." He paused. "You know, I never figured you for a red nail polish kind of woman."

Lyndsey looked at her toes. By the time she raised her head he was gone. She didn't have a minute to think about it. She hurried out of the shower, dried off and dressed so fast that her clothes stuck to her damp body. Skip the makeup. Finger-comb her hair. Tiptoe out of the room and into the kitchen.

Mr. Marbury and Tricia were framed by the glass door in a perfect vignette, a beautiful pinkish sky behind them. She was seated in a deck chair, her head bent forward, her long hair falling over her breasts. Mr. Marbury stood behind her, his hands on his shoulders. He was giving her a massage.

Lyndsey snapped several photos. Then he leaned close to Tricia, his mouth near her ear. She turned toward him, smiling. Their faces were inches apart. Lyndsey kept snapping until Mr. Marbury straightened and stared right at her.

Caught.

Four

The camera was small. She tucked it in her palm, pretended to be brushing her hair from her face, then dropped it into her pocket. She was washing her hands when he appeared at the counter dividing the kitchen from the dining room/living room.

"What were you doing?" he asked.

"When?" *Nerve, don't desert me now.*

"Just now. You were watching us."

"No, sir. I was admiring the sunset. The sun was sinking into the ocean. I don't get to see that very often. Wasn't it gorgeous?" She smiled.

He turned to see the view she said she'd been admiring. Tricia waited, her eyes on them.

Lyndsey checked her menu. *Just forge on. Baffle him with innocence.* "I'm going to start dinner. It'll take about an hour, if that's good for you."

He looked bewildered. "What are we having?"

She read off the notes. "Tomato and mozzarella salad. Penne with spicy chicken, sun-dried tomatoes, shallots, Kalamata olives and feta. Lemon sorbet and Italian cookies for dessert. It makes my mouth water. Can I get you anything while you wait?"

"No." He eased backward for several steps before he turned around and returned to the balcony. After a moment of discussion he and Tricia entered the master bedroom from the balcony and the house went quiet.

Lyndsey leaned against the counter. She did it. She'd pulled it off. The rush was heady. She high-fived the refrigerator. "Yes!"

When Nate returned, she tossed him the camera. He took it into the bedroom to view. A few minutes later he joined her in the kitchen and swiped a few olives as she chopped them.

"Did they turn out okay?" she asked, anxious.

"They're clear. Do you think the client will be happy with them?" He kept his voice to a near whisper.

"There's no kiss," she said. "They saw me before they had a chance to kiss. But if I were married to him, I'd be furious and hurt that he was touching another woman that way. Looking at her that way."

"But is it enough evidence for Mrs. Marbury's legal needs?"

"I would say no."

"You'd be right."

"What now?" she asked, some of her triumph fading.

"We can't manipulate a scene to make it fit."

"I haven't even seen them hold hands."

"Neither have I. I got up a few times during the night and put my ear to their door. I didn't hear anything."

"That's creepy."

"Yeah. I really hoped we could end the investigation this weekend."

She looked up at the resignation in his voice. "What was so important about this job that you agreed to take it when you obviously didn't want to?"

"Charlie Black."

"The P.I. you took the case from?"

"Not *from*. *For*. We worked for Charlie when we first got in the business, until we qualified for licenses on our own. We grew his business way too fast, and he was happy and relieved when we opened ARC and he could go back to being a one-man operation. He's continued to send us jobs that are too big for him, and they often lead to others, but this one was his. Then his wife had a heart attack and he couldn't follow through."

"Oh, how awful. Is she all right?"

"They may do bypass." He leaned an elbow on the counter. "You're a nice person, Ms. McCord, to worry about someone you don't know."

"I think most people are nice."

"Hang around this business long enough and you'll change your mind. Very few people stand up to scrutiny."

She stopped dicing the shallots to focus on him. "I'm sorry you've lost your faith in people."

"You're restoring some of it," he said, his gaze steady.

She waited for a coherent thought to enter her head. "Well, I understand your being frustrated taking this case, but it seemed more than that."

He shrugged. "I was supposed to leave today on my first vacation in years."

"To?"

"Australia."

Australia. The word seemed magical. She hadn't even been as far as San Francisco. "Were you able to postpone it? You can go later, can't you?" *Were you taking a girl-friend?*

"Probably. I'll have to reschedule assignments again. Plus I'd planned to be there over Christmas."

"Alone?" The word came out without a second thought.

"Yes."

"How could you celebrate Christmas by yourself?"

"The point was not to celebrate."

"You…don't like Christmas?"

"And you do. I noticed yours was the only work space in the office decorated for Christmas."

He didn't make it sound like a good thing. She didn't know how to respond. She was sad for him, for anyone who didn't get caught up in the spirit of the holidays. "Do you know why I took this job?"

"Because I railroaded you?"

She hesitated. "Well. That, too. But mostly because I could use the money to bring my sister home for the holidays. This would've been our first Christmas apart."

"Where is she?"

"She's a freshman at Cornell. An architecture major."

"How does a Southern California girl survive the winter in Ithaca, New York?"

"Surprisingly well. She'd never seen snow before and she says she loves it. It helps that she lives on campus so she doesn't have to drive somewhere every day."

As she cooked she told him about how her mother died when Lyndsey was nineteen and Jess was eleven. That Lyndsey had just finished her freshman year at UCLA. How she moved back home to raise her sister.

Then she talked about how she never knew her father, that he'd walked out before she was born, then so did Jess's father when she was only six months old.

"Mom had a problem choosing men with staying power," she said, adding the penne to boiling water. "She was a great mother, though. Fun and free-spirited. Every day was an adventure. It's so quiet now without Jess. Who would've thought I'd experience empty-nest syndrome at twenty-six.''

Nate put together the salad Lyndsey demonstrated. A slice of tomato, a slice of mozzarella, a large basil leaf. Repeat. Drizzle with olive oil. He worked close beside her so he could continue to keep his voice quiet. ''Did you have to give up college?''

''No, but it took me longer. I got my master's in accounting in May, then I took the Universal CPA Exam last month. I'll have the results in February.''

''I can't picture you as an accountant.''

Her back went stiff. ''What's wrong with it? It's steady work. Excellent pay. And I'm good at it.''

Touchy, Nate thought. Protesting a little too much? ''I wasn't insulting you. I'm sure you're good at it, but I do know several CPAs. They don't tend to be people oriented. You are. And you're observant.''

''I'm detail oriented. It's a good trait for an accountant.''

''And an investigator. So are you quitting us when you pass the exam?''

''When I get a job. It's not a secret. Arianna knows. I told her when she hired me.''

''Of course you did.''

''What does that mean?''

Touchier, still. She intrigued him. ''You know that saying about someone having an honest face? You could be the poster child.''

''I've been lying to—'' She angled her head toward the door.

''You've been acting. There's a difference.'' He stepped away from the counter as a soft sound intruded. Their conversation had been barely above a whisper so he wasn't worried they'd been overheard, but it irritated him that Mr. Marbury, or more likely Tricia, was trying to eavesdrop.

"I'll be right back." He opened the door.

Tricia lifted her hand as if to knock. "I—I was wondering about dinner."

"Ten minutes," Lyndsey said.

Nate realized that Lyndsey's imagination hadn't been working overtime. Tricia did look him over like a piece of meat, but he wasn't sure it was born of passion. Her expression was more of a sneer. He kept quiet, putting the burden on her.

"Thank you," she said, her chin notching up. She left.

Nate waited until Tricia's bedroom door shut before closing the kitchen door again. He came up behind Lyndsey and said quietly, "You were right. She wants me."

"What'd she do?"

"Undressed me with her eyes." She was so easy to tease, he almost felt guilty about it.

She stirred the pasta faster, slopping water over the top. "I told you. Besides, she's already got a man of her own. She needs to leave mine alone."

Silence crash-landed in the room.

"I mean—" She fumbled the spoon and her words. "You know what I mean. She thinks you're a married man."

An unexpected wave of tenderness assaulted him. How did anyone that innocent survive in the big, bad world? "She's already with a married man, Lyndsey."

"But he's old."

Nate was still smiling when he served the first course.

Once again they were sent to their room right after dinner, except this time they weren't exhausted.

As dilemmas went, this was a big one. How to spend at least two hours in a tiny room with a man who'd filled her fantasies for months, then had become a pretty good reality, too. Situations like this didn't happen to her. It was like a movie or something: Lyndsey the Ordinary, who stands out about as well as camouflage, is lured into the world of espionage and becomes Lyndsey the Extraordinary. Nate the Great falls madly in love with her. She toys with him, driving him crazy. He begs to sleep with her....

She smiled at the scenario. Begging. Yeah, she liked that.

"What's so funny?" he asked.

He was trying to fix a broken zipper on his shaving kit, his back to her. She'd been enjoying the view as she spun her tale.

Her face burned at being caught. "Do you have eyes in the back of your head?"

He pointed to a mirror on the opposite wall over the dresser.

Oh. "I wasn't smiling at you," she said.

"I didn't say you were."

"Your voice implied it."

"You're reading between the lines, Ms. McCord."

She grabbed a cookie and munched on it, refusing to be drawn into a battle of words with him. Especially when he was right.

He tossed the shaving kit on the bed. "That's hopeless. How would you like to go down to the beach?"

"Now?"

"Why not? We've been dismissed for the night."

"But what if they change their minds and want something?"

"They'll have to wait."

"But what if they do something we should see? Shouldn't we—"

"Let's go." He grabbed her hand and pulled her up.

"You're bossy," she said, but she followed him out the

door, her hand held tightly in his, her pulse pounding at the adventure.

"I *am* your boss."

She kept forgetting that.

Five

There was nothing like a walk on the beach at night, Nate thought as they strolled along the shoreline. They hadn't spoken for the past ten minutes. They were barefoot, their pant legs rolled up. He watched Lyndsey lift her face into the breeze and shake her head. Her hair danced around her.

"We should probably head back," he said into the comfortable silence. He was tempted to put his arm around her as they walked back to the house. He wanted to feel her arm slip around his waist, and her head rest against his shoulder. But she kept a few feet between them.

He thought about how she had assumed her responsibilities, forgoing a time in her life when she should have been free to explore and experiment and raise a little hell.

"How did your mother die?" he asked.

She didn't answer for a minute. "She had an aneurysm. Jess found her in bed."

"And you not only had to deal with your grief, you had to become a parent. Did you resent that?"

"Not often. I knew how to budget money, probably because my mom was horrible at it. It came as no surprise that she only had a small life insurance policy. Along with Social Security payments for Jess, I stretched the money out until she turned eighteen. What saved us—what made it possible for me to keep going to college—was that the house was paid for. My mother had inherited it from her mother."

"You worked and went to college and raised a child. Jess worked, too, I imagine, when she was old enough?"

"No. It's hard to hold down a job and do well in school and have a social life. I didn't want her to miss out. She was already denied a mother. She ended up being valedictorian because she focused on her studies. She was homecoming queen, too."

"That's a hell of a double punch. Did you work while you were in high school?"

"Yes. But I wanted to."

Nate didn't believe her. She wouldn't have insisted her sister not work if Lyndsey had really enjoyed working herself. "What'd you do?"

"The usual. Fast food, sold tickets at a movie theater. Baby-sat. And yes I also got good grades."

"Valedictorian grades?" He looked over at her in time to see her smile.

"Close. Very close," she said.

"Did it hold you back, not being number one?"

"I got into the college I wanted to."

"Were you always an accounting major?"

"Nope. Theater."

He'd expected something different, but not that. "Why'd you switch?"

"Is that a rhetorical question? Look at me. Realistically what were my chances of making it as an actress?"

"I'm looking." *And liking what I see.* Why would she have any less of a chance to be successful in Hollywood than any other woman? "I don't get it."

She looked as if she didn't believe him. "I needed an income I could count on," she said, changing the slant of the discussion. "Everything worked out. I'll be able to pay for Jess's college."

He got it. She didn't want to talk about why she didn't think she was right for Hollywood. "Didn't Jess get scholarships?"

"Not full ride. It costs a fortune to attend a good university. And it's not only tuition and books and dorm room. It's all the other stuff you need. Scholarships and financial aid only go so far."

"Is she working?"

"Not yet."

"She's been there since August."

"I didn't want to push her. It's hard enough adjusting to college and your first time away from home, but especially three thousand miles away." She slowed her steps. "What's with the third degree?"

"Just killing time." He could see she was becoming annoyed at his questions, but he had an endless number of them.

"Well, it's not fair. You're learning everything about me, and I know nothing about you."

"Asking questions is my business."

"That was an interrogation. Now I have a question for you."

"Fire away."

"What did you mean the other night in the office when you said that I fit?"

"Just that. You fit. With me. We look like we could be

a couple." He stopped. "Hang on. They're on the balcony."

Lyndsey focused in the direction of the house. She could barely make out two silhouettes.

"Let's get closer." He took her hand and moved along at a good pace.

"Won't they see us?"

"Maybe." He stopped. "They're looking our way. Come closer."

He drew her into his arms, shifting their bodies so that he could see the house. After a few seconds she let out a long, slow breath and relaxed into him. His arms tightened. So did hers. She loved the feel of his body, the comfort of his embrace. She closed her eyes.

"Are they still there?" she asked, not caring but hoping he would think she was still doing her job instead of thoroughly enjoying being held.

"Yes." He drew back slightly, bent his head toward hers.

He was going to kiss her.

Amazed and expectant she waited. Then she saw his eyes were still focused on the house. It was a ploy. Except...

His body was responding to hers.

"Sorry," he whispered, which struck her as funny.

She started to laugh. He was apologizing for flattering her. Or maybe he was just easy.

"This is supposed to be a romantic moment," he said.

She laughed harder. What an idiot she was, thinking he was really attracted to her. It was just an automatic reaction, that's all.

"Lyndsey?" His tone asked if she'd lost her mind.

She had. Along with her common sense. She wished he wasn't the most fascinating man she'd ever met. Not that she'd been close to very many. Without a father around she hadn't had firsthand experience with the male way of thinking, only her mother's comments about their skewed logic, self-centeredness and lack of responsibility, especially the charmers—and Lyndsey's and Jess's fathers were both charmers. Lyndsey didn't think it was fair to lump all men into the description. To her mother's credit, she never seemed to be whining but was stating the facts as she knew them. She even spoke fondly of both men.

Nate was certainly logical and responsible. Self-centered? Not really.

But she couldn't ignore the obvious: he was charming. He was also sophisticated, attractive and successful, and he probably dated gorgeous women who were slender and equally sophisticated. Lyndsey, on the other hand, was a homebody who frequently forgot to wear makeup, whose curly hair was out of fashion, whose body proved she wasn't a big fan of exercise, and who struggled to make ends meet. Plus she worked for him. How many strikes did she need?

Yet he told her they fit. That they looked like they could be a couple. And he'd come to that conclusion when she was wearing her ugly old black sweater and jeans, no makeup, and her hair was a mess. What was he seeing that she wasn't?

"They went inside the house," he said, stepping back.

"Can we sit for a couple of minutes?" she asked.

He hesitated a few seconds. "Sure, why not."

She stopped trying to figure him out and just enjoyed listening to the surf pound the shore. Voices traveled, laughter, shouts. She didn't know where they came from, only that it meant they weren't alone. She closed her eyes and breathed the salt air, so distinctive, so calming. She pictured Nate on a beach in Australia. It would be summer there. Warm. Balmy. She envied him the opportunity to travel. Sometime she would travel, too.

She'd been thinking a lot about her future and what she wanted. Travel was only one goal. Her work goals were shifting, too. Becoming a private investigator wouldn't have entered her mind before, but the idea had taken hold at some point today and stuck. She was detail oriented, people oriented, and she loved a puzzle. She was tiresomely meticulous, which was why there was never an error in the reports she typed.

Nate interrupted her thoughts. "I can't figure them out," he said.

Lyndsey almost sighed. Back to business. "They don't act like lovers."

He didn't look convinced. "I don't know. There's a certain intimacy between them. I've been in groups of people where a man and a woman are on opposite sides of the room but I know they're together in every other sense. When people have been intimate, you know it, even those who think they're hiding it."

"But what kind of intimacy are you talking about? Aren't there several levels? My sister and I can sit together, our arms touching. There's nothing sexual about it, but it is intimate."

"If it's man/woman, I'm talking sexual intimacy."

"Always?" she asked.

"Ninety percent of the time."

"Maybe on the man's part. For women, intimacy comes from being comfortable, I think, whether it's with a man or a woman."

He looked skeptical. "So you have male friends?"

"Well...no, I guess not. Not close friends. Not someone I confide in."

"Because?"

"Are you just trying to be right? I'm only one woman. Poll a few thousand more."

"I'm interested in your answer. Why don't you have any male friends?"

Because one thing my mother told me I've found to be true—men don't have staying power. They take what they want, then they make a clean break. Not that she'd wanted it any other way. So far she hadn't met a guy she wanted to spend six months with, much less her whole life.

"I don't know, Nate. I guess I haven't met that many men who appealed to me enough to try to make friends."

"We need to go."

She sighed as she stood. She wouldn't soon forget this night, being on the beach with her fantasy man. She shivered at the thought.

"Cold?" he asked.

The man was far too observant. "A little."

He put his arm around her and drew her close. She intended to argue. Really, she did. But she wrapped her arm around his waist instead and let his body heat warm her.

"I think I should be remembering that you're my boss," she said.

"Let's agree for the rest of this weekend that we're co-workers, not boss and employee, although, frankly, I don't think you've given me enough respect anyway."

"Oh, you don't?"

"No. I think you're opinionated, and not deferential at all."

"Which makes me the perfect wife."

She waited for his comeback but none came.

Half an hour later their feet were washed clean of sand, they'd changed into their sweatpants and T-shirts and were lying on the bed watching an old episode of *The Cosby Show.*

"I've been thinking a lot about your sister," he said at the first commercial.

She groaned. "You are a bulldozer."

"Just hear me out."

"Like I have a choice?"

"You could tell me to shut up and go to sleep."

"Like you'd listen? You sure do talk a lot, for a man."

"You like the silent, brooding type?"

"I like the minds-his-own-business type."

He smiled. "Do you also like the he's-looking-out-for-your-best-interests type?"

"For now I'd like a man who doesn't put a question mark on the end of everything he says."

"You would?"

She shoved him. He fell onto his side, laughing. When she did her best to scowl at him, he changed positions so that he could face her and propped himself up on an elbow near her feet. He grabbed her foot through the covers and pressed into her arch. She couldn't help it. She moaned.

"You like that?" he asked.

She nodded.

"You didn't seem to mind that question."

"I'm fickle." She closed her eyes and eased her shoulders into the pillow. She made another sound of pleasure as he pushed his thumb into the pad of her foot.

"Put your feet outside the covers," he said.

Because she could and still keep her eyes closed, she did. She didn't want to see his face. She just wanted to feel his touch. It'd been so long since someone had taken care of her.

"Are you falling asleep?" he asked after a while.

"And miss out on this? No way."

"About Jess…"

She laughed and groaned at the same time.

"Lyndsey."

"Oh, all right. Get it over with."

"I realize I've never met your sister, so I'm basing my opinion strictly on what you've told me."

"Duly noted."

He stopped the foot massage. She grudgingly opened her eyes and pushed herself up to sit cross-legged. He sat up, too.

"I've seen it time and time again. The kids who are given everything by their parents end up the most screwed up."

"My sister wasn't given everything. She *lost* everything. She never knew her father. Her mother died when she was eleven. Eleven!"

"And you stepped in and did an admirable job. But she's an adult now, and you're not helping her grow up by giving her so much, by not making her work for what she gets. You made it on your own, even with the extra pressure of raising her. Jess could—and should—too. She'll not only appreciate what she earns, she'll learn how to take care of herself. That's important."

"You don't understand."

"Maybe not, since I haven't been in your position. But I do know there comes a time when letting go is the best gift you can give someone, even when that someone doesn't think she needs it."

It wasn't as if Lyndsey hadn't debated the issue with herself many times—and even come to the same conclusion. It was just that it was so hard to let Jess go. To let her make mistakes. To let her struggle or falter—or fail. Would Jess hate her then? She couldn't bear that.

She saw sympathy in Nate's eyes and resented him for it, without knowing why. "You're right. You haven't met my sister. You don't know what a terrific person she is. I haven't spoiled her. I made her crummy life a little better, and I will continue to. Because I love her. And because she's all I have." Her voice trembled. It made her mad.

"Don't cry." He said the words hard and fast, with something like panic in his eyes. Physically he retreated.

Lyndsey wouldn't have cried even if he hadn't reacted so violently to the possibility. She'd stopped crying years ago. Better to just suck it up and move on.

"I'm sorry," he said.

She didn't want him to apologize. She wanted him to keep pushing her until she accepted his help, because it would mean he cared about her, like he was encouraging her to do with Jess. But he wasn't pushing. He was apologizing. It infuriated her, she who rarely lost her temper, who always gave people the benefit of the doubt. "You have no right to tell me how to live my life."

"You're right, I don't."

She crossed her arms. "I've managed just fine for seven years."

"Okay."

"What's that supposed to mean?"

"I'm agreeing with you."

"I don't need any help."

"Everyone needs help now and then."

"Not me."

"Even you." Nate inched closer as she drew back. He knew she was so used to going it alone that she didn't know how to share the burden. He wanted to be her sounding board. He wanted to do something wonderful for her, something unexpected, something that would make her smile that glorious smile.

"Don't," she said.

"Don't what?"

"Whatever it is you're planning. I see it in your eyes."

He put a hand on her arm, felt her muscles bunch. "I'd like to help you."

"How?"

He resisted smiling at her continued belligerence. "What would make you feel better?"

"Nothing."

"So you're just going to stay mad at me?"

"That's right."

"Are we having our first marital spat?"

She tossed her head. "I guess the honeymoon is over."

"Maybe not. We could kiss and make up." Why the hell had he said that?

She stared at him for several seconds, hesitancy in her eyes. He waited for her to say no, to tease him a little about it. Instead she looked serious and contemplative.

He remembered the moment on the beach and his instant reaction to holding her against him. He wanted to finish what they'd started. *Just say no, Lyndsey.*

She nodded. How could he back down without hurting her feelings?

"Are you sure?" he asked. *Just say no.*

She nodded again.

A few choice swearwords swirled in his head. "Will you accept it as my apology?"

"Oh, quit asking questions and do it."

He smiled at her impatience. Stalling, he pulled off her glasses and set them aside, trying to slow himself down because, when she looked at him like that, with all that need in her eyes, he wanted to rush. And he wanted to run.

"You have the most expressive eyes, Ms. McCord. They're always saying something."

"You can't tell anything through my glasses."

"Is that why you wear them? To hide?"

"To see."

"You could wear contacts."

"Look, if you don't want to do this…"

"What's your hurry?"

"We're not supposed to go to bed angry." Her eyes dared him.

"I've always found that theory flawed," he said, running a finger down her cheek, along her jaw, across her lips. "It's better to go to bed angry than to say something you'll regret or can't take back."

"Do you ever shut up?"

He loved that she was irritated. Loved that he upset her equilibrium. Because she sure as hell was upsetting his.

He meant to kiss her lightly, just enough to fulfill the dare. But she made a sexy little sound when his lips touched hers, as if she'd been waiting for him forever. Her lips were soft, her tongue warm, her breath sweet. He wanted to devour her.

Slow down. Slow…down.

The commands went unheeded. He wrapped his arms around her and shifted her to lie under him, levering his weight off her with his arms. Her hair tumbled around her head. Her eyes were half-closed. Her mouth, her incredible mouth, was slightly open, her breathing irregular.

He dipped his head, touched his lips to hers tenderly. She whispered his name with such longing. He nestled more comfortably between her legs. She moaned, drawing her knees up, letting him closer. He hadn't meant for things to go so far but he couldn't seem to stop. He buried his face against her neck, kissed the tender flesh under her ear, moved his hips rhythmically against her. She tipped her pelvis, accepting him.

Then he stopped thinking. She rocked under him, lifted into him. He thought he would burst. A long, low moan came from her. He blocked the rest of the sounds with his mouth. Her climax went on and on, until he was sweating from holding back.

He wanted to bury himself in her—

"Did you bring protection?" she asked, her voice strained.

Nate froze in the arctic remnants of her words. What had he done? What the hell had he done?

He loosened his hold, rolled onto his side. "Lyndsey, I—no, I didn't bring protection." Which was a lie. They were in his overnight bag, as always, but this wasn't the time or place for them.

She came to awareness in a flash and backed away from him, eyes wide and cheeks flushed. "Oh, my God," she said. "I—I don't know where that came from." She slid off the bed and hurried into the bathroom.

Well, you pretty much screwed that up, he told himself. He shoved his hands through his hair, locked his fingers behind his head. He'd only meant to apologize for butting into her personal life. How had it transitioned into…that?

Hell. They barely knew each other. He was her boss. And he may be only six years older but he'd lived at least a lifetime longer.

He should've seen it coming. No one had looked so adoringly at him since…since his ex-wife. He'd made sure since then to choose women who didn't.

He looked blindly around the room. Hell, he could make split-second decisions about life and death situations, but he didn't trust his judgment about women like Lyndsey.

Nate eyed the closed bathroom door and wondered when she would come out. Deciding to make it easier on her, he went into the living room. He couldn't go onto the balcony since it connected to the master suite, so he stood at the plate-glass windows and watched the night.

A door opened. Tricia came out, wearing a long, lacy black gown. No lights were on in the house but enough spilled in from outdoors.

"What are you doing?" she asked sharply.

"I heard a noise. Just checking it out."

She moved closer. She was his usual type, he realized. Tall and slender, with a toned body and long, straight hair. His Barbies, Arianna called them. His reward for success, he countered back.

"Do you see anything?" She stood close to him. Close enough he could smell her perfume.

"No."

"I was just getting some cookies," she said, but didn't move.

He scanned the horizon, avoiding looking at her. Her nightgown was cut low, exposing a lot of breast. Lyndsey was ten times sexier in her T-shirt and sweats and those funky little glasses that her hair got tangled in. "Is there something you need, ma'am?"

She touched his arm. "Some advice?"

"I'm just the help." He took a step back, politely shrugging off her hand. "If you'll excuse me."

"Lyndsey…your wife said she expects fidelity. Do you think such a thing is possible in marriage?"

He clenched his jaw against the truth—*not in my experience*—but he believed that Lyndsey believed it. And since he was married to her—for this assignment—then he believed it, too. "Of course I do," he said instead, playing the role of a happily married man.

"I think I'm about to be proposed to. I'm not sure how to answer."

"I can't help you with that."

She sighed. "It's a complicated situation. He comes with a lot of baggage."

"Don't we all. Good night, ma'am." He couldn't get out of there fast enough.

The lights and television were off when he opened the bedroom door. He padded across the floor, lifted the blanket and climbed under. She was faced away from him. He doubted she was asleep.

"We both got carried away," he said to her back. "Let's not let it damage our relationship."

"Okay. G'night."

Okay. There was that word again. The word that meant nothing—or everything.

Six

The next morning Lyndsey waited until Nate left for his run before she opened her eyes. She was mortified. Not only had she assumed erroneously that he wanted to make love with her, but now he must also think she was easy.

She pressed her hands to her face and stifled a groan. He didn't know she'd been building up to this for months. She was primed to fall for him, but the fall had come harder and faster than she could have imagined.

He never should have offered sympathy and an available shoulder. She'd been too long without either. And how were they supposed to pretend to be the happy couple now? That would require dusting off every old acting skill she possessed.

The bedroom door opened, startling her. Nate strode across the room like a man on a mission and sat on the bed beside her.

"I thought you were going for a run," she said, bewildered.

"I was. I am. I figured you were stewing about what happened. I want to clear the air."

"Okay."

He smiled, but she didn't know why. He reached for one of her hands. "I like you."

"I like you, too." Geez, was that ever an understatement.

"You've not only been fun to work with, you've been professional. Considering you had no experience, you've done an amazing job."

"Most of the time I've just kept my mouth shut."

"That's a skill most people don't master. You got it right from the beginning."

"Oh, I'm so glad." Especially now that she was thinking of changing professions. She would talk to him about that later, though.

"Don't think that entitles you to a bonus."

She smiled because he did. Then she relaxed. She'd already gotten her bonus, last night in this very bed.

"Are we okay?" he asked.

"Definitely."

"Good. I'll be back in an hour."

When he returned an hour later he brought with him the substantial Sunday paper to add to the coffee tray then went off to shower. As Lyndsey prepared a zucchini frittata, toasted bagels and fruit, she hummed, almost dancing around the kitchen.

Her decision was made. She'd found her calling. She would make use of all her skills by becoming a private investigator. Surely her accounting background would be invaluable, as well as her acting ability. Plus, she loved the kinds of work it involved. Loved the challenge. She'd typed enough case files to know a lot of the job was routine, but a lot wasn't. There was always paperwork. Computer research. Phone calls. She was good at it all. However, she excelled in people skills. Because she blended into the background, she'd always been a people watcher and thought she understood human nature well.

When he took her home tonight she would talk to him about making a career change.

Should they also talk about what had happened in bed? She felt her face heat. She'd actually...lost control. With very little effort, too. With all their clothes on, too. That was a first. What had he thought about that?

"Lyndsey," Tricia said from behind her.

She turned around, putting a smile on her face. "Good morning. Isn't it a beautiful day?"

Tricia glanced toward the living room windows, where gray, overcast skies filled the view. She looked skeptical. "I guess."

"Your tray's ready. Just let me pour fresh coffee for you."

"You're making Cobb salad for lunch?"

"That's what the meal plan calls for. Is there a problem with that?"

"No." Tricia put her shoulders back a little. "Michael wants you to prepare the salads after breakfast and put them in the refrigerator. You and your husband can leave right after."

A few seconds of startled silence followed. "What about cleaning up?" Lyndsey asked finally.

"A housekeeping service does that. You were here to cook and run errands, if we needed anything. I thought you knew that."

"Of course we knew that," Nate said, stepping into the kitchen. "You're just catching us off guard, having us leave early."

"We figured you'd like some time together, given your busy schedules, and there's little left for you to do here, anyway. Happy three-month anniversary. Here, I'll take the tray myself today.''

Lyndsey stared at Nate. He shook his head a fraction.

"This is great," she said conversationally. "I've got that paper to finish for class tomorrow.''

He nodded. "Anything I can do here?''

She wished there was. At least they could whisper about their early dismissal. "No."

"I'll go pack.''

Lyndsey fretted. Had they done something wrong? Had she tripped up somehow? She thought over her conversations with Tricia. Nothing. They probably just wanted privacy. She still couldn't figure out why they just hadn't had food delivered. Much cheaper, and all the privacy they wanted.

She would never understand the rich.

Nate backed out of the garage. It was all he could do not to burn rubber as they left. He'd never done a job where he had accomplished so little.

"I don't get it," Lyndsey said after a minute.

"What's to get? They didn't want us hanging around any longer.''

"I gathered that, but why aren't we staying nearby, like at the beach? We could take the camera.''

"The chances of anything happening that's worth photographing are too slim to bother. At least this way we know we've got time before he goes home. We can see the client and show her what we have and talk about where to go from here.''

"How do you justify your fee when you don't produce anything of value?''

"You do the job. Its outcome is out of your control.'' Like anything about this job had ever been *in* his control.

"Do you think you'll do more surveillance on him?''

"If Mrs. Marbury requests it. Getting results is rarely a one-time opportunity. Sometimes you work for months on a case before you come up with the documentation. Sometimes you never do." He rationalized his failure because he felt he should have gotten something over the weekend. A kiss, even a hug between the subjects. Something that could be offered as proof. Anything to wrap up the case.

"What if there's nothing to find?" she asked. "What if we're all wrong and there's no affair?"

"Look at the facts. Tricia was proprietary with him. Most men in his position wouldn't let a woman who wasn't his lover speak for him."

"She's also his assistant. That gives her a comfort level beyond the normal."

"Good point," he said. "But she also came out of the bedroom wearing a low-cut negligee."

"But we never saw evidence they were sleeping together. There's a couch in the office."

"You're really playing devil's advocate with that one."

"Well, it's possible," Lyndsey said. "She wouldn't let me in the bedroom to make the bed. I never set foot in the bedroom or the office except when we took our own tour before they arrived. Did you?"

"Just the bedroom briefly twice. The bed was never made." He drummed his fingers on the steering wheel. "He gave her a massage, and there was that moment where their faces were close. Too close for a 'just friends' relationship."

"I know." She sighed. "It's all very confusing. Too many mixed signals."

"Exactly."

"If you're interested in my opinion, I still say they aren't lovers."

"I'm interested in your opinion, Lyndsey."

"But you think I'm wrong."

"I didn't say that. Either way adds up. It's going to take more work to find the truth. Look, can we drop this for a while? The client's going to be interrogating me soon enough."

"Sure."

He appreciated her silence. Once again he noted how quietly she sat, her hands in her lap, her thoughts her own. She didn't chatter for no reason. She answered questions, and she kept up her end of a conversation, but she didn't talk just to fill the silence.

He was grateful, too, that she hadn't brought up last night, yet another screwup. He had to figure out something to say, however, sometime soon.

He phoned Mrs. Marbury when they were a few minutes away. Still she kept them waiting for fifteen minutes before joining them in the sitting room. She looked as if she hadn't slept since they'd last seen her.

"Why are you back so early?" she demanded.

"We don't know," Nate said. "There was little left for us to do."

"Were they suspicious of you?"

"They were guarded." He looked at Lyndsey. "We both felt there was more to their relationship than they showed us, but they maintained strict privacy and discretion."

"You said on the phone that you have a picture."

"Yes." He opened his computer and brought up the series of photographs. "As you can see, there's no real evidence."

She shrank a little with each picture, until she dropped into a nearby chair. Nate sat as well. "What do you want us to do?" he asked.

She straightened her back. "What are my options?"

"We can continue surveillance whenever he leaves his office. Has he been coming home at night?"

"Yes, but late. Very late."

"Does he say he's working?"

"He doesn't say."

And you don't ask? "Do you call him at the office?"

"Not often. He doesn't like me to. The only way I'll get proof is if you get it for me. I can't do it."

"You want us to continue, then?"

The door opened and Mr. Marbury strode in. Nate stood and moved toward Lyndsey. Her eyes went wide. She seemed about to leap out of her chair. He put a hand on her shoulder.

"Ah, the loving newlyweds. And my adoring wife."

"You weren't supposed to be home for hours, darling," Mrs. Marbury said, sounding bored. She leaned back and crossed her legs, bouncing one foot.

Nate was stunned by her level of control.

"I had them followed. I wasn't far behind." Mr. Marbury turned to Nate. "Tricia recognized you from a party she attended last year. You were playing personal bodyguard to Alexis Wells."

Not playing, but doing his job. The Oscar-winning actress had received death threats and needed protection. But, dammit, he knew that as the most publicly visible partner of ARC he had a chance of being recognized. He should've let one of the junior investigators do the job. Because it was for Charlie, he hadn't trusted anyone else. And he'd screwed it up more than anyone else could have.

"I hired them," his wife said, her gaze following him as he came up to the computer and looked at the image there, the one of him and Tricia almost kissing.

"Obviously." He clenched his fists. Only the mantel clock made any sound. Nate felt Lyndsey's tension in her shoulder. He couldn't do anything but wait and see what Mr. Marbury did, then react to it. The man dragged a finger across the image before shoving the lid down.

"I doubt that's good enough for your purposes, my dear," he said. "Not exactly flagrante delicto, wouldn't you agree, Mr. Caldwell?"

Nate said nothing.

"Trust, once broken, is irreparable," he said calmly to his wife, then he took measured strides out of the room. The heavy front door opened and closed. A car started.

Again there was only the sound of a clock ticking.

"So, there was never a chance of knowing the truth. We were defeated before we started," Mrs. Marbury said. "He gave you enough to tease you. And me."

Lyndsey hopped up and went to her. She knelt down. "I'm so sorry," she said, taking the woman's hands. "If it's any consolation, I don't think—"

Nate surged forward, stopping her. Her opinions were just that. "Let's go."

She hesitated. He put his hand under her elbow and pulled her up. To Mrs. Marbury, he said, "It's one of the risks of the business—being recognized. It's never happened to me before. It may never again. I'm sorry that it did, since it voids an investigation when the subject is onto the investigator. If there's any other way we can be of service, please let us know."

He swept the computer off the table with his free hand and pulled Lyndsey along with the other.

"Nate," she said when they got into the car.

"Not now."

Screwup. How many times had his father called him that. *Never amount to anything.* Even though there'd been truth to his old man's words when Nate was a teenager, he'd grown up and stopped needing to prove anything. There was no reason. He *had* amounted to something. He was among the top in his field, had garnered respect and admiration from clients and peers alike. Now this. This…screwup.

And Lyndsey had witnessed it.

*   *   *

When he insisted on carrying her suitcase and garment bag, Lyndsey didn't argue, since she wanted to talk to him about her future. If she let him carry her belongings it would get him through the front door.

Lyndsey was proud of her little home. Although less than a thousand square feet and having only two bedrooms, it was cozy and welcoming, the furnishings not overly feminine, and on the walls were her mother's art, bold and full of life. She had a passion for red, which was incorporated into every painting, if only her signature.

Nate was so quiet she hardly knew he was there.

"Would you like something to drink?" she asked as they stepped inside.

"No, thanks. Where do you want these?"

"You can put them on the sofa."

He looked around, taking in the boxes stacked on the coffee table and floor.

"My Christmas decorations," she said, apologizing for the mess. "That's what my plans were for the weekend."

He didn't just dislike Christmas, she decided from his expression, it had some kind of bitter hold on him. And painful. He looked at the boxes instead of the beautiful art on the walls. His jaw turned to granite.

Obviously this wasn't the time to grill him about the twists and turns of their assignment or about his profession.

He set down her luggage and turned to her. His eyes were blank.

"This was fun," she said, extending her hand when what she wanted to do was hug him.

He reacted automatically, accepting her hand. Why are you hurting so much? she wanted to ask him. How can I help you?

"You were great," he said. "I'll see you."

That was it. A moment later he was gone, and she was left with so many thoughts spinning in her head. She went into her bathroom and looked in the mirror, expecting to see something different, because she felt different. More self-assured. Stronger.

Prettier. How could that be? She was such an average looking woman with nothing in particular to distinguish her, but at that moment she looked pretty.

Chalking up the difference to the fact she was wearing makeup for a change, she retrieved her luggage and carried it into her bedroom. She checked her answering machine. No messages. Jess hadn't returned her call asking what day she could fly home and what day she would have to be back at school. Lyndsey couldn't make the arrangements without that information. She could e-mail her sister, except she rarely answered those, either.

Lyndsey hung up some clothes from the garment bag and tossed others into the hamper. Then she opened her overnight bag. On top was her pair of red panties and matching red lace bra, folded neatly.

Nate had packed her bag. It hadn't occurred to her....

She plopped onto her bed, the lingerie in her hands. Her face was on fire. He'd tucked one cup into the other in the same way she did.

Whipping off her glasses, she tossed them onto the nightstand. Well. The mystery was over before it began. He would know that she didn't wear cotton underwear and white bras, but bright colors and lace. She wondered what had gone through his mind as he placed them in her bag.

The phone rang. She dragged the receiver to her face. "Hello?"

"I meant to tell you something," Nate said. "Co-worker to co-worker, friend to friend. Before I turn back into your boss."

She'd expected Jess, so she was doubly surprised to hear Nate—and to hear him sounding normal, especially after the mood he'd been in when he left not long ago.

"What's that?" she asked.

"If you're invited to a Christmas party, you should definitely wear the red."

A click followed. Her cheeks burned hotter. She dropped onto her back and stared at the ceiling. A smile tugged at her lips. So, he'd seen her underwear. He'd probably seen sexier. More sheer.

But it was your underwear.

So?

So he's going to picture you in it from now on.

Yes, he is, she thought, satisfied. Yes, he is.

Seven

"**W**hat do you mean you can't come home for Christmas?" Lyndsey almost yelled into the phone. "Jess! It won't put me further into debt. I earned some extra money. It's fine."

"I'm sorry, Lynnie. I am. We never planned for me to come home! You know everyone has to move out of the dorms over the winter break. I sublet an apartment for the month. I told you that."

"You did." Lyndsey rubbed her forehead. "But now you can come home."

"I can't. I signed up for winter session," she said, quiet and fast.

Shock snatched Lyndsey's breath. "Why?"

"Because there's a class I need to take."

"We mapped out your courses so that you wouldn't need to take winter session. It's so expensive." Lyndsey looked around her cubicle without seeing anything. She had just arrived at work when the phone rang, the one line she was supposed to answer at night.

"It's not just that," Jess said.

"Then what is it?"

Her sister didn't answer. Possibilities flashed in Lyndsey's mind, none of them acceptable. "You can tell me anything. You know that." *Just don't tell me you're pregnant.*

"I failed one class. I need to retake it now or I can't move on to the next level."

Lyndsey dropped her purse on her desk and finally sat, weighed down by disbelief. "You're still taking finals. How do you know you failed?"

"Because I do."

"I don't get it, Jess. You're smart without trying."

"This isn't like high school, you know."

"I've been to college. I know it's different. I also know you can handle it. What's going on? Are you partying a lot? You're hardly ever home when I call."

"I go out, just like everyone else. You don't expect me to hole up in my room all the time, do you?" She sounded both hurt and belligerent. "I know I have a job to do here. You drummed that into me."

"Then why aren't you doing it?"

"I am. It's just hard. It's not like I don't want to come home, you know. I miss you, Lynnie."

I miss you, too. She fought to maintain the parent role instead of the lonely sister. "How are the rest of your grades?"

"They're not great, but I'm passing."

Lyndsey knew about the freshman struggle, but she had expected more of Jess, who always excelled in academics.

"Do you go to class?" Lyndsey asked.

"Ye-es." The singsong answer was followed by a huge sigh.

"All of them?"

"Most."

Lyndsey closed her eyes. "Are you sure the winter session will solve the problem?"

"I'm sure. I'm really, really sorry, Lynnie. I'll be home in May, just like we planned."

We planned that before I knew how hard it was going to be not to see you for nine months. "Won't you be lonely?" Lyndsey barely got the words out.

"Lots of kids are stuck here. It'll be okay. Um, I'm gonna need some money to pay for the class. Good thing you earned some extra, huh?"

There went the car repairs, too. By the time she paid the extra tuition, nothing would be left. In fact, she would be even further in debt. Winter session fees were exorbitant.

"You can't do this again, Jess. I don't have money to spare. You have to stick to the program we set up. You have to pass your classes. You're more than capable."

"I know. I promise I'll do better."

"Have you had any luck getting a job?"

"Not yet. I guess I applied too late for Christmas jobs, and everyone will be laying off right after the holidays. People say it'll open up again in February or March."

The master plan had included Jess working full-time during the month-long winter break, even if it meant her taking two part-time jobs. Discouragement settled in. Lyndsey almost wished she hadn't earned the extra money, hadn't gotten her hopes up. "You need to find a job, Jess."

"I will. Listen, I gotta go, okay? I love you!"

"I love you, too," Lyndsey said to a humming dial tone. After a minute she hung up the phone, then her sweater. She noted the time on her time sheet, jumbled the Rubik's Cube for Sam then settled down at the computer, but the swing of emotions over the past few days took its toll. She struggled to concentrate on the reports she needed to type, which always required a great deal of attention.

Hours later she finished transcribing, surprised to find no report from Nate. Surely he needed to file something on the Marbury case.

Oh, who was she kidding? She didn't care about his report. She just needed to hear his voice. She'd hoped all day he would call. Another disappointment. But after the way she'd expected sex from him, she wasn't surprised. It was her own fault.

"You're pathetic," she said aloud.

"I am?"

She recognized the voice and was torn between being embarrassed and delighted that he was there. "I'm pathetic, not you. Although I might have included you if I'd known you were there."

Nate grinned. "Why are you pathetic?"

"There you go with the questions again."

"Occupational hazard. What's going on?"

"You didn't file a report."

"How does that make you pathetic?"

"It doesn't. I was changing the subject."

Nate grabbed a rolling chair from the next cubicle and sat knee to knee with her. "I'm working on it," he said. "The report," he added when she seemed confused. "I had something else to do today."

"Attend a cooking class?"

"Funny." He reached into his back pocket. "I talked with Arianna and Sam. We all agreed you should get your Christmas bonus now." He passed her the envelope.

"I didn't even know there was a bonus. What is it, a coupon for a turkey?"

"We're a little more appreciative of our staff's hard work than that. Take a look."

She pulled out the contents. Her face drained of color. "It's a plane ticket."

"It's a voucher for one, actually. You call the airline, arrange the flight and give them the number right there." He tapped the form. "Merry Christmas." The words didn't stick in his throat, for a change, because he was more concerned about Lyndsey's reaction. She should be flashing that awesome smile.

"Thank you. It's a wonderful gift, but you can keep it. My sister can't come home."

"Why not?"

She shook her head. Her throat convulsed. Don't cry, he ordered silently.

"She has to stay at school. Winter session."

"So use the ticket to go see her."

"What?"

That the idea hadn't occurred to her said a lot to Nate. He took her hands in his. "Sweetheart. Planes fly both directions."

She didn't say anything for a minute. "I've never flown before."

"Never? Didn't you go visit the campus with Jess?"

"We chose not to spend money on that. They have virtual tours online, and we chose by reputation, too." She flung herself at him, wrapping her arms around his neck. "Thank you. Oh, thank you so much. I won't even tell you it's too much for an employee who's only been here for three months."

"You're welcome." As she pulled back he cupped her face and studied her. She smiled. That was all he needed. He grazed her lips with his. His bed had seemed enormous last night after sharing one with her.

"I missed you today," she said against his mouth. "I shouldn't say that, but I did."

He remembered how she felt curled up against him the

first morning. Then during the night, the second night, he'd lain awake looking at her, touching her curls, finding them soft and springy.

He set his hands at her waist and deepened the kiss. She moved closer. He let his hands glide up her rib cage, felt her go still as he cupped one breast, then a sound intruded. Footsteps. He jerked back just before his partner Sam Remington came into view. Lyndsey looked away, resettling her glasses. She picked up a pen and tablet of paper and scribbled something.

"Burning the two a.m. oil?" Sam asked Nate.

"I hadn't filed the Marbury report."

Sam said nothing. He was taller than Nate, and broader, and he had a stern face, which rarely broke into a smile. That face had intimidated the hell out of a lot of people, and now he looked from Nate to Lyndsey and back again.

"How're you, Ms. McCord?" he asked, leaning casually against her entryway.

"Fine. Great, in fact." She tossed him his jumbled Rubik's Cube. "Thank you for the plane ticket. You don't know how much it means to me."

He was focused on the puzzle cube, twisting and turning, eyeing it, then twisting it again, his movements fast and sure. He gave her a brief glance. "Our pleasure. I hope you have a good time."

"Oh, I will. I'm going to see my sister in New York. She's at Cornell."

"I remember. What'd you think of your weekend assignment?"

"I loved it."

Okay, time to go now, Nate thought, standing, needing to get Sam alone. "Got a minute?"

"Sure," Sam said. "Hang on." A few seconds later he

handed the solved cube back to Lyndsey. "Are you done for the night?"

"Except for distributing the case files." Her gaze shifted to Nate. "Unless you want me to stay and type up your report?"

"It can wait until tomorrow. Give me the files. I'll pass them out."

She handed him the stack then fussed with the things on her desk, aligning her stapler, phone and notepad with precision. Sam didn't budge. Nate crossed his arms and looked at him. A tiny smile flitted across Sam's mouth.

"I see you're both wearing new jewelry," he said.

Nate touched his thumb to the wedding ring. He'd forgotten the damn thing. "I figured it was safer on my hand than in my pocket." He slid it off.

"Me, too," Lyndsey said, dropping her ring into Nate's hand.

The ping of gold hitting gold rang like a death knell.

"No scorch marks under that?" Sam asked Nate innocently.

Lyndsey pulled on her sweater and tugged her purse over her shoulder. "Well…good night."

Sam stepped out of the way. Nate touched her shoulder as she passed by. She slowed down for a moment then hurried off.

He wandered to the window overlooking the parking lot. Sam followed. Tinted glass prevented her from seeing them watching her. Her engine ground, coughed, then grabbed.

"What're you doing here?" Nate asked.

"I worked the Hastings party. Decided to pick up some files so I can sleep in and work from home tomorrow. Today."

They watched Lyndsey use a squeegee to wipe the moisture off her windshield, then Nate felt Sam's gaze on him.

"I don't think I've seen a guiltier look," Sam said mildly.

Nate slipped his hands into his pockets. "I'm sure you have."

"I wasn't talking about you. You've mastered the blank expression. I'm talking about Ms. McCord. What'd you do, kiss her?"

When Nate didn't respond, Sam swore.

"Not a good idea, Nathan."

"I know."

"Can't help it?"

Nate shook his head slowly.

"Well, it was bound to happen sometime," Sam said.

"What was?"

"You know what. You've protected your heart for a long time."

"My heart's intact."

There was a long pause before Sam said, "Then you'd better think long and hard about what happens next. First, you can't toy with an employee. You've investigated enough harassment cases to know that. Second, she won't rebound like other women. If you think she'll lose interest and patience like the others, you're dead wrong."

Sam pointed to the parking lot. "Look at her. She squeegees her damn windows. She backs her car out of the parking space even though she could just drive straight through the space in front of her. There's no car there. What does she think would happen?" He shook his head. "She's a rule follower. She'll expect you to play by the book. Her book. The one she's created for herself about men and life."

Nate wanted to tell Sam he would put an end to it, but the words wouldn't come.

"I know you've been burned, Nate. I know you don't

have faith in happily ever after. But she does. Remember that.''

''You're a fine one to speak.''

''I don't go from woman to woman.''

''No, you just stay hung up on the same one, year after year. I hear she's finally available. Why don't you go after her?''

''That's my business.''

''Right. And Lyndsey is mine.''

Sam drew a deep breath then rested an arm on Nate's shoulder. ''So, we gave her a plane ticket, did we?''

Sweetheart. He called her sweetheart.

A ball of fire surrounded her heart then spread heat through her body, which was a good thing, since her car heater had died. She had to squeegee her windows and hope to make it home without needing her defroster.

She was going to New York. She would fly in a plane. She would see for herself how Jess was doing. Her sister's decreasing level of communication since she left home was both understandable and frustrating as she spread her wings, but at least now Lyndsey could talk to her in person. She could watch Jess open her Christmas present, a gorgeous leaf-green sweater. They could drink hot chocolate and talk late into the night, like old times.

They had a Christmas Eve tradition of leafing through the photo albums of their Christmases with their mother. Lyndsey would pack them to take. The angel treetop ornament they put on the tree in honor of their mother would have to wait for next year.

This would be her first year without a tree.

She thought about how Nate hated Christmas and wondered why. People didn't hate the holiday for no reason.

He'd kissed her. In the office. More than once. Then he'd touched her, just barely. If Sam hadn't come by…well, that was probably as far as it would've gone, anyway.

It struck her then that she couldn't talk to Nate about her becoming an investigator, because she would be putting him on the spot, given their as-yet-undefined relationship. Why risk messing it up? There were other ways to get answers.

Lyndsey pulled into her garage. She admired the wreath on the front door as she let herself into her house. How did Nate handle Christmas cards, she wondered? Would he open one from her? She'd have to find a funny one.

She turned on her computer to go online to check flights, but before she logged on, her phone rang, startling her.

"I hope you weren't in bed yet," Nate said.

As if that matters. "No. I was about to check flights."

"That's why I'm calling. Since you haven't flown before, I'm volunteering to make the arrangements."

His voice seemed different to her now. No longer the smooth, efficient professional but the man who'd kissed her. Teased her. Satisfied her but not himself.

"I accept, thank you," she said. "I was figuring on an early-morning flight on Saturday and then a Monday morning return."

"Why so short?"

"What choice do I have? I'm not eligible for vacation—and don't you dare tell me to take extra time. That puts a burden on someone else in the office to do my job as well as their own. I won't do that."

"But—"

"I mean it, Nate. You've done enough already."

"*But*…didn't you get the memo about having Monday and Tuesday off?"

She was sure she would have remembered that. "No. I understand why we get Monday off, since Christmas is on Sunday, but why Tuesday?"

"Because the Christmas party is on Saturday. So that means you can come back on Wednesday and not miss any work."

Four days. "That's terrific. And I meant to ask you to-night—" *but I got distracted when you kissed me* "—about your P.I. friend's wife. How is she doing?"

"She had a quadruple bypass this morning, but she came through the surgery okay. Charlie's just barely keeping it together. I spent the day with him. That's the real reason I didn't get around to doing the Marbury report."

"Did you tell him about it?"

"Oh, yeah. Gave him his only laugh of the day."

He didn't sound like it was funny at all. Was he that upset that the case hadn't gone as he'd hoped? He probably wasn't used to things going wrong. "I'm glad she's doing well."

"Me, too."

She didn't want to hang up. She wanted to lie on her bed and talk for hours. She'd learned that sometimes when people weren't face-to-face, they talked about things they wouldn't otherwise. Like why he hated Christmas, and how she really did resent her sister's freedom a little, since Lyndsey had never had any freedom herself.

And that she was falling in love with him.

"Don't finalize the flight plans until I've spoken with Jess, okay?" she said instead. "I wish I could surprise her but I don't dare."

"I'll make reservations but put them on hold for twenty-four hours. Let me know after you talk to her. You have my cell number, right?"

"I do."

"Lyndsey, I really wish you would take some extra—"

"No. Thank you."

"You're stubborn."

"It's not a bad trait, you know. You just make it sound bad."

"How late do you sleep?" he asked.

"When I work nights I'm up by eleven at the latest, usually closer to ten. I'm in the office by seven. My sister's a little hard to get answers from, however. She's developed an independent streak that's hard to break through."

"I remember the feeling myself. Only I rebelled by joining the army. And before you say anything, remember I was eighteen. It made sense at the time. My dad was a Marine. If I wanted to tick him off—and I did—it meant choosing a different branch of the military."

Lyndsey did get comfortable on her bed then, hoping the conversation would last. "Why the military at all?"

"Rebellion, pure and simple."

"Did you regret it?" She hadn't had time for rebellion, although she'd felt it often enough.

"I don't regret it much. I met Sam and Arianna in the army, and life is good because of that."

"You didn't get to go to college?"

"I used to blame my dad for that, too. Now I just wish he'd acknowledge my success."

Grief welled inside Lyndsey at his words. Her mother would never be able to acknowledge her success, but had she lived, she would've been president of Lyndsey's fan club. "Lack of college hasn't slowed you down any," she said to Nate. "In fact, it doesn't seem like the firm could handle any more business."

"Maybe. But I wish I'd done some things differently. I admire you, raising your sister on your own, sticking with college."

"We do what we need to."

"I should let you get to bed."

"Okay." She heard him laugh quietly. "What's so funny?"

"I just enjoy you. Good night, Lyndsey."

"G'night."

It was hard letting him dictate the relationship, but she needed to let him. He was comfortable with her, that much she knew. He was attracted to her. She probably shouldn't read much into it. They'd gotten close because of circumstances. He'd probably slept with and dumped a million women.

But all the reasoning in the world couldn't stop the pitter-patter of her heart when she was with him. Or the daydreams. Or the secret wish that he might fall as hard for her as she had fallen for him.

Eight

Nate's cell phone rang as he jogged along the beach near his house. He didn't usually take the phone with him, so the sound jarred, even though he was expecting Lyndsey to call. He glanced at the screen, saw it was her number.

"Good morning, Ms. McCord," he said, not missing a stride.

"Hi."

Her voice was different. Forced. He came to a stop, tried to control his breathing so he wouldn't pant into the phone. "What's wrong?"

"I hope you can cancel the ticket without any penalty."

"Sure. Why?"

"Because my sister lied to me." Anger and hurt coated her words.

"About what?"

"She doesn't want me to visit. She never did want to come home, either. She's—she's going to Vermont to ski. With her boyfriend. I didn't even know she had one."

He started jogging toward home. "I'm coming over."

"No. I'm going out to buy a Christmas tree. I'm okay. I just wanted you to cancel the flight."

"I'm coming over. It'll take me forty-five minutes."

"It's not necessary."

"Do not leave before I get there." He disconnected before she could argue, then he sent a few choice words toward the East Coast.

Nate was beginning to understand her and her independence. She would go out of her way to show she didn't need him. Hell, he wasn't even sure why he was going there.

Maybe he didn't want to examine why too closely, either.

Less than an hour later he knocked on her door.

"I'm fine," she said without preamble as she held the door for him. "Honest."

He surveyed her as he passed by. She wore blue jeans, and a red blouse covered with smiling, leaping reindeer. Only the top button was undone. When had buttoned-up become such a turn-on for him? Maybe because of the prospect of unbuttoning it? He had a hard time reconciling this woman with the one who had held nothing back the other night. "I'll bet you told your sister you were fine, too."

"I'm glad you're here, but I don't want to talk about my sister."

"Or your disappointment?"

"That either."

"Just one question?" he asked.

She crossed her arms. "Choose wisely, Question Man."

He smiled. "Is Jess really signed up for winter session?"

"That much is true. But she has time off between the

end of finals and the beginning of the session. She could've come home.''

''In her defense, until yesterday she didn't think she could, so she took care of herself. That's good, isn't it?''

She narrowed her eyes at him then broke into a reluctant smile. ''Oh, quit being rational.''

He put an arm companionably around her shoulder. ''You wouldn't want her to sit around, lonely and bored, would you?''

''Like me, you mean?''

''I didn't say that.''

''Would you like something to drink?'' she asked when he stepped away.

''I thought we were going tree shopping.''

Lyndsey stared at him. Had she heard him correctly? ''*I* was. I didn't figure you'd be interested.''

''I brought my pickup.'' He dangled his keys.

She really didn't need a truck for the size of tree she would buy, but she wasn't about to stop him from coming with her, not when she'd been given an opportunity to change his mind about Christmas. ''That would be nice, thank you.''

''However, there is one condition,'' he added.

''There are strings attached?''

His gaze softened. ''Aren't there always?''

''No. Not from me, anyway.''

''Why doesn't that surprise me?'' He cupped her face, brushed his thumb along her cheek. ''I was only going to say, enough with the thank-yous.''

The tender look in his eyes erased any uncertainty she had. ''How about this instead?'' She twined her arms around his neck and pulled herself up on tiptoe, bringing her mouth near his.

''This is good,'' he said, gathering her close.

''This is dangerous,'' she said in return. They hadn't

kissed yet, but she could feel his breath, warm against her face.

His hands slid down over her rear and pulled her snugly against him. "You seem daring enough."

She would've laughed at the idea if she weren't so distracted by the feel of his body against hers. Daring? Not until a few days ago. "Please stop talking." *Before I lose my nerve.*

His kiss fulfilled dreams then promised even more, changing from soft and tempting to bold and demanding. He pulled back after a minute, looked entirely unsure of himself, then came back for more, slanting his head the other direction, asking more of her second by second. His hands went on a journey of exploration, dragging up her sides, his palms pressing into the sides of her breasts, awakening, arousing, urging. He lifted his head and she wanted to whimper. *Not yet. Don't stop yet.* He read her thoughts, kissed her again, deeper, hotter, demanding more. She stopped thinking as his tongue swept her lower lip then dipped inside her mouth to mate with hers in a fiery dance.

She felt him against her abdomen, hard and thrilling and flattering. Her bedroom was so close….

"You taste like cinnamon," he said, easing back.

"I—I just made Snickerdoodles."

"What's that?" His fingertips danced along her spine, low.

She arched. "Cookies," she managed to say. "Want some?"

"Do you know how sexy you are?" He nuzzled her neck.

Me? She was proud of herself for not saying the word out loud and incredulously. "I dabbed vanilla behind my ears. It's supposed to drive men crazy."

She felt him smile.

"Did you?" he asked, sniffing, sending chills through her.

"No, but the theory is supposed to be true." She wanted to stop talking and let things heat up between them, but she sensed a hesitation on his part. She wasn't going to make the same mistake as the last time and jump to conclusions. They would sleep together when—if—the time was right.

"I'll pack some cookies to take with us." She started toward the kitchen.

"Lyndsey."

At the serious tone in his voice she faced him reluctantly, her fears echoing in her head. *Please don't leave. Don't be afraid of what's growing between us.*

"Can you make that a dozen? I haven't had breakfast."

Relief flooded her. "I'd love to fix you breakfast." *Every morning.*

"You would?"

He so obviously wasn't surprised that she gave him a little shove, but it was like pushing granite. He caught her hands and pressed them to his chest, over his heart.

"As I said, you're a very nice person, Ms. McCord. In return, I'll—"

"Stop. I don't want anything in return. I want to fix you breakfast. I like your company. And we might as well get something else straight before we go, too. You're not buying me a tree."

"Hold on a second, Stubborn. I was only going to say that in return for you making me breakfast, I'll eat it."

Oh, he could put the most innocent expression on his face. She didn't know whether to believe him. "You were not."

"That's my story and I'm stickin' to it."

She didn't have a comeback, so she said what was on her mind instead. "Thank you for being here, Nate." *For cheering me up. For the hours of anticipation you gave me when I thought Jess and I could spend Christmas together, after all. I thought I was resigned to being apart, but I realize now that I wasn't.* She smiled. "I'm okay now. I've accepted that life is changing faster than it used to. I've caught up."

"Good."

He swept her into his arms, and he felt wonderful. Warm and safe. She ended the hug before he did. "How do you like your eggs?" she asked.

"Cooked."

"Ah. Just as I suspected. You're easy."

"You can't decorate a tree without a mug of hot chocolate," Lyndsey said. "It's tradition."

"We're having a heat wave. It's eighty-five degrees." He had situated the four-foot-tall Douglas fir in its stand and was untangling a string of colored lights while Lyndsey sorted through her ornaments.

"You don't have to help me decorate, you know," she said, eyeing him dubiously as he fought with the lights. The lights were winning.

"You worried my work won't pass inspection?"

He was teasing her, as he had while they shopped, calling her the Inspector General of Trees and telling her he'd seen parachutes packed with less fanatical attention to detail.

"I can always redo it after you leave." She smiled sweetly at him.

He grunted. "I still don't understand why people put so much time and effort into Christmas."

"Because it's a joyful time of year. People are happy."

"People always looked stressed-out to me."

"Then they're not celebrating it the right way."

"What's the right way? What was your best Christmas?" he asked.

The memory swamped her, taking her back eighteen years as if it were yesterday. "The year I was eight. Mom came home from the hospital with Jess a week right after Thanksgiving. She was such a good baby. She hardly ever cried, and I loved holding her."

He'd succeeded in untangling half of the strand and looked as if he was resisting the temptation to stomp on the rest so that he could just go buy new sets as he'd wanted.

"You have strong maternal instincts," he said.

"I liked girl stuff. Dolls and clothes and playing beauty parlor. Jess was my living doll." She grabbed the other end of the cord to help him straighten it. "Plus that year Jess's dad was living here. It was my first and only taste of 'real' family. There were lots of presents. I adored him. He was like a big kid, and my mom laughed all the time."

"And he just walked out?"

"Memorial Day. I remember because he was supposed to take us to a picnic in the park. He went to get some sodas. We waited here for hours. Finally Mom spread a blanket on the living room floor and unpacked the cooler right there. We ate. I went to bed. She found a note from him on her pillow when she pulled down the quilt that night."

"A man of honor, obviously."

She shrugged at his sarcasm. "Everyone's got their own burdens. You, too, I would guess."

"Actually, eight was a pivotal year for me, too."

"In what way?"

"*Star Wars* and Elvis."

"Sounds like a bad country song."

He grinned. "Well, my dog didn't die the same year or

it could've been. And don't you be maligning country music. It's better than opera.''

"What happened?"

"My dad was home on leave in June—he was, is still, a Marine—and he took me to see *Star Wars*."

"You liked the movie, I gather."

"Oh, yeah. But more than that, it changed my relationship with my dad.'' The lights were finally untangled. He started arranging the bulbs on the tree as Lyndsey kept the cord straight. "We finally had something in common."

"Why weren't you close before?"

"For one, he was gone most of the time. My mom refused to follow him from base to base, so we had a house in Baton Rouge, and he came home when he felt like it." He kept his hands busy and his eyes on the tree. "My older brother, Greg, and I walked on eggshells around him. We weren't used to any kind of discipline from Mom, so we couldn't wait for him to leave. But that year I was eight was different. We'd finally found a connection. When he left I figured things would be different after that. Then Elvis died. My mother was fragile to start with, but his death was her undoing. She went into mourning so deep that she barely functioned, and she cried all the time. I mean, all the time."

Lyndsey recalled his panic when he thought she was going to cry the other night. Now it made sense.

"I'd never heard my dad yell until he came home for Christmas that year," he continued. "He was always a quiet dictator. The commands were in his eyes and his posture and his choice of words. Not this time. Everything he held against her came out. She had a complete breakdown. He put her in a facility, sold the house and most of the furnishings, then took my brother and me to where he was stationed in California."

So, he associated Christmas with his mother being taken

away, and his father taking over after years as an absentee parent.

"I never forgave him for moving us away from home, especially away from Mom."

"You mean you never saw her again?"

"We saw her. About six months later she was released, and he made her come live with us. I thought it was cruel, but he wouldn't let her go. She functioned, but her spirit was gone. They lived in the same house until I graduated from high school. They got a divorce, then I got even by joining the army, as I told you."

"Do you see your parents?"

"Not often. Dad remarried. I've got nine-year-old twin half sisters. He's happy, I think. Mom moved back to Louisiana. She battles depression all the time, but she seems relatively content. I see her several times a year, but I don't stay long. We don't have much to say to each other."

Nate finished putting on one string of lights and reached for another. "I shouldn't resent my dad, I guess, because Greg and I didn't have any kind of discipline until he took charge, and we needed it, but he handled it all wrong. He was like our drill sergeant instead of our father. I hated him most of the time. According to him, I couldn't do anything right. We yelled a lot."

"I can't imagine you yelling."

"I don't anymore." He didn't invest that kind of emotion. Keep it light. Keep it simple. Keep it short-term. That was his motto when it came to relationships.

"Here," she said. "Let me show you how to untangle those lights without a fight." She gave him one end of the cord; she took the other and walked away. It unrolled easily.

"You couldn't have shown me that the first time?" he asked, grateful to end the discussion about his past. He chose not to look back, but to learn from his mistakes and move on. He didn't understand why he'd confided so much to her, since he'd never done that before, except once with Sam and Arianna, and that situation had been unusual—because they weren't sure they were going to live to see another day. The bond they'd formed that day while they faced death was the strongest he had.

Nate and Lyndsey stepped back a while later to admire their work. The tree sparkled and shimmered with mostly handmade ornaments and colorful lights reflecting off shiny red balls.

"Just needs two things," Lyndsey said. She tucked a red and green tree skirt around the base then opened a box, folded back some white tissue paper to reveal a delicate angel treetopper. "Jess and I picked this out the year Mom died, to honor her. It's always the last decoration we put on." She hesitated. "Would you close the blinds, please?"

She slipped it onto the top and straightened the white satin skirt, then her halo and wings. She stepped back, her arms folded across her stomach. Nate watched her a minute and saw sadness swamp her. He came up behind her, wrapped his arms around her. She leaned against him.

"You would've liked her," she said softly. In the darkened room the tree took center stage. "She was so much fun. Spontaneous and loving and generous. Young in her thinking. Daring. Just not very responsible."

"You made up for that."

"I guess."

"You guess? *Responsible* is your middle name." He enjoyed the feel of her hair against his jaw. One loopy curl fell into the vee of his shirt, brushing his skin. What was it about her that was so different? He should feel safe with her because she wasn't the kind of woman he was usually attracted to, but he didn't feel safe. And she wasn't overtly sexy, but that just made her sexier. She didn't hang on his every word, either, and flatter him unnecessarily. Nor did she want him to take care of her or help her out in any way—which made him want to even more. She was independent yet traditional.

And she never mentioned the Marbury case and how he blew it. He appreciated that.

"Are you hungry?" she asked. "I've got time to fix us dinner before I go to work."

"Let me take you out. Nothing fancy."

"Dinner out would be fun. I need to shower and change first."

"Go ahead."

"Make yourself at home."

"Is there anything I can do?"

"If you'd like to put the empty boxes out in the garage, that would be great. I won't be long."

He gathered the boxes then stacked them neatly in the attached one-car garage, maneuvering himself around her car, noticing the dings and dents and faded paint. He thought about his cars. Overkill. Outward signs of success that he needed for himself. Recognition mattered to him, especially since he didn't get any from his parents.

He looked around the orderly space, seeing her life and history in marked boxes. Lyndsey, school, one said. Jess, school. Mom. Grandma Joan. Great Grandma Alice. No wonder Lyndsey was so independent. There didn't seem to be a history of any men sticking around long enough to leave memorabilia, not even in earlier generations.

Dammit. How could he get involved with her when all the men in her life walked out? Or weren't they invited to stay? That was a possibility, too.

The problem was, he couldn't seem to stay away.

But Sam had made a good point. Nate dated women who understood the rules—simple and short-term. He always stepped back when the relationship turned serious, making it easy for a woman to walk away. He hadn't had to break up with anyone. He just forced their hand. No emotional scenes that way.

Nate returned to the house. He couldn't hear the shower running, but the bathroom door was closed. He pictured her in there, naked, damp, flushed.

The phone rang.

"Would you get that, please?" she called out.

He picked up the phone reluctantly. "McCord residence."

"Nate?"

Arianna. He swore under his breath.

"What are you doing at Lyndsey's?"

"Helping her decorate her Christmas tree." Did that sound casual enough?

Silence. Absolute silence. "This is Nate Caldwell?" Arianna asked finally.

"Funny, Ar. How'd you find me?"

"Your cell phone's turned off. I tracked you through the GPS."

Sam, Arianna and Nate had global positioning system on all their cars as a precaution. "What's going on?" he asked.

"I could ask the same of you. Your phone is never turned off. Never."

"I'm on vacation."

A brief pause. "She's an employee, Nate."

"I like her. And she could use a friend. What's up?"

"Someone took a shot at Alexis Wells."

He came to attention. "She okay?"

"Scared but okay."

"It's been a year since the last threat. We relaxed about it. Dammit. Where is she?"

"At home. She's leased a jet to take her to her place on Maui. She wants you to come along."

"Yeah, okay." He glanced at his watch. "Tell her I'll

meet her at the airstrip in an hour. She knows the precautions to take in getting there. Find out which LAPD detective is handling her case.''

''All right. Nate—''

''I'll call you from the jet, before we take off.'' He hung up, not giving her a chance to say anything more.

''Is something wrong?''

He turned around. Lyndsey stood in the living room doorway wearing a white terry-cloth robe and a frown. She looked dewy and fresh. And irresistible.

He walked to her. ''I have to leave town.''

''For how long?''

''I don't know. Depends how fast the police do their part of the job.'' He rubbed her arms. Her warmth seeped through the fabric. ''I'm sorry about dinner.''

''Is it dangerous?''

''Hard to tell yet.''

''Who's the client?''

''I can't say.''

Lyndsey drew back. ''I'll be transcribing the case files.''

''Not this one. Some clients demand premium confidentiality. Those files are handled differently. Filed differently. I'll call you when I can.''

''Promise?''

''Yeah.''

She stepped closer and flattened her hands on his chest, missing him already. ''Thank you for the beautiful day. I had fun.''

''Me, too.'' He stared at her mouth, lowered his head and found her lips, not gently but urgently, as sound and taste and sensation joined exultantly.

A volcano of desire flowed hot through her veins, weighing her down. If she seemed a little desperate, so be it. She needed him. She was a little afraid for him. The combination churned in her stomach, pounded in her blood, stoked a fire in her heart. She wanted to curl up inside his skin and go with him. How could that be? How could she feel so much for him after knowing him for such a short time?

"I have to go," he said finally.

"You'll be careful?"

"Yes."

"Promise me one other thing?"

"What?"

How could she think when he looked at her like that? Like she was something important or…precious. "Promise you won't revert to being Scrooge because I'm not there to reinforce the joy of Christmas. Look around. See how pretty the world is right now."

"I'll try, sweetheart."

He left, the endearment sitting there like a gift with a big red bow.

Lyndsey let herself into the office at seven o'clock and was surprised to find several people still at their desks. Occasionally one or two investigators worked late in the office or came in after hours, but never this many, since they worked in the field the majority of the time. She counted five, most of whom she'd never met. She introduced herself as she made her way to her cubicle, glad to put faces to names.

She put away her sweater and purse, signed in and picked up Sam's Rubik's Cube. The note underneath indicated he'd taken two minutes and forty-six seconds to solve the last time. He must've had a lot on his mind, because he rarely took that long. She always felt guilty about being paid for the fun of jumbling the cube, so Sam solved that by officially writing the task into her job description. She played with the cube for several minutes, finishing up as she walked toward his office to set it on his desk.

"Lyndsey?" Arianna called out from her office as Lyndsey passed by.

She stopped in Arianna's doorway and smiled. "How're you?"

"Good, thanks. Would you come in for a minute? Shut the door, please."

Arianna Alvarado was a beautiful woman with long, dark hair, intense dark eyes, flawless skin, and a figure that made men stare and stumble. Like Nate and Sam, she was thirty-two. Lyndsey had seen her turn on the charm full force for a client once and envied her ability to be professional and feminine at the same time.

"Nate filled me in on the Marbury case," Arianna said, settling into her leather chair. "What'd you think?"

"I think I'd like to become a private investigator."

Arianna's rare speechlessness made Lyndsey smile. "I caught you off guard."

"Well, yes."

Lyndsey leaned forward. "I can't tell you how much I enjoyed the assignment. I was revved up most of the weekend. It was incredible."

"It was new."

"Totally. But I was good at it…I think." *If you don't count my saying too much to the client and almost getting us into big trouble.*

"So Nate said. However, there's a difference between following instructions and taking charge."

"You don't think I could do it?"

"Don't put words in my mouth." She toyed with a pen. "It seems like a fast decision."

"Yes and no. I got my degree in accounting because of the job stability. I needed to know I could support my sister and myself. But I don't have a passion for it. I've been dreading doing it full-time to the point of not applying for many positions yet. The investigative work grabbed me and didn't let go, even though things didn't go smoothly, maybe even because they didn't. And I figure that my accounting background can only help. I know ARC takes on fraud and embezzlement cases. I figure the salary's got to be competitive with entry-level CPA.''

"Do you know what's involved in becoming licensed?''

"I looked it up on the Internet. Three years of compensated experience in investigative work, two thousand hours each year, under the supervision of a licensed investigator.''

Arianna didn't respond immediately. She drummed her pen on her desk and stared at Lyndsey until she squirmed under the scrutiny.

"Have you talked to Nate about this?'' Arianna asked.

"No, and I don't want him to know.''

"Why not?''

"Because I don't want him to have influence either way. This is my career. My life. It has to be my decision.''

"He shopped for a Christmas tree with you today. And you—'' Arianna cocked her head. "You're glowing.''

Lyndsey hesitated. How much should she say? "We got close over the weekend. It's not surprising, is it? We spent all of our time together. It accelerated a...our friendship.''

"Are you sure you know what you're doing?''

"No,'' Lyndsey said honestly, excitement building at the changes ahead. "I'm going along for the ride because I've never ridden anywhere like it before. Everything is happening at once, so I'm not trusting my emotions completely, but I'm sure about one thing. I love this work. I want to keep doing it. I want to get good at it.''

"You're sure this career change has nothing to do with Nate? It can't have anything to do with him, Lyndsey. Nate's not—'' She stopped, as if she'd said too much.

Not someone I can count on? Lyndsey filled in the end of the sentence. Maybe Arianna was right. But maybe Lyndsey could change it. Maybe she needed to take that risk.

"I really want to do it, Arianna." Was that a good enough answer? Evasive enough? She couldn't answer it with total honesty because she didn't know for sure herself. "I haven't been this excited about anything in a long time."

"Okay." Arianna closed her eyes for a moment. "Okay. Here's what I'll do. I'll work with you for a couple of weeks. I'll give you case files to study and we'll discuss them. We'll test your instincts, because the right instincts are critical, especially for a woman, because people look for you to fail. Most people find more comfort with a man guarding them. You do know we do security as well as investigation?"

"Yes, but does every employee? I'm not sure that's something I'd be good at."

"Everyone here does. We have a reputation to maintain. Frankly, I would require you to train in martial arts. It not only fine-tunes your body but it sharpens your mind and speeds up your reaction time. Then would come weapons training. Are you still sure about this?"

Lyndsey nodded. To a nonexerciser it sounded like her definition of hell, but she could do it.

"You'll also be assigned some of the most boring work you could ever imagine, Lyndsey. Some days, some months, it's just tedious. It's reading page after page after page of information looking for one key word or number. It's boring and frustrating. Then there'll be situations where you'll need to extricate yourself from predicaments by using only your wits. It's long hours and hard work. Sometimes it's scary work. Occasionally it's potentially life threatening."

"I'm a hard worker."

"I don't doubt that. Do you have guts? Are you fearless? I'm not saying you couldn't do an adequate job. A lot of it would be easy for you, but I have a feeling you don't want to just do the job. You want to be extraordinary."

Hope fluttered inside Lyndsey. A new dream took flight. "I want to be like you."

Arianna laughed. "I'm flattered."

"I mean it."

"I see that you do." She studied Lyndsey for a few seconds. "All right. I don't have time to spare right now. We're swamped."

"I know."

"You want a job here at ARC, I imagine."

"I want to work for the best."

"I can't guarantee a position. That's a decision all three partners make, and in the past we've only hired experienced investigators, ones who already have their licenses so they can work independently."

"I plan to do this, no matter where I have to go or what I have to do. You'd be missing out on a great employee."

"I expect you're right," she said with a smile. "For now let's just concentrate on finding out if you have what it takes. We'll start right after Christmas."

"Thank you. Thank you so much." Lyndsey stood and resisted the temptation to hug her. She got to the doorway and turned around. "You won't tell Nate?"

"I won't tell Nate. Or Sam, for that matter. First things first."

"Thanks. Oh, and thank you for the airplane ticket. You all are so generous." She almost danced to Sam's office to leave the Rubik's Cube. Her life was coming together in ways she'd merely dreamed of.

The only problem was, if she went forward with her

plans and stayed on at ARC, how would that change her relationship with Nate? He knew she planned to leave. What if she told him she wanted to stay? Would that change everything?

And for better or worse?

Nine

"Lyndsey, we hired people to do that," Arianna said above the din of the company Christmas party, where thirty employees were consuming large quantities of food and drink.

"I can't help it. It's the old caterer in me." She eyed the food table. "I see a serving tray and I have to pass it around."

Arianna dragged her away. "You're a guest. Enjoy yourself."

"I have been. It's wonderful meeting everyone in person. What an eclectic bunch."

"That's a nice way of putting it. What are you doing tonight?"

Christmas Eve. It was an odd day for a company party but the only day when most people could attend. The mid-afternoon celebration would finish early enough for family time.

"Christmas Eve is full of traditions for me," Lyndsey said evasively, watching the door, hoping Nate would walk through it—and hoping he wouldn't. She'd worn a red dress just for him, to show him what he'd missed. To prove she wasn't pining.

Arianna leaned close. "He won't be here."

The words hit her like a punch in the stomach. "I thought the case was over."

"Did he tell you that?"

"I haven't spoken to him since he left." How could he kiss her like he did, and look at her like he had and then ignore her? "But I'm guessing he was guarding Alexis Wells. Mr. Marbury's assistant remembered seeing them together last year—that's how she knew who Nate was. I heard on the news this morning that the man who'd shot at Alexis was caught yesterday near her house on Maui, so he'll have to be extradited. Is that why Nate won't be here?"

"No, that's police business. Nate never attends the Christmas party."

Disappointment swamped Lyndsey, which really made her mad. She was already furious with him for not calling. Why was she investing so much energy in a man who liked to keep her dangling?

She took a sip of mulled cider, tried to keep her voice level. "Is he back in town?"

Arianna didn't answer.

"I shouldn't have put you on the spot," Lyndsey said, apologizing.

He'd been gone eleven days. Not one call.

Out of the corner of her eye she saw someone come into the room from the lobby. She clenched her glass, preparing to act as if she hadn't missed him for one moment.

But it wasn't Nate. It was an enormous Santa Claus carrying a bag over his shoulder. "Ho, ho, ho," he bellowed, assuming the classic Santa pose, legs spread and boots planted, a fist propped on his hip and his belly shaking.

"Oh, no," Lorraine from payroll cried. "Run, ladies. It's Grabby Claus."

"C'mere, you," Santa said, catching her and dragging her to a chair. "Sit on my lap, little girl, and tell Santa what you want for Christmas."

Lorraine laughed while fending off his wandering hands. "I want the same thing as last year and the year before, Santa."

"Me in your bed?" he roared.

"Have you met Abel?" Arianna asked Lyndsey.

"That's Abel Metzger? Oh, I should've known his voice. I didn't realize he was so big."

"He can plough through a crowd like no one else. Abel does this every year. Just go along with him. It'll save you from being hunted down and yanked into his lap."

"Do you?"

"Are you kidding? He gives out Godiva truffles."

Lyndsey laughed as he enticed one woman after another to his lap. Then he crooked his finger at Arianna, who moseyed over, settled onto his thigh and looped her arms around his neck. Lyndsey noticed he wasn't as hands on with Arianna as he was with the rest of the women. His voice wasn't so huge, either, and his cheeks pinkened like the real Santa.

Lyndsey decided she could learn a thing or two about female power by watching her boss.

"Have you been naughty or nice, little girl?"

"Naughty. Very naughty."

"Ho, ho, ho! That gets you two boxes of chocolates."

Arianna kissed his cheek. "Thank you, Santa. I'll try to be even naughtier next year."

He looked relieved when Arianna stepped away, then

he zeroed in on Lyndsey. "And who's this vixen in the red dress?" He patted his lap. "Your turn, little lady."

For someone who wasn't used to being the center of attention it was a big step, but she took a page out of Arianna's book and approached him as if she was the one in control.

"Have you been naughty or nice, little girl?"

"Nice." She toyed with his beard, twining a long white strand around her finger.

"Can't earn your candy that way. What would you like for Christmas?"

"A chance to be naughty." She batted her eyes as everyone laughed.

"Ho, ho, *ho*. Got anyone in mind?"

She was about to say *you,* just to see him blush, but a silence came over the room. She looked around and saw Nate. He looked ready to turn and run.

And he looked gorgeous in his gray suit and black T-shirt.

"Got room here for you, little boy," Santa said, patting his other leg. "Even got you a present. This one's lookin' to be naughty."

"I think our harassment premium just went up," Nate said with a sigh, but he took a seat, his legs bumping Lyndsey's.

"So you got my letter, Santa," Nate said, giving Lyndsey a wink.

She could barely hear over the blood pounding in her ears. *Don't you dare be sweet. I'm mad at you.*

From nowhere, Santa produced a sprig of mistletoe and held it aloft. "Someone's waiting for a kiss, little boy."

Nate's smile turned decidedly wicked. Lyndsey held her breath. Here? In front of everyone? She let her eyes ask the questions.

He winked again then he turned to Santa and planted a

big, smacking kiss on his lips. Everyone roared. Nate and Lyndsey were shoved off his lap. Nate caught her by the arm before she stumbled.

"Cooties," Santa exclaimed, sputtering.

"You've got enough alcohol in you to kill the plague," Nate said. He stroked Lyndsey's arm with his thumb before releasing her.

Santa stood and whipped off his fluffy beard and hair. "Well, somebody get me a whiskey, straight up, anyway. Just to be sure."

Nate turned to Lyndsey. "You okay?"

She nodded. He couldn't read her. He might as well have been a stranger the way she looked at him.

"Welcome back," she said simply. "Excuse me." She headed to the bar, leaving him standing there, which was the smart thing to do in front of their co-workers.

He kept her in sight as he made his way around the room, greeting everyone. She got into an animated discussion with Julie, the receptionist. After a while he ended up next to Sam.

"So," Sam said, not needing any other words to convey his surprise at Nate showing up for the party.

"Yeah," Nate replied, not needing any other words to convey his own surprise back. They'd known each other too long and well.

"Good job on grabbing the shooter," Sam said.

"It was satisfying taking him down."

"Joe Vicente, the LAPD detective, told Arianna and me about the guy's apartment."

"Sick," Nate said. They'd found every inch of wall space covered with Alexis's photos, which wasn't all that unusual. But they'd also found instruments of torture. He'd never intended to kill her but to incapacitate her and drag her off to his place. "Speaking of Vicente, you met him, right?"

"When he came to look at our files from last year's threat. He and Arianna danced around each other a bit."

"No way."

"Could've knocked me over."

"He's a cop. LAPD, at that." Nate spotted Arianna talking with several of the investigators. "I liked him. But we both know *that* would be impossible. She wouldn't go out with him. Ever."

Sam shrugged. "So, have you got plans for tonight?"

He took a sip of merlot and sought Lyndsey with his eyes. "Why? What're you doing?"

"My usual Christmas Eve tradition. Put my copy of *It's a Wonderful Life* in the video and get quietly drunk. Wanna join me?"

Nate eyed him. "Do women get your sense of humor?"

"Sometimes." Sam cocked his head toward Lyndsey. "She's gotten a little more withdrawn every day you've been gone and trying not to show it. Arianna will probably ream you out about it."

People started coming up then, thanking them for the party, saying their goodbyes. Designated drivers were given their charges, the caterers packed everything and left. After taking Nate into her office and giving him hell for whatever he was doing to Lyndsey, Arianna took off to spend the evening with her family.

Apparently Nate had to make amends with Lyndsey, although maybe it would be best to let their relationship die a natural death now, while she was mad at him.

He noticed that she kept herself busy. She took down Christmas decorations, which Arianna had told him Lyndsey had put up, complaining that the office lacked spirit.

"That didn't have to be done today," Sam told her as she closed up the box.

"A lot of people don't like to see the decorations when Christmas is over."

"Well, thank you. Merry Christmas, Lyndsey." He gave Nate a "be careful" look and wished him Merry Christmas, as well.

"I'll walk out with you, Sam," she said abruptly. "Let me get my purse."

Sam raised his brows at Nate.

"Would you mind waiting a minute, Lyndsey?" Nate asked.

"I'm kind of in a hurry."

To do what? "This won't take long."

Nate waited for the front door to close behind Sam. She didn't move, didn't look at him, but stood there, her box of decorations in her arms, her purse over her shoulder.

"You're mad at me."

Her smile was brittle. "You have to care in order to be mad at someone. I stopped caring, oh, about five days ago."

"Why?"

"Why do you think?"

"I don't know." Not for sure, he added to himself. He could guess.

"Because you don't care about *me*," she said, her eyes cool, her mouth hard. "It's okay. Sometimes I'm a little slow when it comes to men. Must be in the genes. Can I go now?"

"I do care about you."

"You have a funny way of showing it."

She was right about that. He'd intentionally not called her, not only because of the job but because every time he was with her, he stopped following his own rules, like no serious relationships, no heartache, and no scenes.

Especially no scenes. He argued, debated, with Arianna but he hadn't argued with another woman for as long as he could remember. He didn't invest that much emotion, because he didn't want it in return. He'd learned from his mistakes.

He and Lyndsey were headed for a scene, and he didn't know how to stop it except to walk out. He couldn't do that.

"You're mad because I didn't call?" he asked, already knowing the answer.

She dropped the box on her desk and faced him, hands on hips. "Are you really that dense?"

"I don't want to make assumptions."

Her color was high. In heels she was several inches taller, which felt strange to him. She seemed to match his height.

"Yet you assumed I wouldn't expect a call from you?" she asked.

"I was working a hard case."

"In eleven days you never had a minute to say hi? Nate, you could've left me a message on my answering machine and I would've been as happy as a cat rolling in catnip. You said you would call." Her voice got softer and softer. "You promised."

"Do you think I didn't think about you?" he asked, heating up. *Don't you cry.* "I'm here, aren't I? I'm sure you heard I never come to the Christmas party. I tried to stay away. I couldn't."

"So now you're mad at *me* because I make you do things you don't want to do?" She scooped up the box again and started to leave.

He grabbed it and tossed it down. "Now who's making assumptions? Do you always walk out in the middle of a fight?"

"It's better to go to bed angry than to say something you'll regret or can't take back," she singsonged, parroting his own words at the beach house.

"I thought it would make you happy knowing that you

tempt me that much. That I have no willpower when it comes to you."

"Not when it makes you mad. Why should that make me happy?" She shook her head. "I'm leaving. You're way too…too—"

"Screwed up?" *Tell me something I don't know.*

"No." She looked at him oddly. "Is that what you think about yourself?"

"I missed you. There. Does that make you happy?"

His blood was singing. He loved that she kept giving him hell. How idiotic was that?

She walked away.

"Lyndsey." He couldn't get any more words out.

She turned. "I don't want to hurt you, Nate."

"Then don't go."

After what seemed like an hour she let her purse fall to the floor as she walked toward him, something unidentifiable in her eyes. She didn't stop but went right into his arms and kissed him. And kissed him. And kissed him some more. Nothing had tasted so good, so warm, so right as she did. Her lips were soft and busy. Her tongue as demanding as his. And all those throaty little sounds…

He maneuvered his hands between their bodies and unfastened the row of buttons down her dress, as he'd been aching to ever since he walked into the party. He slipped his hands under the soft fabric and molded her rib cage, moving her backward into her cubicle until she sat on the edge of her desk. Her eyes spoke volumes, but mostly they said yes.

He separated the fabric, revealing her bra underneath, and a lot of skin.

"You wore the red."

"I can be very obedient."

"When you want to be?"

She nodded. "I missed you so much."

The words burned him. Her eyes never leaving his face, she pulled his shirt free and shoved it up. Her hands, hot and curious, moved over his chest, his abdomen, and beyond, tracing his hard flesh with her fingertips.

He couldn't talk. It scared him, these feelings. Everything was going so fast. The physical chemistry was strong. Overwhelming. His head and heart were doing battle about who should be in charge, and now a more insistent part of his body joined the debate. There was no contest. He wanted her. Now. He dragged his tongue between her breasts, along the lace edge of fabric. Her fragrance, warm and spicy, assaulted him. He suckled her through the lace, her nipples hard and tempting. He couldn't wait to get her naked and writhing under him. He wanted to see her, all of her. Touch her. Explore her. Bury himself in her.

Find home in her.

He raised his head and kissed her again, all the while bunching her skirt above her hips, stepping between her legs, opening her wide. He sought her with his hand, discovered soft, silky panties that he slipped his fingers under, finding incredible heat and inviting dampness. She said his name—

The phone rang.

They jumped. As it continued to ring they stared at each other, breathing hard.

He swore. "We can't do this," he said, dragging his hands through his hair. She was already fumbling with her buttons. Her cheeks were almost as red as her dress.

"Let's—"

"Stop," she said, low and harsh. "Just stop. No one's forcing you."

She ran out.

He should've gone after her. She'd misunderstood. But maybe it was for the best.

Are you out of your mind? his sensible self screamed. Go after her.

He was too late. He got to the parking lot in time to see her drive off. He watched until the taillights of her car disappeared.

She hadn't backed out of her space but had driven straight through the one in front of her.

She'd broken a rule.

Because of him.

Ten

Barefoot, Lyndsey paced her living room. Her frustration and pent-up energy needed an outlet, and pacing was the only thing she could do inside her house, short of throwing or punching things. But then she'd just have to clean up something and replace it. And feel like an idiot.

He wasn't worth it. He was not worth all this grief. She'd been just fine before he came along and she would be fine again. She would show him.

Her doorbell rang. She picked up a bag she'd set on the sofa and opened the door. She tried to smile.

It wasn't who she expected, however.

"Don't you ask who it is before you open the door?" Nate asked, frowning.

"Not that it's any of your business, but I was expecting someone."

"Yo, Lynnie." Her nineteen-year-old neighbor, Benito Gonzales, came up the walk. His timing was perfect. He walked like he owned the world, dressed like a thug, and had been Jess's unpaid guardian through high school. Lyndsey adored him.

"Smokin' dress," he said, giving her the once-over.

She felt Nate's attention spike. "Thank you," she said, then introduced the men.

"Yo, man," Ben said, giving Nate some kind of secret handshake. Lyndsey gave him credit. He didn't fumble.

She held out the bag to Ben. "Merry Christmas."

He patted his stomach. "I'd already packed away those others you brought over. Thanks."

"You're welcome."

"Later," he said, waving a hand as he sauntered away.

"Those were your cookies," she said to Nate.

"Mine?"

"That's right. I baked them for you." She crossed her arms. "Why are you here?"

"You misunderstood," he said, looking serious and sincere. "Back at the office, when I said we couldn't. I meant that we couldn't do it there. Too many people have keys. What if someone walked in?"

"So what do you want now?"

"For you to accept my apology."

"Is that all?"

He nodded.

"Okay." She started to shut the door.

"No." He blocked it with his arm. "No, that's not all."

The ice around her heart began to melt. She could see how hard it was for him, telling her how he felt. This was not a man often in touch with his emotions.

He lifted his head and looked into her eyes. "I want to make love with you. I want to sleep beside you. I want to spend Christmas with you."

"Okay." She barely got the word out.

"Okay?"

She nodded, stepped back and held the door for him. He swept her into his arms, pushed the door shut with his foot.

"I'm sorry I hurt you," he said.

She tightened her hold on him until the urge to cry went away.

"You gave away my cookies," he said, lightening the moment.

"Only two dozen. I baked you ten."

"Ten dozen?"

"I packed them in freezer bags so you could keep them on hand for whenever you wanted them."

"You think they'd last long enough that I'd need to freeze 'em?"

He seemed to be stalling. She wondered if he was nervous. It seemed amazing that he would be, and even more amazing that she wasn't. Nothing had ever felt so right as this.

He won't stay around. Lyndsey ignored the caution calling out in her head, even though the truth stung. She wanted to sleep with him. He would probably break her heart, but she was going to risk it for the chance to be with him, to make memories, to feel cherished.

"I'd offer you a tour of the house but you've already been here," she said.

"I didn't see your bedroom."

Finally. She smiled before she lifted her head from where it was tucked against his neck. "Follow me."

He didn't budge. "I have to go to the car first."

"Why?"

He half smiled.

"Oh." Protection. "I've got some." At his raised brows, she rushed on. "Well, I was hopeful. I mean, unless you have to have your own. Some super jumbo size or...something...."

He looked as though he was trying not to laugh, then he held her hand as they walked to her room. She tried to see it as he might. An antique sleigh bed and highboy dresser that had belonged to her grandmother. Her mother's amazing art on the walls. A quilt of bold colors, which she tossed back, revealing white sheets. She lit a candle beside the bed and turned to him.

"Now, where did we leave off?" she asked.

"You were sighing," he said, taking a step closer.

"Was I?"

"Or maybe moaning." Closer still.

"Probably."

He undid the top button of her dress. Another. One more.

"What were you doing?" she asked.

"I was believing in heaven."

She waited for the last button to be undone. "You're shaking," she said in wonder.

"You should see what I'm seeing. Feel what I'm feeling."

He couldn't have paid her a higher compliment. She didn't feel the least bit shy or hesitant with him. This was right. Meant to be. Destined. He made her feel beautiful.

Soon her dress fell to the floor. He ran his fingers along her collarbones, over her shoulders, down her back. He unhooked her bra and pulled it away, tossing it aside, leaving her only in her red panties.

"Beautiful," he murmured, testing the weight of her breasts and the shape of her nipples. He drew one into his mouth for what seemed like forever, then the other even longer, until her knees started to buckle.

Still it was going too fast, she thought. Slow down. Savor. Remember.

He knelt in front of her as she stepped out of the dress then threaded her fingers through his hair, drawing him closer. His mouth touched her abdomen. He dragged the tip of his tongue down until he reached fabric, then he molded his hands over her rear and tugged her panties down and off. He didn't lift his head but cupped her from below, his thumbs stroking, opening, separating, arousing her beyond anything she'd experienced. Slowly, tenderly, he put his lips to her, touched her with his tongue.

"Now *you're* shaking," he murmured, his breath blowing hot against her. "Your bracelets sound like sleigh bells."

She made a sound she couldn't believe came from her. He nudged her until she landed on the bed. "Lie down."

"No."

"This is no time to be stubborn, Stubborn."

"I want it to be together." She reached for his belt, unzipped his pants, pushed them down. He got rid of them, along with his shoes and socks. She pulled his shirt over his head, learned the contours of his chest with her hands and her mouth, felt his muscles twitch. Finally she pulled off his boxer briefs and admired him.

"You're beautiful, too," she said softly, hardly able to believe he was hers. He was such an ideal, all broad shoulders and muscular chest and flat abdomen. Long, sturdy legs, strong arms. And that most masculine part of him, bold and powerful. She put her mouth to him as he had to her, tenderly, her tongue exploring gently.

He grabbed her head. "If you want this to be together, you need to stop doing that. God, Lyndsey. You're driving me crazy."

She felt strong and brave. She leaned across him, opened her nightstand and pulled out a condom, passing it to him.

For all that he normally talked a blue streak, it was strange that he was so quiet now as he eased her onto the mattress. But what he didn't say with words he said with his eyes and his hands and body. He slid the bracelets off her wrist one by one and set them aside. His kisses started soft, intensified, then overwhelmed. She'd never known that kind of passion, as if he'd been waiting for her for all his life. She knew she'd been waiting for *him*.

She let her mind go blank so that only this experience would fill it, nothing else. She welcomed him into her heart and her body eagerly, willingly, lovingly. He filled her, stretched her, took her. There was no time to go slowly, no time to build. He'd barely joined with her when they dug their fingers into each other, pressed closer, moved faster and found paradise in a quick, hard climb that went beyond the summit, bursting through the clouds. The sensation lasted seconds, minutes, hours. A slow return to earth, then collapse.

She refused to let him move off her but held him tight, tears threatening because it was so beautiful. She didn't dare cry—it had been so long since she had that she would probably have a complete meltdown. More important, he hated tears.

Finally he rolled onto his side, taking her with him. "I'm too heavy for you," he said, drawing back enough to look at her, brushing her hair away from her face.

I love you. She didn't say the words out loud but heard them in her heart. Even though they were whispered, they flooded her with hope and despair. It was too soon. She was superstitious. She'd heard the best way to lose a man was to tell him you loved him before he was ready to hear it. She had no intention of making that mistake.

So for now she would hide her feelings, a big task for a woman who apparently had an honest face.

"Are you hungry?" she asked.

"You are such a hostess." He smiled at her. "I had plenty at the office, but thank you. Are you cold? We can pull the sheet up."

She shook her head. She was a little chilled, but she

wanted to lie naked with him, to look at him, to have him look at her. *He thinks I'm beautiful.* She drew circles on his chest leisurely, still hardly able to believe he was there. With her. He'd made love with her.

He rolled away from her. "I'll be right back."

She heard water run in the bathroom, then she had the pleasure of watching him walk back into the room and get back into bed. It was only six-thirty. They had the whole night ahead of them.

At some point they moved from the bedroom to the living room. Lyndsey wore her robe. Nate had on sweatpants and a T-shirt he'd gotten from a gym bag he always kept in his car. The tree lights were on, Christmas songs played low in the background. He had his head in her lap enjoying a scalp massage and decided he would be hardpressed to remember a better night in his life.

"Would you prefer to open your Christmas present tonight or tomorrow?" Lyndsey asked.

"You didn't have to get me a present just because I got you one."

Her fingers stopped moving. "I—I didn't.... You got me a present?"

He opened his eyes and looked up at her, seeing that she was serious. "You don't know?"

"Know what?"

He sat up. "Did you think those tires appeared by magic?"

"Tires?"

"You didn't even notice?" He started to laugh. The joke was on him. He held out his hand. "Come on."

"Where?"

"To your garage."

She grabbed the lapels of her robe and tugged them closer. "I can't go out there in my robe. With you."

"Ah, the scandalous Ms. McCord. I'm sure you've given them plenty of fuel for the neighborhood gossip fire through the years. What's one more log on the fire?" he teased, pulling her out the front door.

"Well, old Mrs. Brubaker across the street will be more thrilled than scandalized. And Benito's been telling me for a long time there was nothing wrong with me that some hot sex wouldn't cure."

"Was he offering to play doctor?" He ignored the unfamiliar jab to his gut.

"No, he keeps trying to set me up with his cousin. Why, Nate. Are you jealous?"

"Not in my nature." *Usually.* He opened her garage door and pulled on the overhead light.

She crouched down, ran her hand over one tire. "It has tread." She looked up at him. "I knew something was different. I noticed it, night before last? But it was raining, so I chalked it up to that. I hadn't left the house during the day. You know, I leave for work in the dark and come home in the dark. But I should've seen them today. It was daylight. I didn't notice."

He waited for her to say she couldn't accept the gift. That it was too much. That she could take care of herself just fine, thank you very much.

"When I heard rain was forecast, I got worried," he said in his defense, beating her to it. "I didn't want you out on the road with bald tires."

She stood up, her eyes glistening suspiciously.

"Somebody needs to take care of you, Stubborn." He took a step toward her. "It's okay just to say thank-you."

She came into his arms. "Thank you."

"You're welcome." He tucked her closer.

"How did you manage it?"

"While you were working. The mechanic was supposed to park his van so that you couldn't see your car if you happened to look out the window.'' He paused. ''A man would've noticed them that night, you know.''

''I'm a woman.'' She fluttered her lashes.

''I never would've guessed.'' Hand in hand they returned to the house. ''I figured you'd fight me about it.''

''One fight a night is all I can handle.'' She lifted a large box from under the tree and gave it to him without comment.

He was never comfortable opening presents. What did you say? How did you act? He rarely gave traditional gifts, either, not wanting to watch people open them. When he gave a gift, it was offered unwrapped and casually.

He opened the box to find not one item but an assortment.

''Since you couldn't get to Australia, I brought it to you,'' she said, looking pleased with herself.

There were videotapes on the country, a piece of coral, a baggie of sand, sunscreen, a stuffed kangaroo, a bottle of Australian wine, and a bikini bottom. He dangled it from one finger. ''I hope this hot pink number is yours and not something I'm supposed to wear.''

She laughed. ''I heard there are topless beaches there. Just thought I'd give you a mental image.''

He pictured her in it. ''My house is a block from the beach. Would you like to go tomorrow? Wear this? With the top.''

''It's December. Not exactly bikini weather.''

''It's supposed to reach seventy-two tomorrow.'' *I need to see you wearing it.*

''That hot, huh?''

''It'll be nice in the sun.''

She sort of shrugged, but he couldn't tell whether she was saying yes or no.

''What's wrong?'' he asked.

''Nothing.''

He studied her. "Yes, there is. Tell me."

"It's just…being in a bikini."

"Yeah?"

"My skin is so white. And there's—" she fluttered her hands "—you know. My body."

He didn't know what to make of her. "What's wrong with your body?"

"Oh, never mind."

It struck him then that she was really uncomfortable. How could that be? "I've seen you naked," he said softly. "I like you naked." Which was an understatement. She had curves, generous but firm. Mouthwatering. There was nothing about her he would change.

The phone rang. Nate figured out from the conversation it was her sister calling to say Merry Christmas. Lyndsey's face lit up. Nate could hug Jess for calling Lyndsey tonight. He had a picture of her little sister in his mind, cute—he'd seen her photographs—a little selfish and self-centered. Typical eighteen-year-old discovering independence. But she needed to remember Lyndsey and how important Christmas was to her. So he was glad she called.

He wandered over to the Christmas tree while they talked. When they'd decorated it, he purposely hadn't paid much attention to the ornaments. Now he studied them, examining each of the homemade objects, some with their names on them, others with photos. He and his brother had made some ornaments as children, but that had stopped when his mother had her breakdown. His father had thrown out their box of decorations when they moved to California.

Christmas in the Caldwell household was only a slightly different day from the rest of the year. There were a few presents but no tree. A wreath on the front door so that the world would think they celebrated, but no decorations inside. He'd hated it. Hated pretending to be happy with the new socks and underwear and one game. He'd desperately wanted a bicycle one year and had badgered his father for months. He got one—secondhand and rusty. He was too embarrassed to ride it. His father was furious and hauled it to the dump without saying a word.

Nate never had learned to ride a bike.

Then when he'd married, he thought it would be different. He and his wife could start their own traditions. What a joke.

He had to get out of the house, let the thoughts blow away. "I'll be back in a few minutes," he mouthed to Lyndsey, then he went out the front door.

Lyndsey had been watching him while she talked to Jess. There'd been such sadness in his face as he'd looked at her ornaments. Beyond the fact his mother was taken away from him at Christmas, what else haunted him? If she'd never come home, Lyndsey could understand the bad memories he associated with the holiday, but his mother had spent more years with him.

"Are you alone for Christmas?" Jess asked over the phone.

"No. I'm with a friend."

"A male friend?"

"As a matter-of-fact."

"Tell me about him."

How could she describe him? "He's tall, blond and handsome. He's thoughtful and generous." *He puts my satisfaction over his own. His kisses make me dizzy.* "His name is Nate."

"Are you madly in love? You are. I hear it in your voice."

"I'm enjoying his company. Are *you* madly in love?"

"I'm enjoying his company," Jess teased. "And he's telling me I have to get off the phone so he can call his parents. I love you, Lynnie. Merry Christmas."

"Merry Christmas, Jess." A myriad of emotions bombarded Lyndsey when she hung up. Unwavering love for her sister, worry that she would get hurt by this boy, and pleasure that Jess seemed to be maturing and settling down.

Then there were her feelings for Nate. Secret love for him, worry that she would get hurt, and pleasure that her life seemed to be changing in such wonderful ways.

She tucked her legs under her and nestled into the sofa, waiting for Nate to return. When he came through the door, she smiled at him in welcome. He stopped, stared, then stuck his hands in his pockets and moved to the tree.

He touched a bread-dough ornament she'd made in third grade, her school picture glued to it. She always thought she looked like a poodle in that picture, with her wild, kinky hair.

"You were cute," he said.

He seemed exceptionally calm yet at the same time tense. "I was geeky," she said.

"But cute geeky. You should've seen me at that age."

"I can't picture you geeky."

"Oh, I wasn't. I was adorable. Like I said, you should've seen me." He grinned, but it didn't seem real.

What seemed real was when he came up to her, cupped her face and kissed her slowly. Sweetly. His nimble fingers untied her robe and pushed the fabric aside. His clever mouth found new ways to excite her. Within moments they were naked. She urged him down onto the sofa.

"Not here," he said. "In the bedroom. I want lots of room."

For what? she wondered.

Who cares?

He knelt beside the bed and pulled her legs over his shoulders, then used his mouth to make love to her thoroughly, exquisitely, selflessly. He knew where to touch, how to tease, when to torment by pulling back then starting over. She shook, she moaned, she begged. He pressed on, taking her over the top until she thought she would cry out from the intensity, then he rose up and plunged into her until she did.

They fell asleep in each other's arms, welcomed the morning with a slow, leisurely joining, then spent every minute of the next two days together. His house wasn't large but was in a prime location, being a block from the Santa Monica beach. His decorating style was simple. He didn't have much but wasn't home enough to care, he told her. When he had the time he would decorate. Until then, the basics would have to do.

The last evening they sat on his deck drinking wine and eating appetizers she'd thrown together. They were going out to dinner at some point but wanted to watch the sunset first.

"Do you ever take this view for granted?" she asked, settling her shoulders into the comfortable deck chair.

"Never."

Lyndsey hated for the day to end. Tomorrow it was back to work, back to real life. Nate was headed to San Francisco for a few days to do advance security for the arrival of an important politician from Asia. At least this time he would call her. She wondered how he would feel about Christmas from now on. Had his attitude changed?

She took a sip of merlot, savored it a moment, then turned her head to look at him. His profile was strong, like the rest of him. He must have felt her gaze on him because he turned, too, and raised his brows in question.

"Why do you hate Christmas so much?" she asked.

He looked away, took a swallow of wine then another. He was debating with himself, she decided, on what he would say. The truth, she wanted to shout at him. Just tell me the truth.

"On Christmas the year I was twenty-one," he said finally, "I found out my wife was cheating on me."

Eleven

Nate didn't watch her reaction, but he felt it—shock, and maybe even hurt that he'd waited this long to tell her he'd been married. He could use that old dodge that she hadn't asked, but he respected her too much for that. He'd purposely avoided talking about it.

"Your wife," she repeated calmly.

And she thought Arianna was cool under fire? Lyndsey should take a good look at herself. "My ex-wife. Beth."

"Would you like to talk about it?"

"Do you really want to hear it?"

"Of course I do."

He looked into his almost empty glass, swirling what was left. "There's not a lot to tell. We met when I was visiting my dad while I was on leave. I was nineteen and lonely. She lived up the street. We were both out jogging, she flirted, I responded. I was shy back then, especially with girls."

"I can't imagine that."

He wondered what she was thinking. Outwardly she was so cool. "Beth was a year older. She was my first sexual experience…but I wasn't hers. When my leave was up we stayed in contact. She pursued it more than I did at first, but I fell passionately in love." *I was too young and stupid to know it wasn't real.* "A few months later I found out I was being sent overseas as the Gulf War was heating up. I flew home at Christmas, married her, then went to war. I thought she was everything I ever wanted—and she probably was at the time. My father tried to talk me out of it. He backed down when he saw I would've gone to Las Vegas if I'd had to."

"It's hard to change a teenager's mind."

"Yeah. Long story short, I didn't get to come home again for a year. Christmas again. I was going to surprise her. I let my dad in on the plan, and he picked me up at the airport. On the way to our apartment he gave me an envelope. Didn't say a word. Inside were pictures of Beth, not just with one man, but several."

"At the same time?"

He was grateful for the momentary distraction of her reaction. "No."

"Your father took these pictures?"

"He hired a P.I."

"Not Charlie!"

"No. Some sleazy jerk who didn't mind getting up close and personal."

"I'm so sorry."

"Yeah, well, we learn our cruelest lessons the hard way, don't we? Crazy thing was, at first I was mad at my father."

"Shooting the messenger."

He nodded. "She wasn't who I thought she was." She'd

changed from sweet, adoring girl to provocative woman in a year. "I didn't want to believe she'd done it, despite the proof, but she didn't even try to lie. I was gone, she said. She had needs." The same complaints he'd gotten since then from women—he was gone too much. He was unavailable emotionally. He never took their relationship seriously. All of it true. Nothing had changed, nor would it, so he'd adapted. Keep it light. Keep it simple. Keep it short-term. No one gets hurt that way.

"And that's why I hate Christmas…and handling divorce cases, which I've seen far too many of," he said, then looked at her. "So, any ex-husband I should know about?"

She got out of her chair and settled herself on his lap, resting her head against his. "No."

He put his arms around her. He knew her body well now, every glorious curve, every freckle. He knew what heated her up in a hurry, what dragged out her climax, and that she was generous and eager to please.

And honest.

He'd effectively avoided women like her for so long, afraid of repeating the same mistake as he made with his ex-wife, but Lyndsey brought something to his life he hadn't known was missing. He couldn't put it into words. He only knew it existed.

Time to stop thinking about it. "Are you ready to go to dinner?" he asked.

"I'm hungry." She kissed his temple. "For you."

"I would've thought your appetite would be well satisfied by now."

"Is yours?"

"No, but—"

She pressed her lips to his, stopping his words. "What

makes me different? Plus, you're leaving tomorrow. I want to give you something to remember me by.''

Like there was any chance he'd forget. But his curiosity was piqued by the sexy promise in her voice. ''What do you have in mind?''

She whispered in his ear.

He found it fascinating that she was daring enough to propose what she had but couldn't say the words aloud. She was a remarkable mix of innocent and provocative, traditional and modern, courageous and cautious.

He whispered something back, just to see her blush.

Which she did, right before she proved she was a woman of her word.

''I signed up for tae kwon do lessons,'' Lyndsey told Arianna the next evening in the office. ''My first class is tomorrow.'' She'd figured out a way to pay for the lessons. Now she just had to make it happen.

''You're really serious.''

''Completely.''

''And it's because it's what you want. It has nothing to do with Nate.''

''If it weren't for Nate I probably wouldn't have even thought of it, but I think I'll be good at it. I've watched him in action. I've learned from you already. I know there's a reason I have to put in six thousand hours over the next three years—to get experience so that I don't make mistakes like I did on the Marbury case. I'll learn. I don't make the same mistake twice.''

Arianna leaned back in her chair. ''I've been thinking about you a lot. Your innocent look could either get you in trouble or get you answers to questions that no one else is able to.'' She turned her chair around and grabbed a small stack of files. ''Here's your homework. Read them thoroughly. Come in at six tomorrow night and we'll talk about them.''

''I can take them home with me?''

''Just don't lose them.''

''Of course not.'' Lyndsey tried not to be effusive in her gratitude.

''Don't thank me yet. A piece of advice, though?''

''Anything.''

''You might arrange for a massage after your tae kwon do lesson.''

''That bad?''

''Take my word for it.''

Lyndsey already ached from all the physical activity over the past few days. ''Thanks.'' She got up to leave.

''How was your Christmas?'' Arianna asked, her voice pointedly casual.

''Very nice. How was yours?''

Arianna smiled. ''You're already learning. Turning the tables is a good technique. Except I can tell by looking at you that it was more than nice. You carry yourself differently.''

''I do?''

''Straighter. Taller. There's an air of confidence about you that wasn't there. And I don't think I've ever seen you undo more than one button on your blouse before.''

She'd been daring enough to undo a second button. She really didn't think anyone would notice. After Nate dropped her off at her house on his way to the airport early that morning, she searched her closet, looking for ways to jazz up her wardrobe without spending any money. She'd found one solution—wear what she already owned... differently. Mix different combinations. Unfasten an extra button, show off a little more skin, add a necklace.

With the purchase of a couple of items, she could change her look quite a bit.

She didn't want to blend with the background any longer.

"You look happy," Arianna said.

"Which worries you."

"I won't beat it into the ground. You know the risks."

A few days ago Lyndsey had convinced herself that she didn't care if she got hurt. It was worth the risk, knowing that if she didn't let herself enjoy him, she would regret it for the rest of her life. Every girl had fairy-tale dreams. How often did they come true? Rarely, she was sure. But never, if she didn't try.

"I'm only worried about the repercussions here," Arianna continued. "I don't know if we could keep you. Our loyalty has to be to Nate, as the partner. He, Sam and I have worked too hard to stand by and watch our business falter."

"If it comes to that, I'll resign." She tried to sound businesslike but her stomach churned.

Arianna hesitated. "I could recommend you to another P.I....."

It finally struck Lyndsey that Arianna honestly believed Nate could not make a commitment. Ever. She knew him better than Lyndsey did. As well she should.

Lyndsey headed for the door, not wanting to hear anything else. "That would be great. I don't foresee any problems, though."

When Nate didn't call her the next day, she began to doubt.

The phone jerked Lyndsey out of a sound sleep.

"Did I wake you?" Nate asked.

Lyndsey clenched the telephone receiver, shoved her

hair from her eyes and squinted at her bedside clock. "Heck, no. I was doing naked aerobics."

He laughed quietly. "Thanks. I needed that visual to get me through the next fifteen minutes."

She pushed herself onto one elbow and leaned toward her bedside clock. Four o'clock. She blinked, shook her head and looked again. Still four o'clock.

He'd been gone since Wednesday. Now it was Saturday, New Year's Eve. He'd called her at work Thursday night for a short conversation, but that was all.

Oh, quit being selfish, she thought. This isn't high school. Welcome to your first adult relationship. Think about him, how tired he must be. "Have you slept tonight?" she asked sympathetically.

"I'm going to grab a couple hours now. Looks like I'll be flying home this afternoon. Alexis Wells invited us to a party tonight. Would you like to go?"

She sat straight up. The fact he issued the invitation so casually said a lot. He was used to stuff that like. Movie stars, powerful politicians. They were just clients to him. People.

And you'll get used to them, too. The idea made her smile in disbelief. What a turnaround her life had made in a few weeks.

"Are you there?" he asked.

"I'm thinking." There was nothing in her closet worthy of such an event. Plus, while the idea of attending thrilled her, the reality was she wasn't ready for such a leap. "Do you want to go?" she asked.

He yawned. "Doesn't matter. It's up to you."

"You wouldn't think less of me if I say no?"

"I'd think more of you. I'd rather spend the evening just with you, but I didn't want to deny you the chance to rub elbows."

Like she would have something to say to the actress and her friends? "That's not something I need. It would be fun to tell Jess, but that's all."

"Another time, then. How about dinner and dancing instead? I know a great little club. No frills. Just incredible steaks and good music. It'll be jammed, but it should be fun."

A date. A real date. And a guaranteed kiss at midnight to welcome the new year. "It sounds fabulous."

"I'll pick you up around eight. I'm sorry I had to wake you. It really was my only opportunity to call if I was going to give you any notice for tonight."

You can call me anytime, day or night. I'll always want to talk to you. She was proud of herself for not saying the words out loud, for protecting herself a little.

"I can't wait to see you," she said.

There was a long pause, then he said good-night. She snuggled under the quilt, tucked it against her chin. Sleep was impossible. Finally she sat up against the headboard, put on her glasses and pulled the phone into her lap. She calculated the time in New York. Seven-fifteen. A little early but what the heck.

She heard the phone being picked up, then the receiver bounced against something, then silence, then, "H'lo." Husky voice. Irritated tone.

"Happy New Year's Eve, Jess."

"Jeez, Lynnie." She groaned. "It's, like, the dead of night."

"You'll never guess what just happened."

"This better be good."

"I got invited to a party at Alexis Wells's house."

Long pause. "*The* Alexis Wells?"

"*The.*"

Jess screamed. Lyndsey screamed back.

"Ohmigod. Ohmigod. Tell me everything," Jess said, apparently wide-awake.

Lyndsey did.

"You said no? *You said no?* Are you crazy?"

"Maybe. Probably."

"You like this guy a lot, don't you?" Jess's voice softened.

"Yeah."

"He'd better treat you right."

"He got me invited to an Oscar-winning actress's house for New Year's Eve, didn't he?"

"I mean you. Lynnie, the person. You. He better treat you right."

Lyndsey's eyes stung. She loved her sister so much. "I have something else to tell you."

"I can tell I'm not gonna like this."

"You have to get a job, Jess." Silence. Lyndsey forged on. "I need some money to do some things that are important to me. I went on to your university Web site. There are on-campus jobs you're qualified for. If you work ten hours a week, you'll make what I send you in allowance. If you work fifteen, you'll have extra."

"But—"

"No buts. You have to do this. It's important for both of us. I'm cutting you off the second week of the spring semester, so you'd better get your act in gear."

"I don't have any experience."

"You'll get some. You'll do fine, Jess. You meet people well. Once they interview you, you'll have your choice of jobs."

"So you're saying this is for my own good."

"I know you don't think so, but it is."

"I finally got a boyfriend. I won't have time for him."

Lyndsey understood that feeling completely. "Budget

your time. And put your education first. Show Mom you can do it. Make her proud.''

''Like Mom would know.''

''She knows.''

Lyndsey hung up a couple of minutes later. An iron anvil fell off her chest. After all these years of worrying about Jess, mothering her, guiding her, Lyndsey would put herself first now and then. Okay, so she'd used the make-Mom-proud card.

Desperate times called for desperate measures.

Twelve

———

Nate couldn't remember bringing a woman flowers before. He'd ordered them occasionally and had them delivered, but he hadn't personally brought a bouquet until now. He'd kept the florist shop open an extra fifteen minutes while he decided what suited Lyndsey, then tipped the clerk for her inconvenience, wiping the irritation off her face fast.

He'd already forgotten the name of the flower. They looked a little like daisies except their blooms were bigger and deep red-orange in color, a wild look that appealed to him and reminded him of her.

She opened her front door as he got out of his car. God, she was beautiful. He shut the car door, then hesitated. She looked…different. She was wearing a plain black dress, but there was nothing simple about it. It was cut low on top and the skirt landed several inches above her knees. It hugged her curves in a way that made his mouth go dry.

As if she couldn't wait for him another second she stepped onto her porch, then came up the walkway to meet him. Her blinding smile got bigger, brighter. Her eyes—

She wasn't wearing her glasses.

"Hi," she said softly, almost shyly, as she slipped her arms around his neck.

Her body felt amazing. "If I kiss you like I want to, old Mrs. Brubaker will definitely be thrilled."

Her eyes sparkled. "Then it's your duty to the neighborhood, at least."

He brushed her lips with his until hers parted.

"I missed you," she whispered against his mouth, her breath soft and warm.

He pulled her closer, deepened the kiss, felt her shudder. She moved her hips against his.

"So are you packin', Mr. P.I., or are you just happy to see me?"

A whistle pierced the night. "Yo, Lynnie!"

They turned their heads to see Benito saunter by.

"You been cured?" he called out.

"Definitely."

"Okay." He fixed his gaze on Nate. "That's a special lady."

Nate heard the threat in his voice. "Yes, she is," he said in return.

"Okay. Don't do nothin' I wouldn't do." He laughed and kept walking.

Nate handed Lyndsey the flowers. She buried her face in them. He didn't think they had much of a scent, but she sniffed them and smiled her thanks.

He followed her to the house and into the kitchen to find a vase for the flowers. "I almost didn't recognize you," he said, enjoying watching her move around the kitchen. Her legs seemed exceptionally long with the short skirt and high heels. "Did something happen to your glasses?"

"I got contacts."

"Why?"

"It was time," she said enigmatically. "You're the one who suggested it."

"I did?" Why would he do that? He loved her funny little glasses. He loved her in buttoned-up clothes, too. She was sexy as hell. Not that she wasn't now—hell, now he wanted to toss her on the dining-room table and make a feast of her—but it was a different kind of sexy from how she was before. The change made her seem different, not the Lyndsey he knew.

"The lenses are new," she said, "so I can't wear them the whole night, but for now I will." She stood back to study her arrangement. "The flowers are beautiful, Nate. Thank you so much." She kissed him as she passed by, carrying the flowers into the living room, empty now of Christmas decorations. She set the vase on the coffee table. "I told Jess I was cutting off her allowance when the semester starts and that she has to get a job."

Nate tried not to show how pleased that news made him. "How'd she react?"

"She was a little peeved, but she'll do it." She gave him a casual glance over her shoulder. "I started taking tae kwon do lessons."

Stunned was too mild a word for what he felt as she kept heaping on surprises. Sexy dress, contacts, giving Jess an ultimatum, and now tae kwon do? "Why?"

"Arianna raves about it, how it's helped her concentration and reaction time, and keeps her toned. I've been pretty sedentary lately because of my job at ARC, and before that I was studying for the exam."

"Okay, but tae kwon do? Couldn't there have been

something else? Pilates? Spinning? Tae kwon do is a long-term commitment.''

''I like the added bonus of self-defense. It seems sensible in this day and age.''

''There are classes specifically for that. Hell, I can teach you self-defense moves.''

She faced him, frowning. ''Does it bother you?''

It did, although he couldn't say exactly why. ''Why would it bother me?''

''I don't know. I hear you have a black belt in karate. I would think you would encourage others to learn martial arts.''

''I started when I was ten.''

''And I'm starting now.'' She came up to him. ''You seem a little out of sorts. Are you tired?''

Hell, no. He was exhausted. Maybe that's why he felt surly. But this was supposed to be a fun evening. He needed to change the mood, so he put his arms around her waist, slid his hands down her rear and pulled her close. ''You've taken the basic black dress to a whole new level. Let's go show you off.''

Hours later he peeled that dress off her after she'd teased him all night, leaning toward him at the table over dinner and drinks and some of the best jazz this side of New Orleans. She'd propped her chin in her hand, linked her fingers with his on the table and watched him intently as he talked. He was flattered by her interest in his work, but he seemed to do all of the talking because she kept asking questions, while he just wanted to strip her naked and make love to her right then and there.

He'd reached his limit by the time they got back to her house. The dress came off easily. She wore black lace lingerie that he almost tore he was in such a hurry. His need astounded him. He knew he was probably going too fast, coming on too strong. He didn't give her a chance to do more than be taken along for the ride, hardly letting her touch him, afraid he would explode before he satisfied her.

She was different, too, in the sounds she made, the urgent words she spoke, and her complete openness. Whatever traces of modesty she'd had before were gone now, and he welcomed it. Her body was perfect to look at, incredible to touch. Whatever he asked, she did, not just willingly but enthusiastically.

"Nate," she said once, drawing out his name. "Now."

"Soon," he said. But not too soon. Every time she neared the peak, he pulled back, until she turned into something wild. He urged her even higher, let her fall even lower, then took her up again. She clawed his back. Her body shook. He was thrilled by how she arched to meet him, then by the feel of her legs locked around him, and finally by the look on her face when she climaxed. He stopped holding back, drove harder and faster into her and found release in a burst of sensation so powerful he could scarcely draw in air. Worlds merged in a flash of light and thunder, leaving an eerie silence in its wake, darker than he'd ever known, deeper than he'd ever imagined.

He gathered enough energy to lift himself up, found she was breathing as raggedly as he was, and took her mouth in a long, thorough kiss until they breathed as one.

Then he slept, her breasts his pillow, her heartbeat his compass, guiding him home to rest.

Lyndsey wandered into her bedroom about every fifteen minutes. He'd slept through breakfast, the Rose Parade, and the opening half of the first Bowl game. He was so soundly asleep he seemed comatose. Sprawled across her bed and taking up all the space, he rarely moved. She kept checking to see if he was breathing.

He must have been beyond exhausted last night, yet he'd

still taken her out, wined and dined her, kissed her passionately at midnight and made love to her like a man just off a deserted island.

She'd never had this kind of physical relationship. The intensity amazed her. Her lack of modesty was new, too, as was her fearlessness. Her body ached contentedly.

She took a mug of coffee with her the next time she went into the bedroom. He was sitting up, looking groggy and adorable with his rumpled hair and scruffy beard.

"Why'd you let me sleep so late?" he asked, accepting the mug.

"You would've slept through cannon fire." She sat beside him. "You needed it."

He sipped his coffee and looked at her over the rim of his mug. "Would you like to go to the beach?"

"What do you usually do on New Year's Day?"

"Sam and I hang out and watch the games with a few other guys. We're not always in town at the same time, though, so it's not something we do every year. We wouldn't have this year since he's in Boston."

"I'll watch the games with you."

"You like football?"

"Sure."

He smiled. "No, you don't. So I'll ask again. Do you want to go to the beach?"

"We can watch the games today and go to the beach tomorrow."

"I have to go to Chicago tomorrow. I just got a call." He held up his cell phone. "That's what woke me."

How strange. She hadn't heard his phone ring. "What's the assignment? Or can't you say?"

"It's a corporate job setting up a security system for a client who's moving his business to Chicago from L.A."

"I thought Sam was the one to design the security systems. Panic rooms, things like that."

"He's got his hands full at the moment, and this client can't wait. I've got the basic skills, and the final plans will land on Sam's desk for his input. Anyway, I'll be gone two days, three at the most." He tossed aside the sheet, stood and stretched. "If you've got some fix-it jobs I could do for you around the house, I'm pretty handy. Let me grab a quick shower first."

He walked to the door, stopped there and turned around.

She caught her breath at the sight of him. He was hers. That gorgeous man was hers. For now.

He held out a hand. "Yes, you can join me."

How did he know she was about to ask him that?

"You keep looking at me like that and I'm going to get a swelled head," he said.

She laughed and flung herself into his arms. Love me, she pleaded silently. Love me.

Three nights later Nate let himself into the office after midnight. He stopped in the lobby, deciding how to approach Lyndsey. Their relationship had undergone a slight transformation in the past week. He could account for some of it—he'd become more tentative with her. He was waiting for her to walk away, not only because they'd been together for almost a month, the usual life span of his relationships since he never offered any kind of commitment, but because the signs were already there.

First, although she hadn't complained about his work schedule yet, she made comments about it under the guise of telling him he worked too hard. Second, she was changing, had changed a lot since he'd first met her, less than a month ago.

He wasn't surprised. She was experiencing freedom for the first time in years, and she was about to realize her goal of becoming a C.P.A. Her life was in transition.

It occurred to him that she was the same age he was

when he left the army and went to work for Charlie, a situation that had opened up a new life, one rewritten daily with every new experience.

No, he wasn't surprised at her changes, given the circumstances. He was just wary. Plus he liked her the way she was.

Nate didn't try to sneak up on Lyndsey. He called her name as he walked through the office. "I come bearing food," he added. He'd brought dinner with him, thinking if they talked at the office instead of at home they could have an actual conversation. At the office they couldn't just fall into bed.

He heard something fall to the floor, then the sound of paper rustling. She spun around when he walked into her cubicle. Her hands were behind her back. She leaned against her desk.

"You're back!"

Her voice was too bubbly, her cheeks too pink. She looked…guilty. Plus she didn't make a move toward him.

"Are we alone?" He looked around. He hadn't seen a car other than hers in the parking lot, but that didn't guarantee anything.

She nodded.

What was going on? "I don't get a kiss hello?"

"Of course you do." She came toward him, kissed him lightly, then tried to step back.

He drew her into his arms. She felt stiff. Over her shoulder he glanced at her desk, where papers and files were scattered. The times he'd seen her at work, her desk had been organized and neat.

"Is there something wrong?" he asked.

"No. Why do you ask?" She stepped back, blocking his view of her desk again.

"Did I scare you, coming in like that?"

She hesitated. "A little. It's okay. Mmm, that smells good."

He'd almost forgotten he was carrying the bag. "Spaghetti and meatballs from Angelina's. I'll get a chair."

"You know," she said in a rush, "my desk is a mess. Maybe we could eat in your office?"

"Yeah, we can do that."

Her smile was brittle.

"How much more work do you have left?" *When are you going to tell me what's going on? Why aren't you saying you missed me?*

"I'm done. I just have to clean up my papers and distribute the reports. In fact, I'll do it now while you set out dinner."

He left, but he didn't want to. It wasn't as if he could have called her predictable before this, because she frequently surprised him, but her behavior was so far out of character he didn't know what to make of it.

She seemed more relaxed a few minutes later when she came into his room. He had the food out on his coffee table in front of his sofa.

"What do you want to drink? I have water and I have water," he said.

"Water would be nice, if you have it."

"Good choice." He poured it into wineglasses.

"How was your trip?"

"Productive."

His tension built as she didn't make eye contact with him. And the blouse she was wearing had three buttons undone. And he missed her glasses.

Finally he put his plate down. "What's going on?"

"With what?"

"You."

"I don't know what you mean, except I'm happy." She stuffed half a meatball in her mouth.

"About what?"

"That you're back, Question Man. That I got my car heater fixed today. That Jess got a job."

"She did?"

"On campus. She even sounds excited about it."

Which wouldn't account for Lyndsey's unusual behavior, but he let it go for now. It was after two in the morning Chicago time. He was too tired to push her. Tomorrow, after he'd had a night's sleep.

"Are you coming home with me?" she asked as she helped clean up later.

"I'm pretty beat. I'll come by tomorrow afternoon, if you don't have other plans."

"Okay. See you then." She walked away.

He grabbed her arm. Now he knew for sure something was wrong. She hadn't kissed him. "Do you have something to tell me?"

"Like what?"

Guilty seemed to flash in neon in her eyes. He prepared himself for the worst. "Is this it for us, Lyndsey? Are we over?"

She looked stunned. "No! Absolutely not."

No guilt that time, and no lie, either. He was more confused than ever.

She moved in on him, pressed her lips to his. He didn't know what to think. What to do. She seemed desperate for him to believe her. After a few seconds he gave in, wrapping his arms around her, pulling her closer, kissing her. He drew back and stared at her. He wasn't sure he knew this Lyndsey.

"I'll walk you to your car," he said.

"That would be nice, thank you."

They stopped at her cubicle. She grabbed her sweater and…a briefcase?

"New purse?" he asked.

"What? Oh. No. I had a job interview this afternoon before I came to work."

His gut twisted. "How'd it go?"

"Pretty good, I think."

He turned out lights and reset the alarm. The walk to her car seemed endless. "So I'll see you tomorrow. Around one?"

"Perfect."

He watched her drive off. It wasn't until her taillights disappeared that it registered whose file was on her desk. Alexis Wells. Why? And how, since they were locked in a file cabinet that no one had access to except the partners?

Nate returned to the building and unlocked the cabinet. Wells was missing.

He went to Lyndsey's cubicle and opened drawers. No files.

She'd taken it with her.

He dragged his hands down his face and looked blindly around her work space. This couldn't wait until tomorrow.

Fifteen minutes later he knocked on her door. He saw her peek through the blinds.

"Just a second," she said. It took longer than that.

Getting rid of the evidence?

He was stunned by the depth of his anger. He'd trusted her more than any woman, even Arianna, because he'd shared his memories, his failings, his faults. He was trying not to jump to conclusions, but there weren't many possibilities.

Just when he'd let down his guard. Just when he'd decided to trust his judgment that this time he hadn't made a mistake.

The door opened. "What are you doing here?"

"I need to talk to you. Can I come in?"

She backed away. He scanned the room. No file. No briefcase.

"I want the Wells file back," he said.

She'd taken out her contacts and put her glasses on, but he could still see a range of reactions cross her face. Surprise, guilt, then resignation. Without a word she went into her sister's bedroom and came out with her briefcase. She set it on the coffee table next to the flowers he'd given her and pulled out the contents. Not one but five files.

He took them from her, glanced at the names on the tabs. All files from their locked cabinet. "Why do you have these?" he asked, barely able to contain his fury. If it had been anyone else he would've thought she was selling stories to the tabloids, but this was Lyndsey. Lyndsey with the honest face, the generous spirit, the passionate soul.

"I didn't want you to know yet," she said wearily. "Can we sit down?"

Blood pounded in his ears. His heart raced as he took a seat on the opposite end of the sofa from her. She sat like she had the first night, perched on the edge, her hands folded in her lap.

"I want to be a private investigator," she said.

It was so far out in left field he could only stare at her.

"Arianna's been helping me," she continued in a hurry, her eyes beseeching him to understand.

"Arianna has…?"

"She's been working with me the past couple of weeks. I read case files and we discuss them. She comes up with scenarios, and I'm supposed to figure out how I would handle them. She's testing me to see if I've got the instincts it takes. And the nerve. I know it's not the same as actual investigation but—"

He put up a hand, stopping her. "You want to be a P.I.?"

She nodded.

"Why didn't you tell me?"

"Because my decision couldn't have anything to do with you. And you would've been an influence, either way."

"Your decision is made now?"

"It is as far as I'm concerned. Arianna hasn't given me the thumbs-up yet." She pointed to the files in Nate's hands. "Those are my final exam."

He rubbed his temple where his head began to ache. "You expect to work for ARC?" The question came out more harshly than he'd intended, but he felt trapped. If she stayed on at the company she would be around, expecting something from him that wasn't in him to give. The relationship was bound to fizzle out, yet they would continue to see each other all the time. At some point she would have another man in her life. Get married.

Dammit. She was supposed to be safe. She was supposed to leave the company next month, putting a natural end to things. She would walk away, no scenes.

She lifted her chin. Her posture turned rigid. "I'd hoped to work for your company, but I understand that might make you uncomfortable. Arianna said she could recommend me to another P.I."

Arianna, what the hell have you done?

He stood, not knowing what else to say. The files were still in his hands. Take them or leave them? Arianna had given her permission.

"You can have the files," she said, her voice uncommonly quiet. "You're obviously uncomfortable leaving them. I wouldn't be able to focus on studying them, anyway." Her hands clenched, her mouth trembled. She pressed her lips together.

"We'll talk," he said, heading to the door. "Later."

"Okay."

He hesitated at the quaver in her voice but forced himself to keep going. And drove to Arianna's house.

* * *

Lyndsey didn't sleep, didn't even try to. She kept reliving the look on Nate's face when he'd asked if she expected to work at ARC. She'd obviously backed him into a corner, precisely what she'd tried to prevent by keeping her plans from him. She never wanted to put him in that position.

He wasn't pleasantly surprised by the possibility of her staying on at the firm. He was furious.

She sat on her couch all night, hoping he would come back to say he understood. To tell her she would make a great P.I., and that ARC would be lucky to have her. And that he wanted her in his life permanently, too.

Her phone rang at seven-twenty. She snatched it up. "Hello?"

"Lyndsey, it's Arianna."

She sagged. "Hi."

"Did I wake you?"

"No."

"Could you come into the office this morning?"

"Nate—"

"I know. He came over last night. We need to talk about it."

"I don't want to run into him until he's ready to talk to me."

"He's working from home today."

"Oh. Okay."

"I'm heading to the office now. Come anytime you're ready."

Arianna's businesslike tone gave away nothing. Lyndsey didn't have a clue what this turn of events meant.

But one thing was clear. She had to resign.

Thirteen

Lyndsey knew a lot more people in the office since the Christmas party. She got stopped several times as she made her way to Arianna's office. The last thing she felt capable of was idle chitchat but she had no choice.

Arianna's door was open. Lyndsey knocked anyway.

"Come on in. Have a seat. I'll be right with you." She was typing something into her computer.

Lyndsey looked around. Like Nate and Sam, Arianna didn't have photographs on her desk or anywhere else in her office. Were they such loners, then? Is that what her life would be like as an investigator?

No. Several of them at ARC were married and had children. But if you wanted to get to the top, did you have to forfeit a personal life? She didn't think she could do that. She wanted a family of her own someday. Not soon, though. She'd just gotten through raising Jess.

Arianna saved her document, turned her chair to face

Lyndsey, then got up and closed the door. She didn't return to her chair but leaned against the front of her desk.

"How are you?" she asked.

Lyndsey's eyes stung at the sympathetic tone. She blinked and swallowed. "I'm fine."

"Right."

Lyndsey handed her a sheet of paper, her resignation. Arianna glanced at it before setting it on her desk. She didn't rip it up, however.

"I shouldn't have asked you to deceive Nate," Lyndsey said.

"That was a mutual decision made for good reasons."

"He hates me."

"No. If he's mad at anyone, it's me. How did he find out, anyway? He was yelling so much last night I didn't get to ask."

"He was yelling?"

Arianna nodded.

"He never yells."

"I know."

Lyndsey thought about that for a minute. "Um, he found out because he came into the office about the time I was wrapping up. I didn't want him to see the files you'd given me. He knew something was wrong, then I kept making it worse. I never wanted to put him in this position."

"You know you'll face much worse situations as an investigator. You can't lose your cool, Lyndsey."

"I do fine with everyone but Nate. I can't lie to him. He *knows*."

Arianna returned to her chair and picked up the letter of resignation. "I don't want to accept this."

"You don't have a choice. We both know I can't work for him. It would be impossible. I'll stay until you find a replacement."

"You'll stay until you have a job. I know you can't afford to be without an income."

Lyndsey hated that she'd messed things up so badly. Look at what she was forfeiting. A great boss who understood. A wonderful group of co-workers. It was depressing.

"I'm really sorry. You tried to warn me." She must have inherited her mother's genes. She'd fallen in love with a man who didn't know how to make a relationship last. Better to find out now than be left with a baby, like her mother. "Will you still recommend me to another P.I.?"

"Let me think on it. I want the right person for you."

Her intercom buzzed. Arianna pressed a button. "Yes?"

"Sorry to interrupt, but there's a call for Lyndsey from a Mrs. Marbury on line one."

"Thank you, Julie." She pushed the phone across her desk. "You can take it in here or at your own desk."

"Here's fine." She took a settling breath, lifted the receiver and punched line one. "This is Lyndsey McCord, Mrs. Marbury. What can I do for you?"

"I'd like to talk to you. Just you. Could you come to my house?"

"If you can hold on a minute, I'll check my schedule." Lyndsey pushed the hold button. "She wants me to go to her house. Without Nate."

"Are you up to it?"

"I'm not an investigator."

"You're going to be."

The simple statement told Lyndsey everything. She'd passed the test. She couldn't take the time to wallow in it, however. She got back on the line. "I can come right now, if you'd like, Mrs. Marbury."

"Yes, fine. I'll be expecting you."

Lyndsey cradled the receiver. "I'll need to borrow a car.

I wouldn't be allowed in her neighborhood driving my old heap.''

"Take mine." She opened a drawer and pulled out a set of keys.

"I meant one of the company cars."

"I'm not territorial. It's the dark blue BMW. Have fun."

Lyndsey stood. The keys felt heavy in her hand, like a ton of responsibility. "I'll come straight back."

"I'm sure you will. Lyndsey?"

"What?"

"This isn't the time to take backward steps."

"What do you mean?"

"The night you met Nate you went toe-to-toe with him and held your own. Undo that second button again. Put your contacts back in. Show your confidence. You're doing fine."

Lyndsey kept Arianna's words in mind as she drove. By the time she'd been taken to Mrs. Marbury's sitting room, she felt in control again.

"Thank you for coming so promptly," the woman said, extending her hand.

She didn't look any better than she had when Lyndsey last saw her weeks ago. "How can I help you?"

"You started to tell me something when you were here before, but your partner stopped you. What was it?"

After a brief debate Lyndsey decided to be truthful. The poor woman's circumstances couldn't get any worse by what Lyndsey had to say. "I watched your husband and Tricia all weekend. I don't think he's in love with her."

Mrs. Marbury clenched the chair arms. "What makes you say that?"

"Because except for the shoulder massage there was no physical contact between them. Maybe there was a reason for that. It seems to me that it's all circumstantial evidence. Then the way he looked at the picture on Nate's computer screen and what he said about trust once broken being irrevocable…I don't know. It just doesn't fit. Why would he be angry at you about broken trust if he was the guilty one?''

''Are you saying there's nothing between them?''

''I don't know for sure. They were playing games, trying to trip us up, so who knows what was real. I can't even tell you for sure if she slept in his bed or on the couch in the office. What I can tell you is that he wasn't looking at her the way a man looks at a woman he's in love with. Or in lust with, for that matter.''

Mrs. Marbury broke down. She buried her face in her hands and started to sob. Lyndsey looked around the room, then finally went to her, knelt down and held her until she'd drenched Lyndsey's shoulder with tears. Empathetic tears welled up in Lyndsey's eyes, too. Her throat burned. She had her own troubles.

''I love my husband, Ms. McCord.''

''Lyndsey.''

She nodded. ''I did trust him—until he started acting secretive. He won't talk to me, not even on the phone. I need to talk to him. Please, can you convince him to see me just once? I need to explain.''

Lyndsey made a quick decision, not because Mrs. Marbury asked, but because Lyndsey believed there was much more to the story. ''I'll try. That's all I can say. I don't know whether he'll see me.''

''Make him. Please.''

''I'll try,'' Lyndsey repeated. She stood. ''Do you have children, Mrs. Marbury?''

''Lucinda. And, no, I don't. Michael does from his first marriage. I knew when he married me that he didn't want any more. I just always hoped I could talk him into it. If he loved me enough…'' Her voice trailed off as she cried again.

Lyndsey let herself out.

Arianna met her in the ARC parking lot as she pulled in. "Perfect timing," she said. "I've got an emergency."

"Should I wait around to talk to you about the Marbury case?"

"I'll call you at home when I get back in." She shut her car door and left.

Lyndsey thought about Lucinda Marbury while she drove home and decided she couldn't see Mr. Marbury alone. Lucinda had said before that he thought women didn't have any place in jobs he considered a man's domain, like private investigator. Plus she was part of a deceit against him. He probably wouldn't speak to her.

Even so, what would she be trying to prove? That she was a skilled investigator who didn't need help? She wasn't…and she did. Even if her instincts were good, she couldn't see the man by herself. This job belonged to Nate.

But she didn't want to be cut out of it, either. She'd been there from the beginning. She wanted to see it through.

Which settled it. She had to call him. They had to go together.

Nate sat in his deck chair, his laptop resting on his thighs, his gaze on the horizon. The security system for his L.A.-to-Chicago client was designed. In a minute he would e-mail it to work to be printed and put on Sam's desk.

He closed his eyes, worn-out, but all he saw was Lyndsey's face when he'd left her house last night. This morning. Whatever. He dropped the lid on his laptop and set it aside.

Her lips had trembled. Her eyes had darkened to almost black. He didn't know what it all meant. He couldn't believe she'd gone behind his back like that. If she'd talked to him instead of Arianna, he would've—

Hell. What would he have done? Discouraged her, maybe. Probably. He didn't want her around after their affair was over.

His cell phone rang. He hesitated when he saw it was Lyndsey.

Coward.

He pressed the start button, said hello.

"I'm sorry to bother you at home," she said, sounding businesslike.

"No problem." His pulse picked up tempo. He resented it.

"Lucinda Marbury asked me to come see her today. With Arianna's permission, I did. I want to report what happened." She went on to describe their conversation.

"We're not marriage counselors," he said, then was met with silence.

"Maybe this time we need to be," she said finally, coolly.

"What makes you think Marbury will see us?"

"Tricia."

"You talked to Tricia?"

"I got us an appointment at four o'clock, pending your availability."

Her efficiency prompted his first smile of the day. "I assume you would go on your own if I refuse? If I say you can't go, either?"

"Absolutely."

"That's insubordination."

"I'd tell you to fire me but I already turned in my resignation."

He sat up. "When?"

"This morning. Look, are you coming with me or not?"

She quit? "I am."

There was a long pause, then, "Good."

She quit? "How are you going to handle it?" he asked.

"I doubt Mr. Marbury would talk to me. You're the boss."

Was he? No one could tell that based on this conversation. "If you were going to handle it, what would you do?"

"If they had children, I would've played to the abandonment issue. But they don't, and it probably wouldn't have worked anyway because he has children from his first marriage and that didn't stop him from getting a divorce."

"Which leaves?"

"The fact she loves him."

"You think it really is love and not money that motivates her?"

"Yes, cynic, I do."

"And love conquers all."

"No." Her voice got quieter. "But it helps."

Time to end this conversation. "I'll pick you up at three-fifteen."

"I'll meet you in the lobby of his building at three-fifty."

The line went dead.

Fourteen

Lyndsey was worried about being late, so she arrived early, finding parking in the three-story garage attached to the Mar-Cal building. She signed in at the security desk then took a seat to wait for Nate.

When he walked in, she went numb. She'd seen him in action before, but not in this role, dressed in a suit and tie, looking powerful and in control. In charge.

She wore the only suit she owned, the one she'd bought for job interviews. Black jacket and pants, which she paired with a white silk shirt—with two buttons undone. She rose to meet him. *Steady. Steady. He's just a man. The man you have to stop loving.*

"Have you already signed in?" he asked as he approached the desk.

She nodded.

After Nate signed the register, the guard called Mr. Marbury's office for approval to send them up. They walked in silence to the elevator. Nate pushed the button for the eighteenth floor. The doors slid closed. Quiet descended. Sixteen hours ago he would've taken advantage of the opportunity to kiss her, she thought.

"You look very professional," he said.

"So do you."

He half smiled at that.

Stupid, she thought. So stupid. Of course he looked professional. Why wouldn't he?

She hated that she was nervous now that he was about to see her in a different light. He knew she wanted to be an investigator. She wasn't just his accessory, brought along to cook. He would be critiquing her words and actions. She couldn't afford to mess up, even if it wasn't a real investigation job.

As the doors opened she looked at him, admiring his profile. She missed him already. Missed touching him. Sleeping beside him.

Tricia greeted them at the elevator. Lyndsey was glad she'd already broken the ice over the telephone.

"He's on a call," she said, leading the way down the corridor. "He's upset with me for giving you this appointment. You won't find him pleasant or cooperative."

"Thanks for the warning," Lyndsey said. "I'm sure he won't be upset with you for long."

"It doesn't matter. I've already given my notice. Tomorrow's my last day." She held up her left hand, where a large diamond winked. "I'm getting married."

Lyndsey was swamped with something she decided was envy. "That's…wonderful news," she managed. "Who's the lucky man?"

"His name is Paul. Actually—" her voice got lower "—he's president of Mar-Cal's biggest competitor."

"He's who you were talking about at the beach house?" Nate asked. "The one with all the baggage?"

"He's been married twice. It made me reluctant. But I decided to have faith in his love, because I don't want to live without him." She paused before glass double doors. "Here we are."

Tricia left them standing in a luxurious office suite. A woman typed at a computer. Tricia's replacement? Lyndsey wondered. If so, on the surface she was a good choice. Older than Mr. Marbury, well groomed but not slim and beautiful. No potential as a trophy wife.

"Come this way," Tricia said, holding open the door to the inner sanctum.

Lyndsey met Nate's gaze briefly. Reassured by the encouraging look in his eyes, she relaxed. What was the worst that could happen? Mr. Marbury could order them out. They waited to be invited to sit, but he seemed determined to keep them standing.

Nate moved to a chair in front of the massive desk and sat. He motioned for Lyndsey to do the same.

"I'm not going to stand on ceremony," Nate said. "We aren't here as investigators."

"Why are you here?"

"Your wife wants to talk to you."

"I'm aware of that. She can talk to my lawyer."

Oh, he was a cool one, Lyndsey thought. He leaned back in his chair, his hands folded in his lap. He stayed focused on Nate, never once letting his gaze drift.

Nate leaned forward. "Before it comes to that, don't you think you owe her the courtesy of a conversation? You've got ten years invested in this relationship."

Startled, Lyndsey tried to keep a businesslike expression. How could he be so logical with Mr. Marbury and not with her? Didn't Nate owe *her* the courtesy of a conversation?

"I don't owe her anything. She thinks I cheated."

"Did you?"

He scowled. "No."

Lyndsey wished she could high-five someone. She knew he hadn't betrayed his wife. She knew it.

"If you talk to her you'll understand why she thinks you did," Nate said.

"She has a good reason? I gave her a reason to think that about me?"

He seemed stunned by that news. Lyndsey didn't think he was acting.

"Yes," Nate said.

He spread his hands. "I don't see how that's possible. I've always been faithful to her. Never even been tempted. Hell, I got my—" He stopped. "I still can't believe she thought I would stray."

"I can't emphasize enough that she did think that," Nate replied.

Lyndsey put a hand on the edge of the desk. "You got what for her?" she asked, having seen something in his eyes.

He looked at her, then at Nate. "Is this conversation confidential?"

"Of course," Nate said.

"Lucinda wants children. I had my vasectomy reversed as a surprise for our tenth anniversary."

Lyndsey sat back, floored.

"You'd had it done that day we met you?" Nate asked.

"That morning."

"Which would account for your lack of activity. And the quantity of ice." Nate winced and shifted in his chair.

Lyndsey almost smiled.

"To keep the swelling down. I was so doped up when we got there I didn't know or care what was going on. Tricia recognized you right away and told me. We had to completely change our plans."

"How?" Nate asked.

Mr. Marbury got up from his desk and moved to the window. "I had intended to go to the beach house alone. I didn't need anyone fussing over me, and I couldn't tell Lucinda without spoiling the surprise. Plus, I didn't want to get her hopes up until we knew the surgery was a success. Then I got the opportunity to buy a company I've had my eye on for a long time. Problem was, someone else was also interested, and I only had that weekend to put together a report to present to my board. It's a formality since I own fifty-one percent of the company, but it's good business to get their approval and support.

"Without Tricia I couldn't have done it. That's all we did in the bedroom—work. The ironic thing is, I thought you were corporate spies sent to get a copy of the bid I was proposing. I'd arranged for that Charlie person to cook for me, then he suddenly has a change in plans and can't come, but he found a replacement. I bought it—until I learned you were a P.I."

He glanced over his shoulder. "Tricia and I spent our time trying to act like we were vacationing, when in fact we were working feverishly to assemble the report and keep you from knowing." He gave a bitter laugh. "And you didn't know or care. Irony."

He shook his head and looked out the window again. Lyndsey raised her brows at Nate.

"I hired someone to follow you when you left the beach house," Mr. Marbury continued, "hoping you would lead me to whoever was competing for the buyout. Instead you drove to my house, which baffled me. It wasn't until I saw the picture on your laptop that I realized Lucinda had hired you because she thought I was cheating."

His voice broke on the last word. Lyndsey started to plead a case for him to go to his wife, to bare his soul. Nate put up his hand to stop her.

"Sometimes pride needs to be set aside for something

more important." He joined Mr. Marbury at the window. "Go to your wife. Listen to her. Confide in her. You both made assumptions and mistakes."

Lyndsey would've added something about forgiveness and love, but otherwise she thought Nate said the right things. He angled his head toward the door, indicating to Lyndsey that they were leaving.

"Goodbye, Mr. Marbury," she said.

They stopped to wish Tricia good luck before they left the building.

"Where are you parked?" he asked.

"On the second floor, near the stairs."

"I'm on the third."

Which meant they would walk to the garage together.

"Do you think he'll go to his wife?" Nate asked when they got off the elevator.

"He's probably on his way now."

"You think so?"

"He wanted someone's permission—or kick in the butt—to get him moving. He wouldn't have poured his heart out if he wasn't dying to go to her." She paused. "That thing you said to him about pride? That was perfect. It was exactly what he needed to hear." *And what you need to take to heart, too.*

They left the lobby and took the stairs to the second parking level. An ache began to spread from the middle of her chest. Was this the last time she would see him? She was sure he would avoid coming into the office at night until she left ARC. She supposed there weren't such things as P.I. conventions, where they might meet up again at some point, get drunk and sleep together one last time. She at least wanted closure.

Okay, so that was a lie. She wanted him to be as reasonable with her as he'd been with Mr. Marbury.

She wanted a lifetime.

They stopped beside her car. She unlocked the door and tossed her purse inside. *Stop me from going, Nate.*

"I'll see you get paid for your extra hours," he said.

The pain in her chest intensified. "We got sent home early that Sunday, with full pay. I've already been fairly compensated," she said, offering his own words back as if she were teasing—or maybe not teasing but using her own irony.

The attempt at a joke fell flat. "You'll get paid," he said.

That did it. "To hell with getting paid," she said, her fury clawing its way up from the pit of her stomach. "Be honest with me, instead. Do what you told Mr. Marbury to do."

"What?"

She threw up her hands. "That's it, Question Man. I'm outta here." She started to climb into her car. If this was the way he wanted to leave it, fine. She wasn't hanging around for more heartache.

He put a hand on her door. "I'm not ready for this to end," he said. His eyes said more. They begged.

She couldn't let him get away with giving her a piece of the pie. She was starving for the whole thing. "For what to end?"

"You and me."

Her body reacted to his words. You and me. It was what she wanted. So why wasn't she flinging herself into his arms and saying okay. Me, too. Let's go to my house.

Because it wasn't enough anymore. "Am I supposed to wait around until you are ready?" She was proud of how she got the words out, even though they killed her.

"I didn't mean it like that."

"How did you mean it?"

"I don't understand why you're leaving. Why you quit the company."

"You want me to stay until you get me out of your system? Then what? I'm supposed to be able to keep working with you? How do you think I could work for you after what we shared?" *Figure out a way, Nate. Make it happen.* "Our relationship was a mistake. I told myself the only reason I didn't stop it was because I would be leaving in two months, then we could continue without having the boss/employee issue between us. But the truth is...I let it happen because I couldn't help myself."

She couldn't read his expression. She hated how he clammed up when his emotions were involved. Any other time she couldn't get him to stop talking. She pictured him speaking to Mr. Marbury, heard his words, his understanding. Until now she'd been so worried that he would feel obligated to her in some way that she hadn't shared her feelings. Not this time. He wouldn't have the excuse of not knowing how she felt. She was not letting him off the hook.

"You made some assumptions about me," she said, her head high. "I'm not a sophisticated woman who has a fling then puts it out of her head. When I was with you, I—" She stopped, drew a breath, then blurted out her feelings. "I found myself. And I like myself. I'm proud of what I've accomplished and excited to be heading in a new direction, whether you like it or not. You did that for me.

"I didn't change your life like you did mine, I guess. I didn't open up worlds and give you confidence and treat you better than anyone else ever has. All I did...all I did was love you."

She got into her car, started her engine and drove away. In her rearview mirror she saw him just standing and watching.

Somehow she made it home before she fell apart.

Fifteen

Nate looked at his watch for the third time without registering the time. The staff meeting seemed endless. He had no patience for the recitation of case reports by the various investigators, and he contributed nothing in return. Most of the time he drummed a pen on his notepad until someone either threw something at him or told him to knock it off.

When the meeting broke up, he scooped up the notepad and headed to the conference room door.

"Nate," Sam called. "Hold on."

The last of the staff filed past him. No one talked to him.

"Shut the door, please," Arianna said. "We need a partners meeting."

Sam pointed to a chair, meaning Nate should sit. "What're you trying to do, run the business into the ground single-handedly?"

"What the hell does that mean?" Nate asked.

"I mean every day for the past two weeks someone has complained to Ar or me about you. You're surly. You're not available to brainstorm a case. You're ignoring basic courtesies, like please and thank-you. It stops now."

Nate knew he was guilty. He'd intended to fix it every day, but every day he got worse. "You're right. I apologize."

"An apology isn't enough this time," Arianna said. "Sam and I are ordering you to take that trip to Australia you postponed. Get out of here. Get your head together."

"By the time you get back, Lyndsey will be gone," Sam added. "That should help."

Nate looked sharply at him. "She's not already?"

"She doesn't have a new job yet. Ar promised her she could stay until she found something."

"I've put out some feelers," Arianna said. "No bites yet. I think she started applying for C.P.A. jobs again, just to get away. Anyway, that's not your problem. Your problem is you. Fix it. I'm sure you can find some willing Barbie from Down Under to help." With that unsubtle gibe at him, she left.

"Arianna should learn to speak her mind, don't you think?" Nate said conversationally to Sam.

Sam sat opposite him. "We've both been holding back, hoping things would change."

"I know." Nate looked at his friend, saw understanding in his eyes.

"Why don't you just give in to it, Nate?"

"I can't."

"Because?"

"Because what if it doesn't work? You know what will happen, what always happens. She'll start resenting the time I'm gone. She'll want a commitment. The Marburys getting back together is a rare happy ending. I can't hurt her again. What kind of man would that make me?''

"I can give you a list of good marriages, starting with Charlie and his wife. You're exaggerating because it justifies avoiding Lyndsey.''

He couldn't deny it. "How is she, anyway?''

"Not gonna answer that, Nathan. You wanna know, you find out for yourself. You know what watching you has taught me? That lying to yourself is as bad as lying to someone else. And next summer when my high-school class holds its fifteen-year reunion, I'm going. I'll face my past.''

"Why wait until then?''

"For a lot of reasons.'' Sam looked at his watch and pushed himself up. "Ar and I have to get to that meeting with the mayor. Book your flight.''

Half an hour later his travel agent called with the new flights and hotel reservations. He wasn't leaving until eight o'clock that night, which gave him hours until he had to be at the airport. He might as well go home and pack, because he sure wasn't going to get any work done here.

The intercom buzzed. "Nate? You've got a call from a Roy Gordon on line two.''

"Did he say what it was about?''

"No. He just asked to speak to one of the owners about an employee. Arianna and Sam are gone.''

"Okay. Thank you, Julie,'' he remembered to add before picking up the phone. "This is Nate Caldwell.''

"Good morning, sir. I'm Roy Gordon from Rasmussen, Gordon and Culpepper Accounting. I'm calling about a Ms. Lyndsey McCord. She's applied for work with us and listed your firm as a reference. Could you verify her employment for me, please?''

An accounting firm? Hell, no, he didn't want to verify

her employment. *Do you give up that easily, Lyndsey?* He'd expected more of her.

That he'd had a hand in her situation almost killed him.

"I can confirm her date of hire," Nate said finally, forcing himself past his anger and resignation.

"That would be September seventh?"

Nate didn't know for sure, but he knew Lyndsey wouldn't lie. "That's right."

"She's a transcriber?"

"Yes." *And she types flawless reports and hasn't missed a day. And her kisses are hot and sweet and generous. And she makes love like it's as necessary as breathing.*

"Would you say she's an honest person?"

The man's nasally voice grated on Nate. "By law that's the only information I need to give."

"You aren't going to answer because she's not honest?"

Nate barely stopped himself from swearing. "She's extremely honest. You would be lucky to get her."

"So, you're recommending her?"

No. Hell, no. "Yes."

"Good. That's good. Now, just between you and me, did she cause problems with the men in your office? We've got a lot of men and, you know, she's pretty hot."

It was exactly what Nate wanted—a reason to get mad. A reason to vent his frustrations. He stood. His chair crashed into the credenza behind his desk. His fists clenched. "Expect charges to be filed against you and your firm." He had the unadulterated pleasure of slamming down the phone. He couldn't catch his breath for several seconds. Fury snaked through him, doubling in strength, tripling, until it reached the point of no return.

He left his office, not looking right or left, not answering anyone's query. Nothing could stop him. He was going to make damned sure Ms. Stubborn McCord didn't work for that bastard. If she hated his guts because of it, who gave a damn? How much worse could it get?

Lyndsey set the timer for twelve minutes and started to fill another cookie sheet for the next batch. If she wasn't careful she would gain five pounds in two hours.

Her doorbell rang. And rang. And rang.

She hurried through the dining room and to the front door, then hesitated. "Who is it?"

"Nate. Open up."

She groaned. Of all days. She was wearing her stupid old black jeans and sweater again. She hadn't put on any makeup. Her hair. Well, she didn't want to think about that.

"Open up!"

She jumped, then unlocked the door and opened it.

"You are not going to work for that...Gordon. Where is your sense, Lyndsey? He's a sexist pig. You with all your great people skills can't see that?"

His jaw was rigid, his eyes bright. Lyndsey didn't know what he was talking about.

"And what the hell are you doing applying for an accounting job when you want to be a private investigator? Are you giving up your dream that easily? It makes me question your commitment."

Fascinated by his anger, she just stared at him. She hadn't applied for an accounting job. She didn't know a Gordon.

Arianna. Lyndsey would bet this was Arianna's way of intervening, of forcing him to talk to her. How had she manipulated it?

"Well?" he said.

"Well what?"

"Are you giving up?"

Was it crazy that she liked how he'd lost control? If she wanted to learn the truth, did she need to keep him out of control? *Ah, Nate, I know you so much better than you might think.* "That's none of your business," she said calmly.

His scowl deepened. "It is my business. I care about you."

"No, you're being paternal. You can't order me around."

"Paternal?" He filled the doorway with his fury.

"Yes." She crossed her arms. Her heart pounded hard and fast. "Haven't I made enough sacrifices? If I want to work for Mr....Mr. What's-his-name, I will. What gives you the right to tell me how to live my life?"

"What gives me the right?" He stepped into the room, backing her up. *"I love you."*

She took another step back. He'd yelled at her. Yelled. That he loved her. She wanted to throw herself in his arms. Instead she crossed hers again. "You have a strange way of showing it."

"Because it scares the hell out of me," he said, the words like sandpaper on metal. "I love you. I've been miserable without you. Ask anyone."

His misery shouldn't make her this happy. "Maybe you'd better shut the door."

"Lyndsey, I've never missed anyone before. Not like this."

His eyes were filled with agony. He shut the door with a quiet click, as if his energy was completely gone, then he walked to the sofa and sank into the cushions, subdued. His sudden mood shift confused her. She sat in a chair across from him so that she could look him in the eye. She had to see for herself that he was telling the truth. She couldn't survive another two weeks like this again.

"I've barely slept," he said.

She believed him. She hadn't slept much either.

"I knew you were different. I just didn't know how different." He rested his arms against his thighs and leaned toward her. "I liked you from the beginning, then you started to change. To, I don't know, to blossom. I kept expecting you to leave me behind, like your glasses. Then when you confided in Arianna instead of me about wanting to become a P.I., I figured you didn't trust me. I didn't blame you," he said, when she started to interrupt. "Women have had good reason not to trust me. I haven't made a commitment since my divorce. I never wanted to. I want to now.

"I'm begging you, Lyndsey. I've been an idiot. You have no reason to trust me. But you turned my world upside down, and I didn't know how to function in it. I need you. You make me happy in a way I never thought anyone could, because I didn't think I would ever let anyone even try. You tested every belief I had about women and loyalty and trust. You broke down barriers, brick by brick.

"If you'll give me one more chance, I'll prove it."

Lyndsey swallowed the painful lump in her throat.

"Please," he said, leaning closer.

Her throat closed. She nodded, saw something much bigger than relief on his face.

"Have I told you," he said, his voice shaking, "how I love the way you sit like that, right on the edge of your chair, your hands in your lap like some Victorian lady?" He moved to the side of her chair and slid in behind her, wrapping his arms around her waist, pulling her close, his body trembling. "I want to do this every time I see you sitting like this."

Her back cushioned by his chest, she rested against him. Tears burned her eyes at the tenderness in his voice.

"I want to hold you forever, Lyndsey McCord. Just like this. I love you."

"Nate—" A shrill series of beeps interrupted the moment. "My timer," she said, trying to get off his lap.

His arms tightened more. "Ignore it."

"I've got cookies in the oven."

She felt his hesitation, then he said, "Let 'em burn."

If that didn't prove his love, she didn't know what did. "They could catch on fire," she said. "Smoke. Flames. Firefighters. No sex for hours because we'll have to clean up."

He went still, then he buried his face along her neck, his breath ragged. "Does that mean you forgive me?"

"Yes." A tear trailed down her cheek, then another. "I love you."

He turned her around, settled her on his lap, facing him. Somber, he swiped his thumbs across her cheeks.

"I'm sorry. I know you hate crying," she said, suddenly crying more.

He kissed her as the tears flowed. She kissed him until they stopped. They held each other until they smelled food burning, then ran into the kitchen just as the smoke alarm went off, singing a duet with the timer.

"How would you like to go to Australia?" he shouted over the noise.

"When?" She tossed him some pot holders.

He snatched the tray of charred cookies out of the oven and dumped it in the sink then opened a window. "Tonight."

"I have to work tonight."

He laughed. He reached up and punched the reset button on the alarm. She turned off the timer. Smoke filled the room. The quiet roared in her ears.

"I don't have a passport," she added.

He took her into his arms. "Then for tonight, how about

I take you to paradise instead? You only need a photo ID for that.''

"Let me get my wallet...." And then she kissed him.

* * * * *

And don't miss Private Indiscretions,
*Susan Crosby's next passion-filled read coming
to Silhouette Desire in March 2005!*

CINDERELLA'S CHRISTMAS AFFAIR
by
Katherine Garbera

King of Hearts
by Katherine Garbera

Who's on his hit list?

In Bed with Beauty
Cinderella's Christmas Affair
Let It Ride – February 2005
Mistress Minded – April 2005

KATHERINE GARBERA

lives in central Florida with her husband and two children. They are all happy to be back in their native state after a two-year absence. Her favourite things are spending time with her family, writing, reading and talking about reading. Readers can visit her on the web at katherinegarbera.com.

To Courtney, Lucas and Matt—
thanks for making everything worthwhile.

Acknowledgements:

Special thanks to Julie Wachowski
for suggesting Gejas as a romantic place for dinner.
Also, thanks to the entire Windy City chapter
for being so knowledgeable about everything
and for making me feel like one of your own
even if it was only for a short time.

Prologue

Dying had not been what I'd expected and after successfully matching together one couple I felt a little more confident about this afterlife gig. But this body disappearing thing still freaked me out. I was back in that in-between land that Father Dom had called purgatory.

I'd been a capo in the mob before being betrayed by one of my lieutenants. Five shots to the chest and a dying request for forgiveness had brought me here.

The deal I'd cut was essentially to unite in love as many couples as enemies I'd murdered in hate. So I knew I'd be dealing with this angel broad for a while. Matchmaker to the lovelorn wasn't exactly something I'd been dying to do but life was full of surprises. Come to think of it so was death.

In front of me was a large mahogany desk with a library lamp and a jar of Baci chocolates. I'd been here before. The angel broad was there, still looking like she'd just attended a funeral but her dress this time was puke-green.

She was making notes in a file folder. She didn't glance up and I knew she was playing a game with me. I'd done the same thing a time or two when I'd been a capo. It made me feel like a *cugine* instead of the boss of bosses, which I'd essentially been. I didn't like it.

"What's up next, babe?" I asked.

"Mr. Mandetti, unless you want me to stop this whole exercise now, you will refrain from calling me babe."

I still wasn't used to being called by my real name. I'd been *Il Re* when I was alive. *The King.* Yeah, I had an ego and the attitude to carry off that name. "I don't know your name."

"Didiero. I'm one of the seraphim."

"The what?"

"One of the highest angels of God."

"Oh." She made me feel stupid which wasn't a feeling I liked. But she held all the cards and if I'd learned one thing from my time back on earth it was that I didn't want to go to hell.

And I'd never admit this to anyone but I liked the feeling that came with doing something good. It was the first time I'd ever experienced it.

"Didi?" I asked.

"Are you talking to me?" She didn't look up from the papers in front of her.

"Didiero is a mouthful."

She glanced at me from under her lashes. This one would drive me crazy if I let her.

"So who's next?" I asked.

"You still want to go in order?" she asked.

"Nah, give me that green one halfway down." Maybe the middle of the pile would be easier. I wasn't trusting her to pull out a couple. I'm sure she'd fixed it so I'd had to work hard on my first assignment.

She handed me the folder. I opened it up and groaned. CJ Terrence and Tad Randolph. "Aren't there any couples who can do this on their own?"

"Sure, there are Mandetti, but they don't need your help. There is one thing I should warn you about," Didi said.

"Yeah?" I was leery. Why was she suddenly being all helpful?

"You won't take the same human form each time."

It was like she knew how to push my buttons. "Babe, get to the point."

"That is my point, Mandetti."

She disappeared and I felt my body dissolve. I found myself on the streets of Chicago. *My kind of town.* This assignment was looking up by the moment. I was in front of the Michigan Building on Michigan Ave. In the mirrored glass I saw an old lady and two sharp-looking guys.

Not bad. I could definitely handle being a young

hip guy. Both of them were taller than I'd been. I walked toward the glass and noticed only the old lady was moving.

Madon' that couldn't be me, could it? I gave the reflection the finger. Christ, I was an old broad with a frumpy dress on. Didi was probably up in Heaven laughing. Just wait until I saw her again.

One

Of course the first man she'd had a crush on would be the only thing standing between her and her promotion. CJ Terrence smiled with a confidence she was far from feeling and shook Tad Randolph's hand.

Ten years had passed since they'd last seen each other and she knew she'd changed a lot. She'd dyed her mousy brown hair a sassy auburn, she'd swapped her horn-rimmed glasses for aqua-colored contacts that masked her natural brown color. And the biggest thing of all, she'd lost twenty pounds.

But in that moment she felt like her former self— the chubby girl next door. She reached for the bridge of her nose to push up the glasses she'd always worn back then. Dropping her hand, she reminded herself that she'd changed.

She took a deep breath; assured herself that her physical changes were enough to keep Tad from recognizing her. Of course, she recognized him even though he'd put on at least twenty pounds. All of it solid muscle. He looked exactly how she'd expect the owner of a sporting goods company to look.

It was too bad he couldn't be balding like other guys who were her age. Instead his blond hair was thick as ever and bleached by the sun. He looked too good and she wanted to run and hide.

"CJ Terrence," she said introducing herself. She could only hope that maybe Tad wouldn't be able to identify her as the girl he'd known as Cathy Jane in high school.

He took her proffered hand and shook it for the required three pumps. Shivers of awareness or maybe it was nerves shook her. His hand was bigger than hers, not surprising since she wasn't a big girl—at five foot five inches tall she was average and Tad Randolph had grown into a giant since she'd last seen him.

Calluses ridged his palm and his skin against hers was rough and warm. She wondered how his hand would feel against her stomach. Tremors of sensual awareness pulsed through her body. He continued to watch her with that razor-sharp gaze of his. Had she given too much away?

"Ms. Terrence, where do you want these presentation boards?" CJ's secretary, Rae-Anne King, asked.

CJ dropped Tad's hand and glanced at her new temporary secretary. "Please excuse me."

"It's a pleasure meeting you, CJ," Tad said.

"I've…got to set up," CJ said. Yes she was the queen of intelligent conversation—not!

"Don't let me keep you."

Right. One minute in the man's presence and she'd lost ten years worth of self-confidence. Confidence she'd earned by standing on her own and not depending on anyone else.

Tad nodded and walked to the coffee service that CJ had set up. Normally, her assistant would have handled it but this was her first day working with Rae-Anne. Her temp had proven to be a little inept around the office.

CJ motioned to the easel at the end of the long narrow conference room. Working quickly she set up her presentation and then glanced out the window.

It was a blustery day in early December. Chicago was gray and damp. Though the Christmas decorations along Michigan Avenue tried to instill a little cheer, they failed.

Failure was something CJ understood but she didn't plan to let it rest on her shoulders today. She took a deep breath, muttered her mantra to herself and then turned to face the other people in the room.

Tad touched her shoulder; she started and dropped her cards. *Damn.* This wasn't going to work. Six years of moving her way steadily up in the advertising world was suddenly in jeopardy.

He picked her cards up from the floor and held them out to her. Their hands brushed. His were large and tan. He wrapped his fingers around hers, which were cold. Rubbing his thumb across the back of her knuckles he warmed up more than her fingers.

"Cold hands?" he asked softly.

"Always," she said. Her fingers were never warm even in summer.

"You know what they say about hands," he said.

"Honestly, no."

"Cold hands, warm heart. Do you have a warm heart, CJ?" he asked.

No way was Tad Randolph—the only boy she'd ever allowed herself to have a crush on—flirting with her in the middle of the conference room.

"CJ?"

"Uh...I don't know."

"There's something familiar about you," he said.

She took her cards from his grip and nervously shuffled them. Oh, God, please don't let him remember me. She was never going to be able to do this.

"Have we met?"

She shook her head. God, don't get me for lying, she thought. Just in case she crossed her fingers behind her back. Before she could answer her boss walked in.

"CJ was featured in *Advertising Age* last year as part of their Top Thirty To Watch. Twenty-somethings who were taking the advertising world by storm," Butch Baker said from the doorway.

Butch was forty-eight and had been with Taylor, Banks and Markim forever. He was her immediate boss and observing today as part of the promotion process. CJ was next in line for the directorship of the domestic division of the advertising company. Today's meeting wasn't a make-it or break-it deal, but bagging the sporting goods contract would give her a nice lead over her competition.

Butch and Tad turned aside to discuss mutual friends and CJ turned back to her presentation. Everything was in place. If she'd paid closer attention to her notes then she would have realized that P.T. Xtreme Sports was owned by Tad Randolph.

Normally, her secretary Marcia would have taken care of notifying her of such details. But Rae-Anne had been lucky to find the file on the company before they'd had to come down to the conference room.

She missed Marcia. They'd worked together for four years like a well-oiled machine until Marcia had fallen in love with Stuart Mann and married him. The couple had decided to start a family, which left CJ without Marcia's presence in the office. Not that she begrudged Marcia her family, she just wished they'd had more time to train this temp.

"You nervous?" Rae-Anne asked when Tad's other executives filled the conference room.

"I shouldn't be. This is routine." Sure, it's every day the boy you had a girlhood crush on was the key to an important account...and your promotion.

"Then why are you?" Rae-Anne asked.

"That's the million dollar question, Rae-Anne. Thanks for helping me set up. You can go back to the office now."

"No problem. Good luck, CJ."

"I need more than luck," CJ said. She needed a miracle, but her life had been short on those.

Taking a deep breath, she squared her shoulders and began her presentation. She avoided meeting Tad's gaze. And spoke with all the confidence she'd cultivated since she'd left that small town she'd grown up in, and honed since Marcus had left her.

It would be a lot easier to deal with Tad's reappearance in her life if he weren't so damned attractive.

Remember what he said about you and how it felt to realize you'd put your trust in someone who was so superficial. Remember that Tad wasn't the only one to teach you that lesson. Marcus did as well.

How many times did she have to be hurt before she'd finally learned?

Her career had never let her down. Advertising was safer and required no heartache.

But there was a part of her—Cathy Jane—that wondered what it'd be like to kiss Tad Randolph, high school superstar. A little experiment to see if all the hype that had surrounded Tad during high school had been accurate.

She was no longer the girl with the baggy clothes and frizzy hair. She was a sophisticated city girl who knew how to make men take notice of her and wasn't afraid of their attention. At least in the boardroom she knew how to do it.

Life couldn't get much better, CJ thought. Once she started talking her confidence returned and she realized that even if Tad recognized her it wasn't the end of the world.

"I know you had a long-standing relationship with Tollerson but together we can take P.T. Xtreme Sports to the next level," she said.

"Very impressive. We'll be making our decision at the end of the week," Tad said, wrapping up her presentation.

He had a few words with Butch as CJ cleaned up her presentation boards. Not bad, she thought. She'd made it through the presentation and unless she'd missed her guess, P.T. Xtreme Sports was going to be the newest account in her impressive portfolio.

"Great job, CJ," Butch said.

"Thanks, Butch."

Butch walked out of the room and CJ felt like doing the Snoopy dance of joy.

Slowly the conference room emptied leaving only herself and Tad. Why was he still here?

Nervously, she tugged at the hem of her suit jacket. "I'm really impressed with you, CJ Terrence."

"Thanks," she said. She should just clear the air, tell him they'd gone to high school together and then put it behind her.

He moved closer. There was something sensual in his eyes. Was he attracted to her? He quirked on eyebrow at her as she took a half step backwards.

"Am I scary?" he asked.

"No."

He smiled at her and closed the gap she'd just

opened with her retreat. She tried to reassure herself that he wasn't stalking her. If she wanted to she could back away and give herself more space. But she didn't want to. He smelled good. Closing her eyes she inhaled deeply.

He took her hand again rubbing his thumb over the back of her knuckles. ''Are you sure we haven't met before?''

Oh, God. Not again. Why hadn't she run when she had the chance?

What was she going to say? The truth was she didn't want him to ever look at her and picture the girl she'd been. But having an account manager that lied to you didn't exactly inspire confidence.

The rubbing motion of his thumb was sending shots of awareness up her arm. Her hand was tingling and if she wasn't so reluctant to have her past discovered she'd actually enjoy this time with him.

''Well…Ms. Terrence.''

''Well what, Mr. Randolph?'' she said pulling her hand away.

Time to take control and get the heck out of the conference room.

''CJ Terrence…CJ…Cathy Jane?'' Tad asked.

She was frozen. Unable to think of anything intelligent to say she just nodded.

''Cat Girl, I knew you looked familiar,'' Tad said smiling.

Cat Girl…that's what she'd called herself senior year. CJ wished for a time machine. She wouldn't travel to the future to see the marvels it held, or to the distant past to visit Regency England. She'd travel back to her first year of high school.

She'd find her old locker and destroy the box of HoHos she'd always kept there. Then she'd give her teenaged self a makeover, pointing out gently that baggy clothes didn't make her look slimmer and finally giving her teenaged self the one piece of advice no one else had given her but someone really should have—never call yourself *Cat Girl*.

Even if you meant it tongue-in-cheek, some day when you're almost thirty it will sound humiliating and not funny.

Alas, there was no time machine and she'd just have to muddle through this as best she could. Tad Randolph didn't own the only large sporting goods chain looking for representation, she could find another one. Of course, by then Paul Mitchum, another ad executive, would have beaten her to the punch and her career with Taylor, Banks and Markim would be down the drain. CJ wished that the floor would open up and swallow her.

"That was a long time ago," she said at last. "I'm not that person anymore."

"Why didn't you say something sooner?" he asked.

"Come on Tad, honestly would you want Cathy Jane from Auburndale to represent your company?"

"You're not that woman anymore," he said.

"No, I'm not," she said. She met his gaze. His gray-green eyes had always fascinated her. There was more reflected there now than intelligence and fierce will. Now she saw a man with life experience. A man who tempted her to forget what she'd learned about men and maybe risk her heart on the gamble that this guy would be the one who'd never leave.

"I've got to get back to work."

"I won't keep you."

She gathered her presentation case and walked out of the conference room without looking back.

"CJ?"

She glanced over her shoulder at him.

"Have dinner with me?" he asked.

"Oh, Tad. I can't."

"Why not? Come on, Cathy Jane, for old time's sake."

"It's CJ now."

She was tempted but knew that nothing good came from dwelling on the past. Besides, Tad had been the reason why she'd moved away from Auburndale. After she'd overheard him talking about her to his friends she'd realized that she needed to start over where no one knew her.

And Chicago had seemed the right place for that. Except she'd learned that running away meant nothing unless you changed, too. She'd been the same shy, awkward girl until Marcus had left and forced her to take stock of her life.

She didn't really know how to handle men one-to-one. She started to shake her head.

"I know you've changed but we were once friends and I'd like to take you to dinner."

She couldn't stop her smile. They had been friends. He'd been the only kid her age in the neighborhood that summer they'd both been twelve—popularity and weight hadn't mattered. They'd ridden their bikes all over the city and spent all their time together. She'd forgotten those days.

There was a part of Tad that was very dear to her. Not the teenaged boy who'd been more concerned about his image than her feelings, but the friend she'd had when she'd first moved to the ridiculously small town of Auburndale. "You're bigger than you used to be."

She blushed when she realized how ridiculous that sounded.

"Geez, thanks! Come on. Just one meal. What could it hurt?"

She knew she shouldn't but couldn't resist the temptation he represented. He'd been her secret teenage crush, and he'd never noticed her as a woman...until now. It was a fantasy and as long as she remembered that she should be fine. "Okay, one dinner but that's it. We're probably going to be working together and I don't want things to get weird."

"I like your confidence, Cat Girl."

"Uh, Tad?"

"Yes."

"Don't call me that anymore."

"What's going to happen if I do? I am stronger than you now."

"I'm a third degree black belt in Tae Kwon Do."

"No kidding. I practice that martial art too."

This was creepy. She shouldn't have that much in common with him—the boy who'd broken her heart and made her doubt she'd be a mate to any man. "I'd love to spar with you."

"Call me Cat Girl again and I'll give you a chance. I don't want to talk about old times."

"I don't either. I want a chance to get to know the new you."

She tried to smile as she walked away because she knew that there wasn't much new to her. She still felt like the same awkward person she'd always been.

Two

Tad guessed that CJ had been trying to put him in his place but as he watched her walk away, enjoying the sight of her curvy hips swaying with each step she took, he didn't mind.

Man had she changed since high school. He remembered the lonely little girl who'd made him feel like a hero when he'd bandaged her scrapes after she'd fallen off her bike. He remembered her as a sweet shy girl who'd been too smart for him in high school. He also remembered the girl who'd refused to talk to him after senior prom. He'd always wondered why she had cut him off.

But this woman in the conference room had been a sexy blend of intelligence, savvy and sass. Just what he liked in his women.

His mom had been bugging him to look up Cathy Jane since he'd moved to Chicago five years ago, but Tad had put her off. Kylie, his college girlfriend, had left him saying she didn't want to come in second to a sporting goods store just about the time he had moved to the Windy City. Tad had been kind of sour on women then. The last thing he'd wanted to do was catch up with the girl who'd given him the cold shoulder through the last two months of their acquaintance.

Of course, at the time his mom had been pressuring him to marry as well. Which was a common thing with her. But his business had been in that crucial make-it-or-break-it stage and the last thing he'd wanted was the kind of distraction women offered. And he hadn't been interested in marrying some hometown girl or any other girl for that matter.

Tad had shelved his dreams of wife and family and concentrated on making a success of P.T. Xtreme Sports instead. But his mother's health had been deteriorating in the five years since he'd moved to Chi-town and he knew she'd love to see him settled. In fact, she'd hinted rather baldly on the phone last night that she was the only woman in her circle of friends without grandchildren. And he was honest enough to admit he wanted a family.

He'd created a legacy and he wanted to be able to pass it on to his own kids. But finding the right woman wasn't easy. He wanted a woman who'd look up to him and need him.

Cathy Jane would have fit that bill, but he wasn't

sure CJ did. She'd changed. He remembered long curly brown hair that he'd always tried to accidentally touch. God, it had been incredibly soft. Her auburn tinted tresses had been tucked up today. Was her hair still that soft, he wondered.

Her eyes had thrown him as well. She'd always had the biggest brown eyes behind her horn-rims. She looked good with blue eyes and if he'd never known her as Cathy Jane he might even prefer the blue. But he had known Cathy Jane. Why had she felt the need to change so much?

A small leather wallet was lying on the end of the table. He'd give it to one of the secretaries on his way out. He picked it up and it opened. Staring up at him from a typical DMV photo was Catherine Jane Terrence.

He skimmed her address. Her condo was only a few blocks from his. All this time they'd practically been neighbors and never run into each other. Tad was honest enough to admit he wouldn't have recognized her as his old childhood pal without hearing her name.

Whistling under his breath he left the conference room. A pretty brunette receptionist smiled up at him as he approached. He smiled back at her. "Can you direct me to Ms. Terrence's office?"

She gestured toward the left. Bangles rattled on her wrist. "Down the hall, third door on the left."

"Thank you."

He paused outside her doorway. He could hear CJ talking to her secretary. It didn't sound like CJ was having a great day. Frustration underlined each of her words. He was beginning to think that CJ worked too hard. It wasn't even lunchtime—way too early to be stressed out.

He rapped on the door frame. Both women looked up. CJ's secretary was a middle-aged woman with graying black hair and a few wrinkles. Both women wore identical expressions of frustration.

"Can I help you?" CJ asked.

"You left this in the conference room," Tad said. Oh, yeah he was a smooth talker with the women. Why was it that Cathy Jane made him feel like he was on his first date?

"Oh, thanks. You could have left it up front."

"Yes, I could have." This was going to be harder than he thought. Why was CJ so damned determined to keep things all business between them? Probably because, at this point, there was only business between them. Yet when they'd shook hands earlier in the conference room he'd felt something pass between them that had nothing to do with ad campaigns.

"I have a few questions to ask about your presentation, can you spare me five minutes?"

"Sure. Rae-Anne, why don't you go down the hall and ask Gina to show you around the office?"

Rae-Anne brushed past Tad muttering under her breath about bossy women and—while his Italian had never been good—he thought he heard her curse in that language.

"Your secretary is…different," he said at last.

"She's a temp. Today's her first day and we're still working out the kinks," CJ said. She leaned against the desk, fiddling with the clasp on her wallet. She tucked a strand of hair behind her ear. "What questions did you have?"

He didn't have any. He hadn't had a chance to review her presentation but he hadn't liked being dismissed. He'd learned a long time ago that the only way to achieve what he wanted was to take charge. He cleared his throat. "Just wanted to clarify a few details. We have an in-house production company for educational videos. We usually use them for our commercials as well."

"Come into my office. I want to make some notes," she said, leading him through the connecting door. Her office was a decent size with a large window overlooking Michigan Avenue. Her walls were decorated with awards and plaques of appreciation from companies.

The article Butch had referred to earlier was framed and hanging on the wall. CJ's picture was cool and confident. She hardly resembled Cathy Jane—the girl he'd known. But even then he'd known she'd go on to do great things. She'd been smart and shy but very focused on getting out of Auburndale.

"That shouldn't be a problem. When you make your decision, I'll get a contact name from you and talk to the head of the department."

"I'll do that," he said, leaning back in the leather guest chair. Her office was subtle and relaxing but also spoke of success. He felt a twinge of pride at how far she'd come from the girl she'd been. Despite the way things had ended between them, he'd always thought of her fondly.

"I can't believe you own a sporting goods store," she said.

"You're not the only one. I started college prelaw."

"You look sporty," she said, then rolled her eyes.

He didn't remember her being this funny. But then she'd always been so uncomfortable around him. His friends had teased him about spending so much time with a chubby brainiac. But deep down, he'd always liked Cathy Jane.

"Believe it or not, I am capable of intelligent conversation," she said.

He smiled. She'd always been one of the smartest people he knew. "You're the first person to call me sporty."

"I know you were an athlete in high school. Is that how you got into the business?"

"During college I started to work out more and tried some things I'd always wanted to."

"Like?"

"Mountain biking, rafting, some rock climbing."

"Do you still do all that?" she asked.

He nodded. "I was in Moab, Utah last week."

"You've changed so much," she said.

"So have you, Cathy Jane."

"I'm CJ, now, Tad. Some days it doesn't seem I've changed all that much," she said.

"Good. I always liked the girl you were."

"Is that why you told your friends I paid you to spend time with me?"

Tad hardly remembered the boy he had been until she'd said those words. He'd been more concerned with how he looked to his friends in those days than hurting Cathy Jane's feelings. Honestly, though he'd never known she'd overheard his remarks.

He was embarrassed by them now. No wonder she'd never talked to him after senior prom. "Hey, I was young and stupid."

"Yeah, so was I," she said.

"Does this mean you don't have a crush on me anymore?" he asked, cursing himself for not keeping quiet. Because a crush was the only thing that had explained her behavior back then.

CJ sank back in her chair unsure what to say next. She knew she should have run when she first had a glimpse of Tad Randolph. But his warm gray-green eyes had convinced her to stay before he'd even recognized their past connection. And she'd never had good instincts when it came to men.

When they'd been in high school she'd idolized Tad. She'd spent hours writing his name in her notebooks and dreaming of them together. But now, as a mature woman she understood things that never would have entered her mind then—like relationships were complex and needed both people to be interested.

Though Tad's comments had hurt, a part of her had

needed to hear what he really thought of her. It had given her the courage to break free from the familiar and start over. College had taught her more lessons and Marcus had finished her education when he'd left.

Tad leaned forward in his chair. Bracing his elbows on his knees and watching her with an intensity that made her breathless. She shivered under the impact. What was he thinking?

"Tad…" She stood and paced to the window. How could she explain to him that maybe she'd needed to hear the truth about herself. That his comments, though hurtful at the time, had made her realize that she needed to be strong inside. She needed to get away from her comfort zone and try the things she'd always secretly dreamed of.

She heard him stand but didn't turn. Maybe he was leaving. But then she felt his presence behind her. He patted her awkwardly on the shoulder.

"Sorry I said it that way," he said. His hand slid down her back lingering at the curve of her waist.

His touch rattled her senses and for a minute she wasn't sure what he'd said.

She wrinkled her nose, wishing again that Marcia still worked for her. Her old secretary would have interrupted by now and sent Tad on his way. "I hoped it wouldn't come up."

"I had no right to ask it," he said.

"I guess you did. There's no easy way to say this. I think I'd built you into someone you really weren't," she said.

"What kind of guy?" he asked.

"The kind that looked past the outer shell of who I was and saw me as something more," she said. He'd been someone she could debate the merits of Voltaire versus Molière. He'd been someone who understood that sometimes it was easier to be smart than to socialize. He'd been a safe haven from the other popular boys who teased her endlessly.

He cupped her face and shivers of awareness spread down her body. He had always had that effect on her senses. The first time it had happened in the advanced biology lab she'd nearly freaked out. It still shook her.

"Would it help at all to know that I regretted the words as soon as they left my mouth?"

"*Yeah, right.* You always did have a touch of the blarney in you." It was nice of Tad to try to reassure her. Her reservations about men had started long before she'd met Tad and continued long after she'd left Auburndale.

He shrugged and let his hand drop. "I only wish I'd had the maturity to make that moment right."

"Well, you were responsible for my leaving town and making the life I've made. So maybe I should thank you."

"I knew you went to Northwestern. Was it what you expected?" he asked.

"No," she said. But it had definitely helped her grow up and had cemented her decision to make her career her life.

"You'll have to tell me about it," he said. He crossed back to the guest chair.

"Now?" she asked, walking back to her desk. She wasn't going to tell him a thing about that time in her life or Marcus Fielding.

He shook his head. "I have to get back to work."

"Of course. You rattled me, Tad."

"I know," he said, wriggling his eyebrows. "I have a feeling not many do that, Miss Top Thirty."

"You've got that right. Next time we meet I'm going to be on my toes." Or at least give the impression she was. She knew herself well enough to know that Tad was always going to knock her a little off balance.

It didn't seem fair that the one guy who had that ability should be the only thing standing between her and the realization of her career goals.

"I'd rather you weren't," he said.

She smoothed her skirt and cocked her head to one side. "That's what all the men say."

"Do they?" he asked.

"You know they do. Guys don't like smart women," she said, teasing him.

"Only dumb guys don't like smart women," he said with a cocky grin.

She'd forgotten what it was like to spar with a man. The men she'd dated lately tended to be as career focused as she was. "You never were dumb. Though, I may have to revise my opinion."

"Why?" He took a step toward her.

Although she realized she never should have started

this, she wouldn't back down now. "You look like a jock."

He tucked his hands into his pockets and canted his hips to one side. Her breath caught in her chest. His pose was blatantly masculine and unexpected. He sounded like her childhood friend but there was an aura of sexuality and macho self-confidence the Tad she'd known had never used around her.

"I own a sporting goods company. I am a jock."

"That's what I was afraid of," she said, trying to force him back into that comfortable mold he'd previously inhabited in her mind.

He raised one eyebrow at her in question and cocked his head at her.

"I'm trying to think of a way to put this delicately…"

"You don't have to mince words with me," he said, taking another step toward her.

She edged back stopping only when her desk blocked her retreat. "I'm just afraid that buff body of yours may have cost you a bit of the gray matter."

"You think I'm buff, Cathy Jane?"

She blushed as she realized she did. It was never a good idea to fall into lust with your client. She cleared her throat. "Please don't call me that."

Taking his hands from his pockets, he ran one finger down the side of her face. "Why not?"

"Because I'm not that girl anymore," she said.

He leaned closer to her. His minty breath brushing

her face with each word he spoke. "You're so much more than you used to be, Cathy Jane."

Pivoting on his heel he walked out the door. CJ put her hand over her racing heart and knew she'd just met more than her match. She would have to avoid spending any time alone with him.

Saturday dawned bright and chilly. Tad left his condo and ran along the shore of Lake Michigan. CJ had been ducking his calls all week and frankly he was tired of it. He'd let her have her space but that was all about to end. He was a man of action and winning games was something he'd become accustomed to.

The rhythm of his exercise cleared his mind and soon he was analyzing Cathy Jane. He hadn't realized she'd heard his comments to Bart all those years ago. He'd never meant for her to be hurt and he'd actually gone on to defend her. But guys like Bart never really understood women.

Tad realized he didn't understand them either. Kylie had wanted a rich husband and Tad had worked his butt off to make his dreams of a sporting goods store come true. But Kylie hadn't been satisfied with that. As he worked to build his business, she'd complained that she didn't want a man who worked all the time.

What kind of a mate would CJ be? She was successful in her own right and wouldn't need a man's money to support her. But would she want a man to share her life?

He'd talked to his mom again this morning, casually mentioning that he'd run into Cathy Jane. His mom had asked about CJ and her sister Marnie.

"Nice girls, nice family," his mom had said, and he knew what she'd meant. The kind of girl she wished he'd marry. He'd hung up without saying anymore to his mom about CJ. But she'd planted a seed in his head.

Would CJ be willing to marry him? They were both nearing thirty and their careers were on track.

He'd got her to agree to dinner but little else. She'd hedged and had her secretary send regrets twice. But Tad was used to hard work.

He ran his usual five miles, but altered his route so that he jogged by CJ's building on his way home. He'd always had a photographic memory and the image of her address on her driver's license was etched in his mind. Could he drop by unannounced? He slowed as he approached her building.

Two women were struggling with a Christmas tree. He slowed his pace. He thought it was CJ and an older woman. He still wasn't used to seeing her with auburn hair. In his mind she had thick ebony hair. She looked cute with her knit cap and matching muffler around her neck. Her companion looked like her secretary.

He slowed to a walk to let his breathing slow and even out and then approached her. All he could make out was her long black wool jacket, legs encased in faded denim and a pair of boots that would have done any one in Auburndale proud.

"Rae-Anne, can you lift your end a little higher?" CJ asked. The two women juggled the tree without much success. The six-foot blue spruce was a nice tree—not unlike the one that he'd ordered for his condo. For someone who'd changed so much, they still had a lot in common.

"*Madon'*. I'm trying. I'm not as strong as I used to be," Rae-Anne said.

"Let's set it down for a second," CJ said, bending at the waist to set the trunk on the snow-dusted ground. Her coat slid up and Tad was treated to the full curves of her backside. His fingers tingled with the need to reach out and caress her.

Instincts older than time had his hand lifting before he could stop himself. Her buttocks looked firm and full, but he'd learned the hard way that women didn't appreciate a man reaching out and grabbing something he liked. She straightened, still holding the tree up.

"Can I help?" Tad asked, reaching around CJ to take the trunk of the tree from her.

CJ glanced over her shoulder at him. Her breath brushed across his cheek and he inhaled sharply. The scent that was uniquely CJ assailed him. He was surprised at its familiarity. It reminded him of home and of memories best forgotten.

"What are you doing here?"

"I live up the street," he said, gesturing to his building. "Let me carry the tree up for you."

"Thanks, but we've got it," CJ said, brushing his arm aside. He refused to let her budge his arm.

She glared up at him but he knew she wouldn't make an issue of it in front of her secretary. "We don't need your help."

"*Merda,* I do," Rae-Anne said. She put her hand over her heart and sighed loudly. "Some of us aren't as young as we used to be. And I just stopped by to drop off the Monday files. I finally figured out your last secretary's system."

CJ bit her lower lip, unsure. He knew her well enough to know that she didn't like to give ground. He sometimes wondered, if he hadn't let her beat him in arm wrestling when they'd been twelve, if they'd have even been friends.

Tad took control, grabbing the tree and hefting it with one hand. "I got the tree."

"Very impressive. Do the girls usually swoon when you do this?"

"You're my first, CJ," he said.

"I'm impressed. Are you sure you won't drop it?"

Always the smart-ass, when they'd been teenagers she'd teased him about his choice of girlfriends. He'd forgotten that there'd always seemed to be two different Cathy Janes. The one at school who kept her head down and her nose in a book and the one at home who sassed him. He wondered what she'd do if he kissed her. Her lips were full and he was tempted more than he should be. His plan for a wife was simple and straightforward—filling a void in his life. "I can handle one tree, CJ."

"Of course, you can," Rae-Anne said. "You're not a middle-aged woman."

"Kind of you to notice," Tad said, smiling at the other woman.

"Think nothing of it," Rae-Anne said. "I believe in giving credit where it's due."

"So do I. Machismo isn't something that requires praise, Rae-Anne," CJ said.

"Machismo?" he asked. A man had to have a strong ego around CJ. Unlike Kylie who'd always flattered him...until she'd walked out the door with one of his competitors.

CJ tilted her head to the side and studied him. He couldn't help it. He flexed his abs and stood a little taller. Her gaze moved over him and his blood flowed heavier. He shifted his legs trying to keep her from noticing his stirring erection through the fabric of his sweatpants. "Overabundance of testosterone sound better?"

Oh, yeah, he was going to kiss that smart mouth. To hell with her Christmas tree. "Gallant rescue sounds good to me."

"You always did have a big head."

"You always were a bit of a pain."

"Then why are you here?" she asked.

Because she was the one woman he'd never been able to forget. No matter how many beautiful, intelligent women he'd dated, CJ had always lingered in the back of his mind. "I'm a glutton for punishment."

"Follow me. I'm on the twelfth floor. We have to use the service elevator," CJ said.

"I'm yours to command."

"As if," she said and climbed the stairs to the building.

Rae-Anne and CJ held the doors open for Tad, and in a short time they were standing in CJ's apartment.

"Where's your tree stand?" he asked.

"I can do that. I don't want to take up too much of your time."

"I don't mind."

"Really that's okay."

"You can't do it on your own," he said.

"Rae-Anne is going to help me, right?" she asked.

Rae-Anne had a pile of file folders in her arms and didn't really look like she'd expected to decorate a tree.

"Do you want me to help?" Rae-Anne asked. "My mother used to say many hands make light work."

Tad winked at her, sensing he had found an ally in his pursuit of CJ. And he just realized it was a pursuit and nothing less than complete surrender of the saucy redhead would suit him.

Three

CJ had had enough interaction for the day. Saturdays were normally her favorite. She wanted Rae-Anne to go home and Tad to disappear back into the fabric of the past so that she could once again have control of her life. She'd make herself a nice cup of herbal tea and then climb onto the counter and pull down the box of HoHos she had stored above the refrigerator.

They were for emergency use only and after this day she knew she needed the sweet bliss that only consuming a box of chocolate cream-filled cakes could bring.

She'd talked to Rae-Anne last night and they'd discussed Rae-Anne bringing over the Monday files so they could have a head start on the week. But then

Rae-Anne had called to say she'd be late and CJ had decided to go and get her Christmas tree. Bad idea. She should have gone into the office instead. Nothing was the same with Rae-Anne as it had been with Marcia.

But Tad was a different matter entirely. The purely masculine look in his eyes told her that he was interested in doing more than renewing old friendships and frankly, that made her nervous.

She was glad that Rae-Anne was here because she didn't want to be alone with Tad.

Her weary soul said no more guys with buff bodies and yet she'd always been drawn to them. Marcus had been a marathon runner who'd spent hours in the gym. Even her dad had been a high school football coach.

"I'll make the coffee," she suddenly blurted.

And for some reason being around Tad seemed to reduce her normally quick tongue to banal small talk. More and more she was slipping back into the old Cathy Jane, joke of Auburndale high school.

"I'll make it," Rae-Anne said.

"No offense, Rae-Anne, but you have yet to make a pot of coffee that anyone would drink."

Rae-Anne threw back her head and laughed. "*Madon'*, this woman thing is making me crazy."

"What woman thing?" Tad asked.

"You wouldn't believe me if I told you," Rae-Anne said. Turning to a battered box she pulled out a tangled mess of Christmas lights.

"We've got our work cut out, my friend."

"I think I can handle it."

CJ left them to sort out the lights telling herself there was nothing wrong with escaping to the kitchen. Not long ago she'd vowed to never let a man make her cower again and here she was hiding out in her kitchen. She boiled water in her teakettle and made coffee in her French press. She had a box of cookies in the cupboard and she arranged them on a Christmas plate from the set her mother had given her the year before she'd died.

There was a part of CJ that really hated the holidays. Marcus had broken up with her on Christmas Eve five years ago and he'd changed something inside her when he left.

She'd hoped to marry him and become his wife. She'd had visions of a shared future where they had their own small ad agency and they worked together. But Marcus had needed something else in a wife. He'd been using her to get a promotion and once he had obtained it, he'd dumped her for the right woman. A corporate wife who'd put her husband first instead of her career.

Her father had run off just after Thanksgiving the year she was eleven with an eighteen-year-old cheer-leader. And her mom had been diagnosed with cancer two days after Christmas when CJ was nineteen. So, the holidays always represented not just joy in a sea-son of giving, but also sadness and a sense of loss at what could never be again.

"Rae-Anne sent me to help you."

CJ made a mental note to talk to Rae-Anne. That woman was entirely too bossy for her own good. "I think I can handle coffee and a plate of cookies."

Tad stepped into her "step-saver" kitchen and CJ backed up a pace.

"Did I suddenly develop some communicable disease?" he asked.

She flushed. "No, why?"

"Because you keep dancing away from me. What's up, Cathy Jane?"

She forced herself to stand her ground when Tad came closer to her. It wasn't that she was afraid of him. It was her reactions that made her leery. Not even Marcus who she'd contemplated marrying had made her skin tingle, her pulse pound and her body ache the way Tad did.

"Nothing."

He reached out and caressed her face. Drew his large callused forefinger down the side of her cheek. His wizard green eyes watched her carefully and she struggled to keep any sign of what she was feeling from her face. Marcus had taught her that men wouldn't hesitate to use a woman's body against her.

"I know you better than that."

She shivered again as he took his hand from her face and turned to the plate of cookies. God, she hoped he didn't really know her. Didn't realize that her feminine instincts were stronger than her control. And that at this moment she wanted nothing more than to order

Rae-Anne from the condo and beg Tad to touch her once again.

"Not anymore, you don't," she said quietly. The only element in her favor was that Tad was a stranger.

"The other day in your office you weren't like this."

"Well, we were in my office. You were a client, not a guy in clinging sweatpants lifting heavy things with one hand."

"Did I impress you?" he asked, pivoting back toward her, pinning her between the kitchen cabinet and him.

She had to tilt her head back to meet his gaze and when she did, she wished she'd hadn't. There was a heat there that mirrored the longing in her soul. Nervously she licked her lips. His eyes tracked the movement and he leaned the tiniest bit toward her before stopping.

"Do you want to?" she asked.

"Hell, yeah."

Her blood ran heavier in her veins and she knew that what she wanted—really wanted—was for him to notice her as a woman. No matter how dangerous that attraction would be, she wanted it.

But she hadn't lost her mind. This new Tad was too big. Too "large and in charge" as her ten-year-old niece, Courtney would say.

"I'm not in the ego-building business."

"Cathy Jane, this has nothing to do with ego," he

said. He settled his hands on her hips and drew her closer to him.

''Tad, I really don't think…''

''That's right, don't think.''

He lowered his head toward hers. Her hands rose to his shoulders and instead of doing the prudent thing and pushing him away, she kneaded his shoulders, leaned up on tiptoe and met his hungry mouth with her own. Oh, my God, she thought, Tad Randolph is kissing me.

Tad wouldn't have guessed that her mouth would taste so sweet. She was shy and hesitant and he coaxed her gently into opening her mouth wider and letting him explore her hidden secrets. Ah, yes, this was what he'd been searching for.

She didn't lie passively in his embrace. But she didn't take charge either as he'd expected her to do. At work she was a modern-day Amazon but in his arms he realized there was still a lot of the shy, sweet girl he used to know.

Her touches were tentative on his shoulders and back. Her mouth under his was soft. Her curves were pliant against him. He pulled her more fully into his body and held her for a minute. His mouth pressed against hers in the chaste embrace she seemed to need.

He lifted his head and dropped light kisses on her cheeks and forehead. Her eyes were the remembered dark brown today instead of the blue-green contacts she'd worn that day in her office. She watched him warily and he wanted to reassure her. To promise her that he didn't want to hurt her only show her a passion that he suspected would be Heaven on earth.

"Relax, CJ, let me in. I promise it'll feel good."

"We have to work together," she said.

"That sounds like an excuse."

"It is. God, it really is. But you aren't what I expected, Tad. And I have no idea how to handle this," she said. Her voice rasped over his aroused senses with the same impact as silk over skin.

He didn't have words to reassure her. Wasn't sure that this was a good idea from his vantage point either but he knew there was no way he was leaving the kitchen having only shared one kiss.

"Cathy Jane, you slay me," he said and lowered his mouth once again to hers. This time he took her lower lip between his teeth and suckled. He was so tight and full and needed her more than he'd ever admit.

He slid his hands down her torso, skimming the full curves of her breasts and spanning her waist. He bent his knee and thrust his leg between hers. She grasped his shoulders and her mouth opened with a soft sound.

Holding her head in his hands, he tilted her face back and took her mouth the way he wanted to take her. Fast, hard, deep and so thoroughly that she'd never again touch her lips and not think of him.

She smelled of a sweet floral scent that was wholly feminine. And felt like pure fire in his arms. He slid his hands down her back and around the curve of her waist. Moaning in the back of her throat, she kneaded his shoulders. He thrust his tongue deeper in her mouth. Until she was clutching at his shoulders and returning his embrace fully.

There was something challenging about the woman CJ had become. Something in her eyes and walk that told all men—especially Tad—that she wasn't an easy woman to seduce. But he'd always been a determined man.

He traced the line of her spine down her back to the full curves of her buttocks. Damn, her butt felt as good in his hands as he'd known it would. He wanted to deepen the caress. Her jeans molded to her curves and he couldn't resist tracing the center seam between her legs. She moaned again, scraping the edge of her fingernail around the neckband of his sweatshirt. His arousal grew heavier. Every nerve ending felt hyper-sensitive.

He slid his hands back up her body. She was so womanly. He needed to touch more of her and the only way to do that was to slip his hands under her shirt. She made one of those soft sweet sounds he was becoming addicted to.

He caressed her back and plundered her mouth. Content for now to have her in his arms and be able to taste this small part of her. A part of him knew that he wouldn't be able to stop if he let things continue much longer.

He peppered her face with a few small kisses and slowly slid his hands out from under her shirt. He continued to hold her in his embrace until his pulse stopped racing. His erection was still heavy between his legs but he was old enough to know he wasn't going to die from it.

He stepped back after a minute. CJ fingered her lips with tentative fingers and watched him as if unsure what he wanted from her. He thrust his fingers through his hair and wondered when his simple plan to marry her had become so complicated.

"Um...I better bring the coffee out to Rae-Anne."

She tried to skirt around him but he stopped her by blocking her path. He knew it was childish but there was something about CJ that made him react from the gut instead of from the head.

"This isn't over," he said. He didn't know why she was running but realized that life had changed this woman more than he'd realized.

Crossing her arms over her chest she glared up at him. He felt like a big mean bully and wanted to pull her back into his arms and kiss away her irritation.

"Yes, it is."

"Why?" he asked, not willing to let the subject drop. "It can't be because of one comment in high school."

"It's not."

He waited but she didn't say anything else.

She sighed and then looked at the floor. Finally in a small voice she said, "I don't have affairs."

Now we're getting somewhere. "Why not?"

"Life is easier that way."

Life was going to be damned hard for him until he had her in his bed, writhing under him. "I'm not going away."

"You will."

Her confidence threw him. She'd been the one to leave him all those years ago. "Don't count on it, Cathy Jane. I have plans for you."

"Business plans, I know."

"I'm going to marry you," he said, surprising himself. But the words sounded right in his soul. She was exactly the kind of woman he'd been unconsciously searching for. He'd been thinking of marriage a lot lately.

He wanted her to be his wife. He wanted her to be the mother of his children. He wanted her in his bed and it had nothing to do with the fact that his parents wanted him to give them grandkids.

"What?"

Having blurted out his announcement, he had no choice but to keep going. Damn, this is what happened when he let his groin do the thinking. He should have eased into his announcement but she'd been backing away and he'd wanted to put his mark on her. To claim her as his even though he didn't have the right.

"You heard me. I've analyzed the facts and I think we'd be very successful together as a married couple."

And he did believe that. He'd tried love with Kylie and ended up frustrated and alone. Marriages, the really successful ones he'd noticed, were based on common likes, similar backgrounds and physical compatibility.

CJ thought maybe she'd stepped into one of those alternate realities like they had on *Star Trek: The Next Generation* sometimes—like the one where Tasha Yarr was really alive and married to a Romulan. Tad watched her with that mix of determination and intelligence that she'd come to recognize meant he wasn't backing down.

She was still trying to assimilate all the feelings from him kissing her. It had been a high school dream and something she'd imagined a million times. But the reality had been so much more. Now she knew his taste, his touch. The way his hands felt on her face. And the way he'd closed his eyes just halfway as they'd pulled apart. Dammit. She didn't want to think about the kiss.

Instead she jumped on the one subject that was a powerful distraction. Marriage.

"Are you nuts?"

"No. I'm serious about this."

"We don't know each other," she said. And there was a part of her that was really glad he didn't know her. There were certain secrets she wasn't going to share with anyone—especially a man.

"Sure we do. Plus we have a lot in common."

"Name one thing."

"We're from the same small town."

"That barely counts. And we don't live there anymore. Name something else."

"We both chose the same type of Christmas tree."

"Tad, have you fallen on your head lately? You don't marry someone because they like the same things as you do."

"Just think about how peaceful our Christmases will be."

"There's more to life than Christmas."

"I know. We also live only a few blocks apart and work in the same area of town."

"So do hundreds of other people. That hardly means we're meant to be."

"Yeah, but hundreds of other guys haven't kissed you."

"You hadn't either until today, so I don't see what that has to do with anything."

"Maybe you are the one woman I've never been able to forget, Cathy Jane," he said, quietly.

"Is that true?" she asked. When he called her Cathy Jane it made her feel cherished. Not like a corporate warrior who'd carved a place for herself in the world, but like a woman who'd found a special spot with the right man.

She watched those wizard eyes of his carefully. They revealed no emotion to her and she sensed that he was trying to decide if pretending he was in love with her despite the time that had passed between them would win her. But she'd been lied to by men her entire life and she'd learned long ago not to believe what they said.

"Forget I asked," she said. She'd learned some tough lessons about men. You'd think she'd have enough smarts to stop asking them questions like that.

"I won't forget you asked. I want you to say yes, CJ...."

"But you can't admit that I've been on your mind. I'm not asking you to confess undying love."

"Good. Love is such an indefinable thing."

"It's not a thing, it's an emotion. Do you have those?"

"Sure, I do."

"Just not for me?" she asked.

He gave her an aggrieved look. What had happened to Tad in his past relationships? Something in his tone told her that he was hiding an important detail from her. "We don't really know each other."

"My point exactly," she said. Marriage was... scary. She didn't know that she'd ever be able to risk her heart on happily ever after since every time she'd counted on that, she'd lost.

"Which is why our marriage will work."

"How do you know this? Did you try it once before and fail?"

"No. I've never made it to the church."

He must have gotten close. She wanted to find out more about his past relationship but didn't want to probe too deeply. "Then how can you be so sure?"

"I watched a friend of mine get torn apart in the name of love."

There was a fierceness about him that told her that he did experience deep emotion. For a minute she mourned the fact that she wasn't the person inspiring that emotion in him. But she'd looked in the mirror. She knew her limits.

She was the meat and potatoes kind of girl. A solid meal that would keep you alive. She wasn't the fancy French pastry that everyone craved. It was time she stopped forgetting it.

"I don't plan to ever marry," she said at last. She wasn't settling in her personal life and fully expected to remain single because she was realistic enough to realize no man could give her everything she wanted from him.

"Cathy Jane, forget those dreams you have of a white knight. We can have a nice, comfortable life together."

Screw you, she thought. What was she a pair of bedroom slippers? Sure she knew that she didn't exactly have it going on when it came to being a sexy goddess but that didn't mean she was comfortable.

"No. Thanks."

"No to what?" he asked as she pushed past him and gathered napkins and paper plates.

"To marriage," she said under her breath.

"I haven't asked you yet."

Stunned she pivoted to face him. He watched her

with a calm implacability that made her want to scream. "You are so frustrating."

He gave her a half smile that she was sure he intended to lighten the mood. But nothing could. She'd only seriously considered marrying two men in her life. Tad when she'd been eighteen, which had been pure fantasy.

And then Marcus when she'd been twenty-three, which had been harsh reality. Now Tad was here asking her to marry him and she wanted to say yes but she couldn't...wouldn't. She wasn't risking her heart and soul for another man. No matter how attractive he was or how sincere his offer of forever sounded.

"So are you."

Picking up the cookie platter she hurried out into the living room. Rae-Anne was standing back staring at the tree. For a moment there was a look on her face that gave CJ pause. Her secretary had an aura of sadness around her.

"You okay, Rae-Anne?"

Slowly Rae-Anne turned to face CJ. "Yeah."

"Do you want to talk about it?" CJ asked.

"Hell, no."

CJ set down the cookie tray and Tad was right behind her with the coffee. Her living room was spacious and had a nice grouping of a sofa and a couple of chairs. Rae-Anne took one of the armchairs and Tad stood next to one of the other ones. So CJ sat on the sofa.

She focused on serving coffee and then relaxed

against the cushions. Tad didn't sit down, just propped one hip against the arm of the chair and watched her with that wizard's gaze of his.

She had the feeling he wanted to pursue the topic they'd been discussing in the kitchen. He was going to be disappointed because she wasn't ever going to be alone with him again. And the topic of marriage was *not* going to come up if she had any say so.

"What were you two talking about?" Rae-Anne asked.

"Our marriage," Tad said around a bite of cookie.

"I didn't realize you two were serious. When will the blessed event take place?" Rae-Anne asked.

"When hell freezes over," CJ said.

Four

Tad threw his head back and laughed. Despite CJ's homey living room with the Christmas tree, a part of him wondered if she was going to be worth the battle. He'd lost at love before even though he hadn't told CJ the details. Losing Kylie had changed him. It had made him realize that life was more than winning and that sometimes a loss could cut deep.

She crossed the room to the stereo and put on a CD that played Christmas tunes. But CJ had so much sass and spunk—way more than he remembered Cathy Jane having. He couldn't wait to get her into bed. He had a feeling this glimpse of the real CJ was one not many people saw. "It's certainly cold enough to freeze hell today."

"I'm not kidding," she said, taking a large sip of her coffee. There was a hint of vulnerability in her eyes that he knew she'd regret revealing. There was so much more to his Catwoman than he expected. She'd always been complicated, he just hadn't been mature enough to appreciate her.

He waited until she swallowed then made sure she was watching him. "Good. I like a challenge."

"Is that all this is? A game?" CJ asked.

It was more than a game and more than he wanted to admit to himself. He didn't know why but she'd become important to his future.

The CJ he'd kissed in the kitchen was gone and in her place was the modern-day amazon he'd first encountered in CJ's office. The hint of vulnerability he'd glimpsed in her was now carefully concealed. Would the real Catherine Jane please step forward? "Would you play with me if it was?"

"No, Tad. Marriage is a sacred bond," CJ said.

"Not everyone thinks of it that way," he said, gently. Kylie certainly hadn't. She'd thought of it as a business transaction and the more money he'd brought to the table the more viable a husband candidate he'd been. Only at the time he hadn't realized it. Wouldn't even listen to Pierce when he'd tried to warn him that Kylie was only with Tad because of his bank account.

Pierce was his partner and best friend, a paraplegic who'd endured a lot in the name of love.

"Women do. Right, Rae-Anne?"

"I'm not the best one to ask about this," Rae-Anne said, staring down into her coffee cup.

Tad watched the older woman. There was no ring on her finger. But that didn't mean anything.

"Divorced?" CJ asked.

"I never had the time for marriage."

"Gay?" Tad asked.

"No. I just never took the time to settle down," Rae-Anne said.

"Do you regret that?" Tad asked her.

"Recently, I've started to. But my job used to be the most important thing in my life."

"Well, my job still is. And I'm not going to give it up for some guy," CJ said, standing up and walking toward the bank of glass windows that provided a clear view of Lake Michigan.

Tad set his coffee cup down and walked up behind her. Placing his hands on her shoulders he tugged her back against his chest. Damn but this woman felt right in his arms. "I'm not just any guy."

She tilted her head back and looked up at him. "No, you're not."

He cupped her face in his hand. "Is that the problem then?"

"There is no problem. I'm just not the marrying kind."

"Why not marry Tad?" Rae-Anne asked.

CJ pulled away from him. Tad had forgotten the older woman's presence. He wished he and CJ were by themselves in her apartment. They communicated more honestly when he was touching her than at any other time. He was sure once he had her alone and in his arms, he could convince her to marry him.

"He's a pain in the butt," CJ said.

"Perhaps he just knows what he wants," Rae-Anne said.

Having the older woman as an ally was definitely going to be an advantage. But then maybe Rae-Anne had regrets that she couldn't go back and change. "Thanks, Rae-Anne."

"Why are you on his side?"

"I just don't want to see you end up like me."

"Is that a sin?"

"Some people think so," Rae-Anne said.

Rae-Anne's phone rang and she answered it. After a terse conversation, Rae-Anne disconnected the phone. "Some people just don't know when to leave well enough alone. Do you need anymore help from me?"

"No. Thanks for bringing by my files and for your help with the tree. I'll see you tomorrow afternoon with the rest of the staff for the tree decorating party."

Rae-Anne left and an awkward silence fell between them.

"What have you got against marriage?" Tad asked, propping one hip against the armchair. CJ's apartment was tastefully decorated in a feminine way. Lots of light colors and baskets for magazines. But he felt comfortable here. Something he'd never felt in any other place except his parents' home.

"I'm not willing to give up everything for a man."
She was staring down into her coffee cup.

"That sounds bitter," Tad said.

She shrugged and finally glanced up at him. "Not
bitter—realistic."

He left his perch on the chair and sat down next to
her. Leaning back, he placed his arm along the top of
the loveseat over her shoulders. She started and jerked
away from him. Sloshing coffee onto her hands.

She put the cup on the table and wiped her hands
on a napkin but didn't relax. Just sat there tensely
waiting for him to pounce. Gee, that made him feel
good. What had he done to make her believe he was
the enemy?

"In the kitchen you asked me about love. Anyone
who believes in love can't be totally against marriage."

She started gathering items on the coffee table as if
cleaning up the cookies and coffee cups were the most
important thing in the world.

"Aren't you going to answer me?" he asked.

She glanced over her shoulder at him and he regretted pushing her. He knew one of his greatest faults
was impatience.

"I'll admit I want to find someone to love me—not
just an image that I represent."

"Cathy Jane, you've always been in your own playing field."

"Don't say things like that. You don't mean them,"
she said.

But he did. And convincing her of it would take considerable effort. But then everything worth keeping in his life had taken hard work. Why should CJ be any different?

He thought about his best friend, Pierce, who'd lost the woman he loved when he'd lost the use of his legs. His friend's devastation in the aftermath of losing Karen had confirmed to Tad that he never wanted to feel that way. He'd learned that it didn't pay to let a woman close. Tad had vowed to never let himself be affected so deeply by any woman.

But even that warning wasn't enough to sway him from wanting CJ. She turned away from him and he had the first doubts that his plan for a simple marriage of convenience might not work.

"Come to dinner with me tonight and I'll prove that I'm the only man you want."

"I don't think so," she said, gathering the tray with emptied coffee cups and leftover cookies. She couldn't focus on Tad and his insane desire to have her as his wife. It didn't matter that she was tempted, hell more than tempted to be Mrs. Tad Randolph. All that mattered was that she'd found a way of living that worked for her and she wasn't willing to rock the boat for some buff blond guy.

"I'll help with that." Tad stood to take the tray from her but she turned away.

She didn't want to make this decision with her hormones and just those few minutes in his arms earlier told her that saying no to Tad was the only sane option. She'd learned at Marcus' hands that she was a slave to her body and heart. And she wasn't going to live through that again.

"No, thanks."

He blocked her path to the kitchen. Determination written in every line of his body. Dammit, she wished he were still the ninety-pound weakling he'd been when they were twelve. Then she'd have brushed right past him and outrun him. But now, he looked like he could take on Mt. Everest blindfolded and she felt like she'd be doing good to get through a thirty-minute yoga class.

"I'm not leaving until you agree to have dinner with me," he said, drawing one finger down the side of her face. He toyed with a tendril of hair at the back of her neck. Her hands trembled.

"Why'd you dye your hair?" he asked, leaning forward around the tray. He brushed his nose against her head and breathed deeply. "You smell good."

She was shaking now, the coffee cups clattering on their saucers. Tad took the tray from her and put it on the coffee table. "Answer me."

"What?" she asked, totally rattled. All she wanted was to grab his hand and take him down the rather short hallway to her bedroom. She wanted to push him back on the bed and have her way with him.

"Your new hair color, why?"

How could she explain to this very attractive man that being an average mousy-brown-haired woman wasn't what she wanted the world to see of her? He wouldn't be able to understand that physical image was the easiest thing to change and still the most important to her. It was one more facade between her and the rest of the world.

She shrugged, trying for nonchalance, which she was far from feeling. "I needed to make a clean break with the past."

"Was it really that bad?" he asked.

He was too close. She could smell the sweat that had dried on his body. She wanted to do what he'd done, lean in and breathe in his essence but she couldn't. One lungful of his scent wouldn't be enough.

She wanted to indulge all her senses with him. To forget all this talk and communicate in the most essential way men and women could. Except she knew such communication was the most dangerous of all. "No. It didn't fit with the new me."

"I like the new you," he said, brushing his lips against hers. "But, then, I liked the old you too."

It wasn't enough. That brief brush of lips. She stood on her toes and kissed him. She closed her eyes, held his head in her hands and tasted him. She thrust her tongue past the barrier of his lips and teeth. The flavor of coffee and cookies deluged her taste buds.

She tilted her head to the side, pulling back then returning again to his mouth. He kept his hands at his sides letting her control the embrace. Seeming to know that she needed a chance to be in charge. Or maybe he knew this was the key to her weakness. She backed away abruptly. When was she going to learn?

He licked his lips, crossing his arms over his chest. His eyes watched her and she didn't know what to do next. This situation was not her comfort zone. She wanted him out of her house. *Now*.

"It's been a long time since…"

"Me too," he said, rubbing his thumb over her lower lip.

She ached for him in the most primal way. Her breasts were full and heavy. Her nipples taut. If she leaned forward just an inch she'd be able to rub against his chest. That hard well-developed-buff-sports-guy chest of his that called to her like the HoHos in her kitchen cupboard. But she wasn't ready to surrender everything for him. "I'm not sleeping with you, Tad."

"I don't really want to sleep," he said blandly.

She couldn't help but smile. "Please, just let it go."

"I can't. You're going to be my wife, CJ. You know I don't say things that I don't mean."

"Stop it," she said, backing away from him. He did so say things he didn't mean. He'd been the one to promise her at age twelve that he'd always rescue her and then he'd hurt her.

The next condo she bought was going to have a huge labyrinth of rooms. In it she would be able to stand at one end of the maze and have to yell to be heard at the other.

In such a complex, a six-foot tall man couldn't dominate any one room. She could easily escape not only a person, but the feelings and memories they evoked. "You don't know the real me. I don't think *I* do."

"That might be true. But I'm not leaving until I do."

"Why?"

"Because I know you'll avoid me from now on unless we clear the air."

"Clear the air. Is that all you want to do with me?"

"Hell, no. I want to take you to bed and break down all the barriers you've put between us."

"Tad, go away."

"Why?"

"Because I'm not the girl you want."

"Yes, you are."

"Because I like the same Christmas tree you do."

He gave her a half smile that took her breath away. "No, because you're beautiful and sexy and you've haunted my dreams since the last time I saw you."

She took the tray and left the living room. She couldn't think when he said things like that. When he made her believe that forever and happily ever after might still exist. It was as if everything Marcus, her ex-lover and ex-boss, had taught her disappeared. But she knew better.

"I'm not your dream woman, Tad. I'm no man's."

No man's dream woman. The words echoed in his head and Tad realized he'd unintentionally hurt CJ. The woman he thought had no weaknesses had just revealed one. And it was a deep wound. He felt like he'd callously torn the scab off of it.

As badly as Kylie had hurt him when she'd left, Tad had never been bitter toward women. For one thing Pierce wouldn't let him. He'd said one sour apple didn't make the whole pie bad. And Pierce had been right. There had been other women since Kylie, but now Tad acknowledged that he'd kept them at arm's length. Something he wasn't going to be able to do with CJ.

He knew a gentleman would leave but he'd never held that title. He was a businessman and sports enthusiast. He'd been a farmer and a brainiac. But never a gentleman.

Since she'd reentered his life she'd become his dream woman. He wasn't going to tell her, but other women paled when compared to her. Which was why he'd decided to marry her.

The music had switched off sometime when Rae-Anne left. And it didn't seem very festive in CJ's apartment anymore. But it did feel wintry and cold. And he wondered how he was going to make things right. His father's words rang in his ears. *It's our job to protect the women.*

Tad knew he'd done a poor job of that today. He lit a fire in the fireplace and put on a Bing Crosby Christmas CD.

He didn't like to hear CJ talk about herself like she wasn't good enough for any man. He only hoped his long-ago comments weren't to blame. What the hell had happened to her while they'd been apart?

He wasn't leaving until he had an answer. He pushed his way into the kitchen stopping when he saw CJ leaning against the counter with her arms wrapped around her waist and her head tucked down. His arms ached.

"Are you still here?"

"Yeah, and I'm not leaving until we get some things straight."

"What things?"

"One—I'm not like every other guy you've ever met. Two—you don't have any idea what my dream woman looks like. And three—you promised dinner."

"Not now. Okay?" she asked. The vulnerability in her eyes made him want to find the bastard who had hurt her and tear him apart. He stopped thinking about questions and answers and instead went to her and took her in his arms.

He held her tight, savoring the feel of her against his chest. She kept her own arms wrapped tight around herself.

"We are going to talk."

She drew an unsteady breath and he knew she wasn't going to acquiesce to his wishes easily. Too damn bad. Somehow he was responsible for making the spitfire he'd met in the office into this quivering mass of femininity. He had no idea how to change her back. But he was going to try.

This was precisely why he'd decided on an unemotional entanglement with the opposite sex. A marriage of his convenience and her pleasure. It was simple really.

"Cathy Jane, what's wrong?"

"Nothing."

"Women always like to talk about how men don't communicate but y'all could give lessons."

"You sound like your dad."

"Hell, I feel like my dad must when my mom is giving him the cold shoulder."

"I'm not giving you the cold shoulder. I'm just asking you to leave me alone."

"Same difference," he said. His dad wasn't one to talk about emotions but last spring when his mom had had a breast cancer scare, his dad had told him that he couldn't live without his wife. Tad didn't want to believe that he couldn't live without CJ but he knew that Cathy Jane had touched something deep inside him years ago. Something he hoped was mutual that bound them both together.

"We're not married," she said quietly.

The crackle of the fire and the lighted Christmas tree made him wish things weren't complicated with CJ. Made him wish he could take that afghan off the back of her couch, the one he knew her Aunt Bessie had made, and lay it on the ground. Then he'd lower her down on it and make love to her until the shadows in her eyes had disappeared. "I'd like us to be."

"You are making me crazy. Please don't mention marriage again."

"Give me a good reason not to," he said.

"We don't know each other."

He leaned closer to her and brushed a soft kiss against her lips. "Then let's get to know each other."

He scooped CJ up in his arms and walked back into the living room. He sat in the armchair nearest the Christmas tree and put her in his lap with her legs over one of the arms and her head resting against the back corner.

"This is more like it," he said.

"What is?" she asked, her eyes were glassy and he knew whatever she was battling was overwhelming.

He dipped his head and brushed a soft kiss against her forehead. She made him want to cherish her. He didn't understand it. He'd come into the condo with a plan—convince CJ to marry him, maybe cement that decision in bed. But this tenderness, this damned protectiveness she called from him, he didn't understand.

"You...offered up like a feast."

She gave him a half grin then hauled back and punched him in the arm. "Will you stop it?"

This was his old Cathy Jane. This woman he could handle. But that didn't change the fact that something had happened earlier to hurt her and he didn't have a clue what it was. "What happened before? I've never seen a woman react the way you did to a simple marriage proposal and a kiss."

"Nothing with you is simple, Tad."

"You're making this more complicated than you

need to. What happened to the girl I knew in Auburn-dale?''

''She grew up.''

''Growing up doesn't necessarily mean barriers.''

''Well it does for me.''

''Talk to me, CJ. Tell me what that means.''

''I just forgot something that I shouldn't have.''

''What?''

She bit her lip and looked away. He wished she trusted him enough to tell him her secrets.

''You don't have to tell me now.''

''Tad, this isn't going to work. I'll call Butch and tell him to assign someone else to your account.''

''Don't be ridiculous. I told you I'm going to marry you and I'm still determined to make that happen.''

''I'm not marrying a man who isn't my image of the perfect man.''

''Tell me what the qualities are.''

''It's not a list of things you can go out and buy.''

''What is it then?''

''Just a feeling I'll get deep inside when I know it's right.''

''Love?''

''Maybe. It's kind of this indefinable thing that I'll know when it happens.''

She stood up and crossed to the front door. She opened it and Tad got to his feet reluctantly. ''You owe me a dinner. I'll be back at six to pick you up.''

''Do we really have to do this?''

"Hell, yes. Love is overrated and I'm going to prove it to you."

He bent down, took her mouth swiftly and deeply and walked away.

Five

Christmas had never really been CJ's favorite time of year. Mainly because her mom used to try to make them into the perfect little family during the holiday season. And that had just made her dad's absence more obvious. She knew her mom had everyone's best interests at heart. CJ wondered some times if that wasn't why she tried so hard to make everyone believe she was an image of perfection instead of a real human with faults and weaknesses.

Tad had sent a car and a dozen long-stemmed white roses for her at 6:00 p.m. Standing on the street with a light snow falling, cold wind seeping into her clothing, and a bouquet of sweet-smelling flowers in her arms, she debated getting into the limo.

Tad scared her. More than she'd thought an old high school friend ever could. It wasn't like she really had that many friends from the good old days, she thought wryly.

"You okay, ma'am?" the driver asked.

She hated being called ma'am. For God's sake she wasn't even thirty yet. Way too young to be called ma'am. Except today she felt old and wary. *Very wary.* Hell, too wary for a woman her age. She should be able to enjoy an attraction with the opposite sex instead of being afraid of it.

But fear was part of the allure for her. Her body was pulsing in time with the music in her head. Slow, steady sex music that she'd ignored for a long, long time. Only tonight she didn't want to ignore it and that's precisely why she wasn't getting in the car.

"No," she said to the young driver. "I'm not okay."

She pivoted and walked back in her building past the doorman with the curious expression. The ride up in the elevator was painfully slow, but the car finally arrived at her floor. The condo she called home had never looked more like the sanctuary it essentially was.

She put her key in the lock and made up her mind. She wasn't going to get back on the merry-go-round that had lead to her near destruction with Marcus.

If standing Tad up cost her a promotion at work, so be it. Her sanity meant more than her job. At least right now it did. And she'd started over before. It was actually something she felt she'd mastered.

Her apartment was warm and welcoming after the cold street. She changed into jeans and a thermal shirt and then lit a fire in the fireplace. Glancing in the gilt-framed mirror over the mantel, she scarcely recognized herself. She'd changed a lot in the process of trying to find herself. She'd thought she knew who she was but a wind from the past had shattered her sense of self. Now she saw a woman who vaguely resembled the image in her head and that hurt.

She put on a Christmas CD and puttered around her apartment turning on the tree lights and trying to shake off her mood with seasonal cheer. Not even a cup of apple-cinnamon herbal tea helped. Without thinking, she climbed up on the counter and opened the cabinet above the fridge.

There sat an untouched box of HoHos. Why she liked them she didn't know. They had no nutritional value. They didn't even taste good if you savored them. She pulled the box down along with the un-opened bottle of Bailey's.

Taking the snacks, the liquor and a snifter, she made her way to the living room. Thank God her mother hadn't lived to see her daughter alone and afraid at the age of twenty-eight, reduced to spending her evenings with a bottle of after-dinner liqueur and children's snack cakes.

The music inside her head changed to a frenzied Mozart concerto with layer after layer piled on top of each other. In her mind she knew the layers were job, past, Tad, family and somewhere buried deep beneath the frenetically playing music was Catherine Jane, the real Catherine Jane. Not Cathy Jane or CJ. Just a girl who didn't really know who she was or what she wanted.

After forty-five minutes of analysis she realized she was waiting for something. Waiting for…someone.

She reached for the HoHos box but dropped her hand. She wasn't going to eat her way back to a size 16 over some guy. Except that Tad wasn't just a guy. If he was she'd have gotten into the limo and gone to dinner with him. There was no pressure in dating a man she wasn't attracted to. It was only the men who touched a deep emotional chord inside her that made her quiver with awareness.

She went into the kitchen and started baking. The doorbell rang two hours later when she was in the middle of her grandmother's famous pineapple cheesecake. She hesitated.

Checking the gingerbread cookies baking in the oven, she walked slowly toward the door.

She'd bet money that Tad was on the other side. She'd been waiting for him to come but when she opened the door she found instead a take-out deliveryman.

"I didn't order anything," she said.

"It's a gift."

He opened the heat-sealed container and handed her

a bag of food and a note. She tipped the deliveryman and he left quickly.

She took the bags into the kitchen and opened them. Inside was a meal of Peking chicken and fried rice. The note had been written by Tad.

Enjoy dinner on me, since you wouldn't have dinner with me.

She shivered a little. Felt like a big coward and knew that she'd hurt Tad. Something she'd never really intended to do. But she'd had no choice. She couldn't risk losing herself again to the one man she'd never been able to forget.

Tad pushed himself hard in the weight room in his condo. It took the edge off his anger. Anger he didn't have another outlet to release.

If he'd been at his folks' place in Florida he would have visited one of his high school buddies and started a fight with him. There was nothing like a good fist-fight to get rid of rage. But they were miles away.

He'd known that he was moving too fast for CJ. But standing him up—hell, that ticked him off.

Women confounded him. He'd never really understood what Kylie had wanted from him until she'd walked away. He didn't really understand why his mom was obsessed with grandkids. And most of all he didn't understand why Cathy Jane Terrence—who dressed in suits, looked like she'd stepped from the pages of *Style* magazine and called herself CJ—was afraid to have dinner with him.

The phone rang but he ignored it. Leaving the weight room and going to the kitchen, he filled a glass with filtered water and drained the cup. In the other room he heard his machine pick up. Heard his own voice telling the caller to leave a message and then CJ's voice. Soft and tentative.

He wasn't going to listen to her message. Hell, when she was finished he was walking into the office and deleting it without listening to it. Tad Randolph wasn't a guy she could manipulate whenever she felt like it.

But he found himself walking down the hall in time to hear her say she was sorry. *She was sorry. Damn.* It sounded like she was on the verge of tears and without really thinking about it, he grabbed the handset.

"CJ?" he asked.

She took a deep breath and then in a husky voice said, "Oh, you're home."

He didn't know what to say to this woman who he wanted to marry but wouldn't let himself love. The woman who had more walls than he knew how to scale. The woman who had become the one he wanted. "I was working out."

"Um…I just wanted to thank you for dinner. That was really nice of you," she said.

Tad knew he could hold onto his anger and let this relationship go no further or he could let it go and try to understand why Cathy Jane always ran. "No problem."

Silence buzzed on the open line. Why had she called tonight?

"Listen, we need to talk," she said, as he heard pans clatter in the sink. Then water running.

"I'll say."

"Are you going to listen or be mad at me?" she asked. The water shut off. He pictured her in her kitchen. In his mind she wore those tight jeans she'd had on earlier.

"CJ, I sat at a table for two in a very expensive restaurant waiting for you for over an hour."

She took a deep breath. "I'm sorry."

"Yeah, right. Why'd you agree to have dinner with me?" he asked. But his mind wasn't on his anger. Lust had kindled to life the minute he'd realized she was in the kitchen where he'd kissed her. He could still feel the softness of her curves against his body. His blood ran heavier.

"You were pushing too hard."

Not as hard as he'd wanted to or else they'd both be in his bed right now instead of in their own houses having a tense conversation on the phone. "I was, but you know I wouldn't force you into anything you didn't want to do."

"I guess."

"Are you afraid of me?" he asked. He didn't think she was. The way she'd kissed him this afternoon told him that she didn't fear him on an instinctual level.

"I don't know."

"I'm not the same guy you used to know." Whatever happened now, he refused to leave things in the weird limbo they'd been in since the last time they'd seen each other in Florida. He liked the woman CJ had become. Liked that she was a successful businesswoman. Liked that she was sassy and smart and sexy as hell.

"Well I'm not the same girl either."

He leaned against his desk. What was she driving at? She'd hinted earlier that she'd changed. But then when he'd given her the opportunity to tell him or show him, she'd chickened out. "I know. What can I do to convince you I'm not a monster?"

"I don't think you're a monster."

"Then what's going on here?" he asked.

"I've never been able to deal with desire well," she said in a shaky voice.

"I don't understand."

"I want you."

His groin hardened and his entire body started to pulse in time with his heartbeat. He straightened and paced around the room. "I want you too. So what's the problem?"

"You want to marry me," she said.

"I'm not following," he said. She made him feel like an idiot sometimes.

"I've never been able to handle a committed relationship and have a life at the same time."

"I'm not planning on taking over your life."

"No you wouldn't plan on it. But it would happen all the same."

"Why do you think that? I don't want to run your life," he said. He meant it, too. He'd learned a long time ago that women need their space. He just wanted someone to share the success he'd achieved.

"What do you want from me?"

"The future. Our future. Not one where we live separate lives but one where we're together."

"That sounds so easy."

"It is. Trust me."

Trust him. There was a part of her that wanted to just give in and do whatever Tad asked of her. She'd always liked strong-willed men because life around them was blissfully effortless.

That was why she didn't trust herself. Not Tad. Tad was still the great guy she remembered. But he made her forget who she'd become.

"It's not that simple." She paced the length of her kitchen searching for an escape to the memories Tad's deep voice evoked.

"Sure, it is," he said. His confidence nearly undid her resolve. He'd been right about other things before. Things like which schools to apply to. Which classes to take at the community college over summer.

"Tad…"

"You're weakening. I know you are," he said.

She smiled to herself. The kitchen counter was covered in freshly baked goods and she reached for the royal icing to assemble the gingerbread house from the pieces she'd made earlier.

Her mother, Marnie and she had made two hundred gingerbread houses one year to raise money for presents. God, she'd hated the smell of gingerbread that year. But now it made her feel nostalgic and warm inside. She'd made the house so many times over the years that the work was mindless and she assembled the house feeling her mom's spirit with her as she worked. "What do you want from me?"

"You keep asking me that. I want marriage." He'd been angry when they'd first gotten on the phone. She'd heard it in his voice. But now he was teasing her. He was more relaxed. She was glad. She regretted leaving him alone in a restaurant.

She didn't want to be responsible for him feeling that way ever again. "I'm not going to change my mind."

"Leave that to me."

"Are you sure you want to try?" she asked. Marcus had left her shattered and she wasn't sure she wanted to risk herself again. She didn't want to be back in that emotionally desolate place again.

She'd had to leave her job and start over with another company at the bottom. She didn't want to do it again. And on the emotional side she cared for Tad in a way that she never had with Marcus. Marriage had sounded like a business transaction when Marcus had mentioned it but it sounded so right when Tad did. Maybe that was why she was fighting so hard to keep him at arm's length.

"Hell, yes. The best things in life are the ones you have to work for. Haven't you found that?"

She pushed a row of M&M's into the roof of her gingerbread house. Her career was the only thing she had in her life. She had nice possessions and a house that was the only place where she let her guard down. It had taken her three years of saving and living in a shared three-flat in a so-so neighborhood before she'd been able to move here. "I can be really stubborn."

"I've seen that side of you. And I think I can get around it."

"How?" she asked, absently licking the icing off her finger.

"With a kiss. Babe, you were putty in my arms."

She set down the icing bag and stood up. If he hadn't kissed her today. If she hadn't kissed him then it would be so much easier to walk away. But the powerful desire arching between them was the one thing that had been missing in her life. And she needed him. It scared her. The emotional connection or the physical bond, one or the other, would be okay but not both. "Yeah, I was."

How had he guessed? But then she thought that maybe when you stood a guy up and then confessed to wanting him that he might suspect that you had dating issues. Heck, she had more than issues, she had phobias and she wasn't sure she wanted to explore them with Tad. He made everything about her life seem sharper. She hated lying so she changed the subject. "Will you be in your office tomorrow?"

"I'm not going to stop asking," he warned.

Stubbornly, she refused to say anything else. Finally Tad sighed. "Yes, I'll be in my office. Why?"

"I'm going to send some cookies over."

"Homemade ones?"

"Yes. I've been baking all night."

"Did you figure anything out while you were riding the range?" he asked.

She laughed. That was definitely a Mr. Randolph comment. Tad's dad used to tease her about all the time she spent in the kitchen cooking for Tad when they'd been friends. She'd always liked his folks. They had the kind of marriage that made young girls dream some day they might find their true love and live with him.

"The only conclusion I came to was that I didn't want to hurt you again."

"You can't," he said.

She felt small when he said it. And didn't really know how to respond to him. "Oh."

"I didn't mean it in a bad way."

"There really isn't a good way to take that."

"You're not the only one who's been hurt," he said, softly.

She hadn't thought of that. She'd been so focused on protecting herself she hadn't thought that Tad probably was doing the same thing. Perhaps that was why he'd proposed the marriage of convenience with her.

"Are you sure you want to pursue this?" she asked.

"This? What are you talking about?"

"A relationship," she said, knowing he was being deliberately obtuse.

"I intend to pursue you, Cathy Jane. The rest will work itself out."

He hung up and she leaned back against the counter feeling the first tinge of hope that maybe this relationship would be different from the rest.

Six

"**H**old the elevator," CJ called as she entered her office building. Plagued by fevered dreams of her and Tad making love in her kitchen with gingerbread houses all around them, CJ woke late and had to rush to make it to work on time.

She'd called her office but Rae-Anne hadn't taken the phones off voicemail. She was more than a little concerned that things were going to be a mess in her office on this Monday morning.

A large masculine hand blocked the doors and she entered the car, juggling purse, briefcase and scarf. She glanced up to say thanks and met Tad's bright green eyes.

"Good morning, CJ."

"It hasn't been good yet," she said. Seeing him now seemed an extension of the dreams she'd had last night. The spicy clean smell of his soap surrounded her. He wore an Icelandic sweater that brought out his eyes and made him look like a Norse god. And she wanted nothing more than to move closer and confirm that he felt as good as she remembered. But she was at work and Tad didn't belong here.

"Let me see what I can do about changing that," he said as the elevator doors closed. He tugged her into his arms and tilted her head back.

His warm breath brushed against her cold cheeks and she knew this was something that had been missing from her life for a long time. She refused to think about it, having decided on her cab ride to work that she was going to take whatever Tad offered her physically.

Slowly he lowered his head, taking her mouth with his in a deep drugging kiss that soothed the frantic pace of the morning. She responded eagerly in his embrace, holding him closer to her. Sensation spread throughout her body. He backed her up against the wall of the elevator car, his big body surrounding hers.

She felt small and very womanly in his arms. He groaned deep in his throat and thrust deep in her mouth, tasting her with languid parries of his tongue.

He slid one leg between her thighs and she rocked her hips against his jeans clad thigh. One of his hands traveled down her back and squeezed her hip, urging her to keep moving against him.

Her breasts felt full and heavy and she shivered, needing more. She pushed her hands under his sweater and felt the warmth of his back through the layer of his cotton T-shirt. She scraped her nails down his back and he groaned again. He was hot and hard between her legs. And she wished she'd worn a skirt to work today instead of pants.

The elevator binged. Tad cursed under his breath and moved away from her. Dazed, CJ had no idea where they were for a minute. But it came rushing swiftly back to her. "My God, I'm at work."

Tad picked her purse and briefcase up off the floor and handed them to her. His lips were swollen and his eyes narrowed on her body. The flush of arousal was on his face and she knew he was as flustered as she was.

"You make me forget everything I've learned in the last five years," she said.

"Like what?" he asked. There was an intensity in his gaze that made her shiver.

"That men and work don't mix."

"Same tune different verse, Cathy Jane. You've been saying that to me every time I get too close and I'm still not buying it."

"Do you want an account manager who is so easily distracted?" she said.

"You're right," he said.

His words cut her but then she didn't really expect anything less. "I'll ask Butch to assign someone else."

"I don't want anyone but you. You're very good at what you do," Tad said with a wicked gleam in his eyes.

He gestured for her to exit the elevator and she did, grateful to see that the hall was empty. She hurried to her office but then slowed as she realized it might seem to Tad that she was running from him. And she'd decided to take control of the attraction between them.

She stopped in the kitchen area and selected a decaf cappuccino from the coffee machine. "So, what are you doing here?"

"I'm here for you," he said in his husky morning voice. She crossed her arms over her chest and scooted away from him. He was too tempting. She wanted to say yes to the vague innuendo in his voice and drag him down the hall to her office, close the door and finish what they'd started in the elevator.

The crotch of her panties was damp, her heart was pounding, her nipples tight and only time or a quickie was going to give her a reprieve. And she didn't want anything quick with Tad. She wanted long hours spent together on a comfortable mattress.

"Don't look at me like that or I'm going to kidnap you and say to hell with the contract negotiations."

"Contract negotiations?"

"That's why I'm here."

Dammit. She closed her eyes and tried to will her mind back to business.

"Here's your coffee," Tad said, handing her the foam cup.

Tad pushed a button to select his drink and she suddenly realized she didn't care how cowardly it looked she had to get away from him. She wasn't in any position to talk to him about terms this morning. She edged toward the exit.

"Where are you going?"

"I need some time to get myself together for this meeting."

"You aren't prepared?" he asked.

Great, on top of everything else, now he thought she was incompetent. "I am. It's just you've rattled me."

"Only fair since you do the same to me."

"Tad, we have to work together. Let's put that first, okay?"

"We are but I thought we decided last night to test the waters."

"What did you have in mind?"

"Pierce and I are having our annual rock climbing race at the store this afternoon. Why don't you stop by for that and then we'll go grab some dinner?"

She watched him, afraid to be alone with him, but needing to more than she'd expected. "I'll be there. But this morning let's just concentrate on work."

"For now," he said and started down the hall to the conference room. She watched him walk away and felt the pressure of his presence tightening in her gut. She needed to figure out what she wanted and take control of this thing with Tad before it destroyed her.

* * *

The meeting with CJ's group went well and afterward she'd rushed back to her office without saying a word. Satisfied with the agreement he'd gotten from her in the coffee room earlier, he'd let her escape and returned to his office in the flagship P.T. Xtreme Sports store on Michigan Avenue near Water Tower Place. His office was on the third floor of the building they leased and overlooked the busy retail floor.

They had a rock-climbing wall that was busy with kids and other tourists taking a break from shopping to work out something other than their wallets. He and Pierce were scheduled for their annual rock climbing/light decorating competition.

Despite the fact that Pierce was a paraplegic and had lost the use of his legs during a fall on Mt. Hood, he still climbed. Pierce refused to let his disability change his life. Tad credited Pierce's outlook and drive as the influence that had made him stop feeling sorry for himself and take charge of his life.

Pierce used his massively strong arms and upper body to pull himself up the rock wall. It was incredibly hard to do—most climbers used their legs for balance and strength but Pierce had refused to give up the lifestyle he loved and had learned to climb without the use of his legs.

It was time for the event to start and Tad had a feeling he would be stood up again. This time he wasn't going to be gentlemanly about it. He was going to CJ's house as soon as the event was over and he wouldn't leave until she told him why she kept running away from him.

The local media were here to cover the event and he and Pierce had both been interviewed earlier. They also had a tree-lighting ceremony that featured the state champion long distance runner from a local high school. The entire affair was innocent but then again so was riding in the elevator most of the time.

"Ready, old man?" Pierce asked from the doorway.

Tad was beginning to think it was past time to throw in the towel where CJ was concerned. "Yeah, I guess so."

"What are you waiting for?" Pierce asked.

He grabbed his harness and climbing shoes and walked out of his office. "Not what. Who."

"Am I supposed to understand that?" Pierce kept pace in the wheelchair, pushing it with his muscled arms. The chair rolled past Tad and into the waiting elevator.

"Nah."

"How'd the meeting go with the new advertising company?" Pierce asked. Pierce was in charge of product development and would be working closely with CJ and her team. He had just returned from a two week vacation in Montana where his family owned a large cattle ranch.

"Good."

"I'm still not sure we made the right decision."

"You've seen the presentation boards. I know they'll do a good job."

"If you say so."

"I do. You know I'm always right when it comes to these decisions."

"I know you think you are. Remember last year you said the Bears would go all the way."

"I remember you saying the same thing about the Falcons."

"Better not let this get out or we'll look like we don't know a thing about sports."

"I was right about opening this store."

"So you had one good idea," Pierce said.

His cell phone rang before he could respond. "Randolph."

"It's CJ. I'm on my way to your store but traffic is heavy."

"I wasn't sure you were coming."

"I said I would."

"You've changed your mind before."

"Not anymore."

"Promise?" he asked.

"Promise," she said, disconnecting the phone.

Pierce watched Tad with a shrewd gaze. Tad didn't want to talk about CJ with his friend. Pierce had said on more than one occasion that Tad had horrible taste in women. He didn't want Pierce's opinion on CJ.

"Who was that?"

That was the thing about working with your best friend. Pierce felt free to poke his nose into all of Tad's business. "No one."

"The woman you were waiting for, right?" Pierce

asked. He maneuvered the wheelchair around as they approached the ground floor.

"Pierce, I don't meddle in your personal life."

"Enough said. Ready to get your butt kicked by a handicapped man?"

Pierce had won the past three years. And it wasn't because Tad let him win. Pierce was a fierce competitor who'd honed his body into a winning machine. He spent a good portion of the year winning wheelchair road races. "You bet."

They entered the crowded showroom. "I'll take the media while you set up the gear and lights."

"Gotcha."

"Need some help, *compare?*"

Tad glanced over his shoulder surprised to see Rae-Anne at the shop.

"What are you doing here?"

"Working, believe it or not. I'm supposed to get a feel for your company's work ethic. All of CJ's team is here tonight."

He was surprised to hear it but shouldn't have been. For CJ the job always came first. He had a feeling that if they had dinner tonight it wouldn't be just the two of them. "CJ's a hard boss."

"You have no idea the half of it. Women are…demanding."

Tad laughed. "You should know."

Rae-Anne muttered something under her breath and reached for a string of lights testing them. "What's the point in doing the event?"

"One hundred percent of tonight's profits go to area schools' nonvarsity sports programs. We get a lot of traffic and this gives the customers' kids something to do while they shop."

"I'm impressed."

"Let's hope CJ is too," Tad said.

"Still waiting for hell to freeze?" Rae-Anne asked.

"Yes."

"Anything I can do?" Rae-Anne asked.

"Mind your own business," CJ said, coming up behind them.

CJ knew that old chestnut about listening at eaves but she'd never been able to help herself. Rae-Anne shrugged and walked away. "Talking about me?"

Tad pivoted to face her. His eyes lingering on her lips. She knew he wanted to reach over and kiss her but wouldn't with all the people around them. She was tempted to lean over and kiss him instead. Anything to shake him up in this environment where he was way too confident.

He shrugged and gave her a half smile that went straight to her heart. "Just soliciting help from your faithful secretary."

"You need help?" she teased, moving closer to him. He'd changed and was wearing shorts and a T-shirt. He looked like the buff sports guy he was and she wanted him.

He leaned down, his cologne surrounded her and

when he spoke his warm breath brushed her cheek. "Not really but I figured any extra couldn't hurt."

Awareness spread throughout her body pooling in her center. She wished she could go back in time to this morning in the elevator. She'd hit the stop button and make love to him. Then there wouldn't be this anticipation running through her veins and filling her with excitement. Then she'd be able to concentrate on her job. On learning everything she could about P.T. Xtreme Sports instead of focusing on the sexy co-owner.

But that wasn't going to happen, so she patted his butt and scooted away from him. "I don't think you're going to need anything extra."

He threw his head back and laughed drawing many, appreciative feminine stares.

"You like what I've got?" he asked, closing the gap she'd opened between them.

"What do you think?" She'd forgotten what it was like to play this teasing game. To let anticipation build until it was a fevered pitch and neither of them could wait a moment longer.

"Cathy Jane, you always keep me guessing."

That made her feel in control and more sure of herself than she should around Tad. "Good. You're too cocky for your own good."

"Too cocky?" he asked, arching one eyebrow at her.

She titled her head to the side and gave him the once-over. His athletic shorts revealed his muscled runner's legs. She skimmed her gaze over him starting at his well-worn climbing shoes and not stopping until she reached his head. "Yeah, you know that attitude that says I'm a buff-macho-man-in-control-of-his-environment."

He canted his hips to one side. "I'm giving all that off?"

Now she felt a little silly. "Well, not all that but you know what I mean."

He cupped her face and kissed her quickly but fiercely. She shivered as he pulled away. "I know you make me so hot I can't think of anything else but you."

"Really?" she asked.

"Really."

"Good. It'll keep you on your toes."

He chuckled again, turning to adjust his harness and then step into it. "Better watch that sassy mouth. It's going to get you in trouble."

The vee of the straps on his thighs drew attention to his groin. She could tell she'd had an effect on him. With a wink, she said, "That kind of trouble I can handle."

"Is there any that you can't?" he asked, moving closer to her.

Teasing and lightness were the key to managing Tad. She wasn't sure, but she thought he might be content with the facade she showed the world instead of trying to see the real woman she hid. "None that you have to worry about."

"Who says I'd worry?" he asked, buckling the harness and then wrapping the lights he and Rae-Anne had straightened earlier into a neat coil. He put the lights into a pouch and fastened it to his belt.

He looked every inch the primal man she knew him to be. Tad was the kind of frontier man who would have been able to support his family with no one else around. He was a survivor and that appealed to her because if the past ten years had taught her anything it was that she was a survivor, too.

"I knew all that testosterone had killed the gray matter."

"Cathy Jane, you are playing with fire," he said, leaning close to her once again. She grabbed his harness and pulled him closer. His pupils dilated and she knew she was playing a dangerous game.

Though the store was crowded they were isolated together. They stood on the other side of the barrier that separated the public from the climbing wall.

"What are you doing?" he asked, his voice low and husky.

"Checking to make sure your harness is tight."

"Why?" he asked.

She'd needed to touch him again before he climbed the wall. It was kind of high and she didn't want Tad falling. "Because you've got all the trouble you need right here with me."

"Now that you're here, I can handle anything you throw at me. It's when you're running that you give me difficulty."

"Are you sure you know how to do this rock climbing thing?"

"Oh, I know exactly what I'm doing on the wall."

"What is the point of this?" she asked.

"Climbing to the top stringing the lights and then rappelling back down. All before Pierce of course."

"Pierce is your partner?"

"Yes."

"Is he any good at this?" she asked. What kind of competition was this going to be? From the job perspective this could be just the thing they needed to give Xtreme Sports the edge.

"He's second best," Tad said.

"You wish," a man said.

CJ turned to see a very well-built man in a wheelchair. He had kind eyes and was wearing a harness like Tad's.

"Cat Girl meet Pierce. Pierce, this is Cathy Jane Terrence."

"Cat Girl?" Pierce asked, glancing up at her.

She knew she was going to regret that name from the moment she'd met up with Tad. But as she stared at him, very much at home in his environment she realized she didn't regret having him in her life again.

Seven

"That name is a long story and one that needs to stay in the past. Please call me CJ," she said, taking the hand Pierce held out to her.

Pierce took her hand and brought it to his lips, kissing her hand. "It's a pleasure to meet you. I like stories, tell me about this name of yours."

CJ flushed and Tad realized that their inside jokes were meant to stay inside. And he knew that the name, which had been her rebellion against a group of peers who didn't see beyond her outer shell, was still a point of vulnerability with her. Why hadn't he realized it before now?

"We knew each other in high school. That was her nickname then," Tad said at last.

CJ gave him a surprisingly grateful look. Did she still not trust him?

"I can see where you got that nickname. You are sexy, but I am surprised high school boys would have been able to appreciate the nuances of your charm."

CJ shrugged and Tad remembered how he hadn't made her life any easier during that time. Her expression made Tad want to carry her away from Pierce and the crowded store. He wanted to find a secluded place to apologize once again for the idiot he'd been as a boy. To promise he'd make up for all the hurt she'd endured as a teenager.

"What was your nickname?" Pierce asked.

"None of your damn business," Tad said. Rad Tad had ruled the school and he'd been very aware of his position in the small pond that Auburndale Senior High was. He'd loved being the guy everyone knew or wanted to know.

Pierce watched CJ with more than just passing interest. Noticing Pierce's reaction to CJ, Tad realized he wasn't going to be content to let things develop slowly in the way that CJ wanted. He needed to brand her with his name.

He wanted every man who looked at her to realize they were poaching on his territory. And he knew that screamed of machismo and that CJ would never let him live it down if he gave her any indication of how he felt.

She was his—dammit. On a very elemental level he and CJ had bonded and he wasn't going to let her go.

Tad reached down and tugged her hand free of Pierce's. CJ lifted both eyebrows at him in question but he ignored her.

His past relationships had shown him one thing. He liked the challenge of going after a woman just out of reach. Was that the appeal with CJ? His gut said there was much more involved than that.

Frustrated, he glared at Pierce. As soon as he did, he saw the amusement on his friend's face. All this talk of high school had obviously made him revert to that eighteen-year-old behavior. All the experiences he'd gained with women fell away and he felt exposed and raw in front of CJ.

Being ribbed by Pierce for his behavior was insignificant compared to the jealousy running through him. Branding CJ was the least of the things he wanted to do to her.

Usually Tad was amused by Pierce's old-world manners. In fact, Pierce had flirted all the time with Caroline his last girlfriend and that had only amused Tad.

"CJ Terrence from the ad agency?" Pierce asked.

"The very same," CJ said.

Tad wrapped his arm around her waist and pulled her firmly against him. Her soft curves cushioned against his body, distracting him from the conversation. Too much time had passed since he'd held her in his arms.

"I didn't realize you two were personally involved," Pierce said.

"Actually, Cathy Jane's the woman I'm going to—"

"Say it and I'm going to plant a kiss on Pierce's lips he'll never forget," CJ warned.

"Say it," Pierce urged.

"Forget it, buddy." Tad tugged her back and dropped a quick kiss on her full mouth. He tipped her chin up and stared into her eyes. "Not saying it doesn't change my plans."

"What plans?" Pierce asked. His friend was enjoying this a little too well for Tad's liking.

"Nothing. Let's get this rock climbing thing done. CJ and I are going to dinner."

"Sounds good to me," Pierce said. "I'll go make the announcement."

Pierce rolled away and Tad checked his gear one more time. He hoped the climb would distract him from the new feelings spreading through him. Marrying CJ was one thing, caring for her something else, something he wasn't sure he could control and he didn't like that.

The strong emotions she inspired were intolerable. This was a woman who'd been running from him since the moment that they'd met again a few weeks ago. And Kylie had proven to him that chasing after a woman did nothing but make him look like a fool.

Tad had to be able to let her go. He refused to end up like Pierce had when Karen left him. Sitting alone in a dark room with only a picture album and a bottle of Cutty Sark. Using cheap booze to push away memories that he thought would last a lifetime.

Keep it light. He could do that. Hell, he had a history of keeping things light.

"Give me a kiss for luck?" Tad asked CJ.

She hesitated. "I kind of invited my staff to go to dinner with us."

Tad knew that despite what she'd said to him earlier, she was still running from him. Running from something he made her feel?

"I'll get Pierce to join us as well. What were you planning to discuss?"

"At the time I was afraid to be alone with you. But now…"

"Now?" he asked.

"I think I might have sabotaged myself. Because I can't wait to be alone with you."

"Promise?"

She leaned up and hugged him tightly to her. He forced himself to let her control the embrace but he wanted—hell, he needed—to crush her to him. To keep her close to him so that she didn't change her mind.

"Promise," she said in his ear.

Dinner at the Cheesecake Factory had been a noisy affair. CJ's staff had a million ideas and Pierce had been a jovial host spurring them on. Halfway through dinner Pierce's significant other, Tawny O'Neil had joined them. The leggy blonde had dropped onto Pierce's lap and planted one hot kiss on his lips.

Tawny had been funny and watching her and Pierce together had made CJ long for something she'd never had. A real relationship. One that was based on mutual desire, respect and affection.

Tad by comparison seemed quiet and brooding. And now that they were sitting in his car outside her condo building, she wasn't sure how to proceed. So much had changed between them and yet her fears remained.

"Alone at last," Tad said.

She wanted to smile at him and keep it light. He was just a guy. Just an ordinary guy. But he wasn't. And she'd always known that.

Sleeping with Tad was the biggest risk she could take. Because she was already half in love with him. He embodied so many of the qualities she wanted in her Mr. Right. Cementing their relationship by making it a sexual one was all she'd thought of since this morning when he'd kissed her in the elevator. But he wanted something from her she'd promised herself she'd give no man.

"Second thoughts?" he asked, tracing one finger down the side of her face.

"Not really. It's just that now that we're alone, I'm not sure what to do."

His features were illuminated by the dashboard lights and in his eyes she searched for some emotion that he felt but couldn't acknowledge. She saw tenderness and desire. Was that enough?

She was trying so hard not to let her body control her life again. And she realized that protecting herself from being hurt might be a bigger risk. Was it a risk she was willing to take?

He leaned close to her; his breath brushed her cheek. Her face still tingled from the rough rasp of his fingertip. Awareness spread throughout her body, pooling in her center. She shifted on the seat, clenching her thighs together.

"Invite me up for a cup of coffee," he said. He had no doubts. Maybe she was thinking about this too much.

She tilted her head to the side. Inside her the heavy beating of lust awoke. Each beat of her heart seemed louder and fiercer than the one before it. Her clothes felt constricting.

Tad's breathing was shallow as well. His nostrils flared and pupils dilated. Her mind noted every masculine detail and she realized that there was no turning back. She'd made up her mind earlier in the day.

"Want some coffee?"

"Hell, I want more than that," he said.

"How about something sweet with your coffee? I still have some cookies, pies and cakes I baked the other night. Is that enough to satisfy you?"

"You're all the dessert I need."

She hesitated with her hand on the door. "Am I really?"

Tad framed her face with both of his hands and

brushed his lips against hers. "Are you having doubts again?"

"You already asked me that."

"I want you to be very sure of this, Cathy Jane, because once we make love everything will change."

She swallowed. She knew that it would. And perhaps that was why she was hesitating. But she couldn't live the rest of her life in fear of a man's touch. Afraid that she'd indulge the passionate side of her nature at the cost of her sanity.

"No doubts."

She got out of the car and led the way into her building. The doorman smiled and waved at them as they waited for the elevator. She hadn't brought any man up to her place the entire time she lived here. Finally the doors opened and they entered the car. Tad pressed the button for her floor and as the doors swooshed close, pulled her into his arms.

He smelled good and it felt right to be in his arms. Every sense was attuned to him. His scent embedded deep in her hungry soul. He rubbed his hands down her back, cupping her buttocks and bringing her body more fully against his.

He possessed her with a complete attention to detail that left her burning for more. She turned her face toward his, seeking his mouth but he evaded her. Stroking his lips over her face.

His mouth settled on her neck. Teasing her with soft biting touches that made her forget everything but him. Her world narrowed to just the two of them.

When the doors opened on her floor it seemed natural that he'd lift her in his arms and carry her down the hall.

He set her on her feet in front of her door. He watched her with narrowed eyes. He was aroused and wanted her with an intensity that warned her her time for running was over. Her body said good, she was through with running. But her heart warned her to be careful. That the price to be paid for passion was a high one.

"Open the door, CJ," he said. His voice was deep and raspy and she knew he was on the razor's edge as well. That for him reason and caution were being superceded by instincts older than time.

Knowing she wasn't alone in these tumultuous emotions reassured her. She took her key from her purse and unlocked the door.

Glancing over at him, she wondered what he would do when he realized that she wasn't the innocent girl he remembered. When he realized her fears stemmed from perhaps too much knowledge of herself and not an uncertainty of what sex with him would be like.

"Last chance to run," he said.

She wasn't running from Tad anymore. Or from herself. The past few years had been cold and lonely and she wasn't going back to them again.

Taking his hand in both of hers, she opened the door and pulled him inside. She pushed the door closed and backed him up against it. She brought his mouth down to hers and laid both of their fears to rest.

* * *

CJ took his mouth in a kiss that was deep and carnal. She tasted him with languid strokes of her tongue, exploring him as if she meant to leave no secrets between them. As if she meant to uncover all of his desires. But he wasn't eager to play the passive role.

He returned the thrusts of her tongue with his own. Tilting his head to the side for better access, he cupped the back of her neck, supporting her while he savored her mouth. She moaned deep in her throat and shifted restlessly against him.

His erection lengthened and he nudged his hips forward, thrusting one leg between her thighs and nestling his too purple flesh against her. Frustrated by the barrier of clothes between them, he pushed her coat and his to the floor.

Reaching between their bodies, he unfastened her blouse. Her bra was lacy to the touch and her nipples hard little stones. He tore his mouth from hers and stared down at her in the dim light. She was exquisite. Her body pale alabaster.

Her fingers worked busily at his shirt as well. Raking her fingernails down his chest, she gave him a smile as old as time. He let her explore his chest for a few moments, savoring the arousal spreading throughout his body. She leaned down to nip at the skin that covered his pectoral with her teeth and then went lower to suckle both of his nipples.

Her mouth on his nipples sent a pulse of pure fire through his groin. His erection tightened, becoming painfully full. This wasn't going to be a soft gentle seduction. He needed more. And he needed it now.

Using his hand under her chin, he tipped her face up to his and kissed her again. And then she was rocking against him, her breath coming in short gasps. He pulled away.

With one hand he unfastened the front clasp of her bra, but didn't push the cups away from her skin. He felt her breath catch in the back of her throat. Knew she was anticipating his next touch.

He wanted to bend down and take her hard nipples in his mouth. But he waited until he was sure she was aching as much as he was for the touch. He circled the areola carefully, watching her squirm as he did so.

"Like that?" he whispered against her neck, right below her ear.

"Oh, yes," she gasped.

He slid his mouth down the column of her neck stopping at the base to suckle against the wild pulse beating there.

She grasped the back of his head and held him to her. Her lower body gyrating against his. "Tad…"

He bent and moved lower. Nibbling along her skin until he encountered the cups of her bra. He traced the edge where fabric met flesh with his tongue. Goose pimples spread across her chest. And her grip on his head tightened.

He cupped her breast in his hand. Molding and lifting the globe, he turned his head and blew lightly on the tip. She shivered again.

He hovered over her aroused nipple letting his hot breath bathe her flesh. When he touched her with the tip of his tongue, she moaned his name again.

She was on the brink of orgasm and he wanted to see her go over for him. Wanted to see the moment when pleasure infused her entire being. He unfastened her pants and pushed them down her legs.

CJ unfastened his pants and pushed her hand inside, stroking her hand down his length finally cupping his balls. She squeezed gently and he almost came. But he wanted their first orgasm together to be hers. He lifted her in his arms and carried her to the couch.

He set her down on the soft cushions. She leaned forward and he could feel her breath on his groin. He groaned. He wanted her mouth on him. "Not yet."

Gently he pushed her panties down her legs and then arranged her so that she was spread out on the couch for his consumption. He slid one of the pillows under her hips so that she lay before him like a scrumptious feast.

"This is what I call dessert," he said, reaching between her legs, he fondled her humid flesh with long slow strokes.

Carefully he pushed one finger into her channel and she moaned, her fingernails digging into his shoulders. He slipped a second finger inside to join the first.

She was so wet and ready for him. But he didn't want this to end too quickly. He dropped openmouthed kisses on her stomach and abdomen. Then trailed his mouth lower. Her hands were in his hair once again.

He glanced up at her. Some women didn't like a man's mouth on them in such an intimate way.

"Okay?" he asked.

She bit her lip and nodded.

She smelled musky and womanly and he couldn't wait another minute to taste her. He parted her with his thumbs. Her pleasure center was thick and swollen and he teased her with his breath and lips. He continued working his fingers inside her body.

With his other hand, he plucked at her nipples and stroked her from neck to waist and back again. Her hands moved restlessly up and down his back and as her tension grew her touch became more frantic. He stopped caressing her body and held her hips with both hands. Tasting her deeply until he felt her clench around his tongue.

She cried his name out loud and her body shook in his hands as she came.

He lifted his mouth from her and stood. Then lifted her and carried her down the hall to her bedroom. He placed her on the center of her bed and removed his clothes before climbing in next to her and pulling her into his arms.

He pushed her open blouse and bra from her body and savored the feel of her in his arms. His stroking hands rekindled her desire. But when he tried to roll her under him, she pushed against his shoulders and he let her force him onto his back.

She straddled his hips and rose over him. His sex was still rock hard and he could feel her wetness against him. Thrusting upward he teased himself with her warmth. He moaned out loud. He needed to be buried hilt-deep inside this woman. Now.

"Not so fast, Rad Tad. It's time for my dessert."

Eight

"**D**essert, am I?" he asked with a mock frown.

Leaning over him, CJ licked her lips. "You are more tempting than anything in my kitchen."

She had Tad in the one place she'd always wanted him—her bed. Even though he'd brought her to climax on the couch, there was still an unnamed emptiness inside her that only complete possession would satisfy.

She wanted him to fill her. She wanted to engage his senses the way he had hers, sending him beyond anything he'd felt with any other woman so that he'd always remember her. She wanted to brand his soul the way he was marking hers.

But she wanted to do it on her terms so that she could protect the woman deep inside her. The woman who'd always been susceptible to her appetites and who'd never really learned to say goodbye to her dreams. The woman who was very afraid that Tad was going to realize one day that CJ was no more than a facade.

She wouldn't allow herself to be that vulnerable. She caged his wrists in her hands, holding them on the pillow next to his head. Tad said nothing only watched her through narrowed eyes. His penis stirred against her moist center, letting her know he enjoyed the change in roles.

She lowered her body until they were pressed together, propping herself on her elbows she stared down at him. His eyes were languid as if he had all the time in the world and there was no urgency. But his heart told a different story, beating frantically beneath her chest.

She leaned down and kissed him. Taking her time and finishing what she'd started at the front door. He tried to take control of the embrace, lifting his hands. But she forced them back to the bed.

CJ nipped at his bottom lip in warning. He returned to his supine position but she knew that it wasn't her will dominating him but his desire to let her dominate him.

She hadn't meant to tease him when he'd given her such pleasure earlier. "What do you like?"

"With you, everything."

She smiled. That was one of the nicest compliments she'd ever received. "Good. Lace your fingers together and keep your hands under you head,'' she ordered.

He did as she commanded. She rocked back on her heels, still straddling his body. He was a strong man with an athletic build. ''Wait here.''

''I'm not going anywhere,'' he said.

She hurried into the bathroom and grabbed her massage oil and a box of condoms from the medicine cabinet. She also picked up a box of matches and lit the candles on her dresser when she reentered the room.

Tad had propped three of the pillows on the bed under his shoulders and now reclined on the bed like a pasha awaiting his harem girl. It didn't matter that she'd told him to wait there for her, his presence dominated the room.

She placed the box of condoms on the nightstand before sitting on the bed near his hips. She lifted the small brown bottle that contained a sandalwood scented liquid.

''What have you got there?''

''Just some oil. Do you mind?''

''Not at all.''

She poured a small amount into her palm and rubbed her hands together. Then leaned over him. Rubbing the soothing lotion into his skin. His muscles under her hands were hard and strong. But he was putty in her hands.

She massaged her way down his torso, taking the time to explore his bare upper body. The hair on his chest tapered down to his groin. She poured a small puddle of oil low on his abdomen and then rubbed it downward. His body twitched as she moved lower. She teased him by massaging his thighs and then working her way further down his left leg.

She massaged his feet and then moved back up the right side of his body. His hips moved restlessly as she neared his groin again. This time she shook two small drops onto the swollen flesh. His breath rasped between his teeth as she worked her hands over him rubbing until all the oil had been absorbed into his skin.

Straddling him again, she bent over him until she could caress him with each undulating twist of her body. His penis was hot and hard between her legs. Each circular motion of her hips brought him closer to her entrance. She felt him tense underneath her each time she brought him closer and closer to her center.

"I need more," he said.

"How much more?" she teased, rubbing the tips of her full breasts against his chest. He moaned and rocked his hips up towards her, seeking entry.

She stretched over him to reach the box of condoms. While she fumbled to get one from the box, he latched onto her nipple and suckled her. She dropped two condoms before she finally had one. She reached between their bodies and put the condom on him. Then stroked his length a few times until he sat up and grabbed her hips.

Holding her still, he thrust upward and into her. She gasped at the size of him, he was bigger than she'd expected. Her sheath stretched to accept him but she felt too tight.

"Come on, baby, you can take me," he said. He rubbed her back in large circles and soon her body had adjusted to the too-tight feeling of having him inside her.

"I can't wait any longer," he growled against her neck.

He thrust upward into her, pulling her hips down to meet his. His pace increased until they were both frantically striving toward the pinnacle. Her nipples abraded his chest with each thrust. He suckled at the base of her neck, whispering hot sex words against her skin and urging her on. Telling her she was beautiful and sexy. The most woman he'd ever held in his arms.

She held his shoulders and caressed his back. He slid his hands from her hips to her mound, touching her exactly where she needed to be touched. And sending her over the edge. She cried out his name as he gripped her hips harder and thrust up into her once, twice and then came with a shuddering growl that rocked her bed, body and her world.

She lowered her head and rubbed her cheek against him. His heart thudded under her ear and she closed her eyes for a moment savoring his closeness and memorizing his scent.

The scent of sandalwood still lingered in the air when Tad opened his eyes the next morning. CJ was full of surprises and secrets. He hadn't expected the sensual massage she'd given him or her aggressive behavior in bed. Taking a strand of her hair in his hand, he brought it to his nose and inhaled deeply. Arousal spread slowly through him. They'd made love twice more in the night and though he should be satiated he wasn't. If he had his way he'd keep her in bed for at least a month.

His stomach growled. He knew it was close to dawn because of the sunlight creeping in under the closed window blinds. He scanned her room for a clock but couldn't find one.

Her bedroom was an oasis of calm prints and Asian inspired furniture. The candles she'd lit last night were thick chunky ones in muted tones. And the large mirror over her dresser showed the two of them on the bed. He leaned up on his elbow to see them better.

The expression on his face was fierce. He looked like a predator. By contrast CJ looked like prey laying underneath. Cursing under his breath, he rolled to his back.

He stretched his arms over his head. The more he came to know CJ the less he really understood her. She was complex and deep, revealing the important details of herself grudgingly.

But last night had opened his eyes. He'd come to realize that CJ used more than dyed hair and contacts to keep the world at bay. She'd also hidden the sensual side of her nature.

A woman who hid from the world. A woman who was trying to protect herself.

Had he played a part in that? Had his careless comments more than ten years ago wounded her in some way that she'd never recovered from?

He glanced over at her, she faced away from him. Her long hair curling on the soft cream-colored pillowcase. The feminine curve of her back called to him. He reached out and traced a pattern over her skin.

She was so soft and so fragile, he thought. Sleeping next to him her guard was down and her vulnerability was apparent. Rolling onto his side, he pulled her toward him, wrapping his body completely around her.

He wanted to wake her up and vow to be her protector. To make a noble speech the way knights of a more chivalrous age had. But he wasn't a chivalrous knight. He was a twenty-first century man who had vulnerabilities he didn't want the world to see.

Marrying her seemed more dangerous now than it had before. The first time he'd proposed it had been straightforward. He liked her, he wanted to sleep with her, she was someone his parents would adore. But these new protective urges she was inspiring puzzled him.

She moaned a little in her sleep, shifting in his arms. Her buttocks rubbing against his hardening shaft. He swept his hands over her body, and she mumbled in her sleep again, undulating against him.

"Wake up, sleeping beauty," he said, nuzzling the vulnerable curve of her neck.

"Tad?" she asked.

"Who else would it be?"

"No one else," she said. She rolled over to face him. Her hands came up to cup his jaw. Her fingers stroking over his beard stubbled cheeks.

She was pliable right now, still more asleep than awake. Leaning down he kissed her. She twisted against him, bringing her thigh up over his hip. He thrust against her center. Not entering her just letting them both feel each other.

He rocked them both back and forth, bodies moving together until they climaxed. It wasn't a huge world-rocking orgasm like the one they'd shared in the night, this one was more suited to the soft morning. He tucked her closer to him.

"This can't be real," she said.

"It can be."

She groaned, opening her eyes. "Please don't bring up marriage now."

"Why not?"

She tried to push away from him but he refused to let her budge. "Tad."

"I'm not letting go until you talk to me. I know there's more to your hesitation than the flimsy reasons you've given me."

"How do you know that?"

He shrugged. He wasn't sure of the right words to use. The ones that came to mind felt crass and too harsh for the woman in his arms.

"Why is this so important to you?" she asked turning the tables.

He didn't want to talk about himself. But she stared

at him with those deep brown eyes of hers. "Uh...it's complicated."

"My point exactly."

"I'm not like you—afraid of marriage. It's just that...I'm going to sound like a sap when I say this."

"I won't think you're a sap," she said, leaning up to kiss him.

At least she wasn't trying to leave the bed. He took a deep breath. "Have you been home lately?"

"Not in four years. Marnie lives in St. Louis and my mom's buried in Orlando so there's no reason to go to Auburndale. Why?"

"My mom's been having some heart problems, she spent three weeks in the hospital last summer."

"I'm sorry to hear that. What does she have to do with your wanting to marry me?"

"My parents are tired of waiting for grandkids and are always bugging me to settle down. Until my mom went into the hospital I didn't take it seriously. I felt like I had all the time in the world, but I don't. My folks are older and this would make them happy."

She leaned up on her elbow. "What about your happiness?"

He grabbed her and pulled her down on his chest. "I'm happy with you."

"Really?"

"Really. You're so open, honest and fun-loving."

"You sound like a personals ad."

A niggling thought at the back of his head warned him that things weren't going as smoothly as he thought they would. He knew he should tell her more—maybe let her glimpse that dream he had in his head of her as his wife and two little kids playing at their feet. But instead of being quiet he said, "You're just what I want in a wife."

She pushed out of his arms and stood next to the bed. "But I'm not any of those things."

She pivoted and walked out of the bedroom into the connecting bathroom, slamming the door behind her.

CJ stared at herself in the bathroom mirror. She scarcely recognized the naked person reflected there. It had been a long time since she had love bites on her neck and beard burn on her breasts.

Her thighs were pleasantly sore and her center was still a little dewy from her latest orgasm with Tad. He was a generous and skillful lover.

She'd known that if she slept with Tad everything would change between them. She'd been prepared to let him see a part of herself she normally hid from the world. What she hadn't been prepared for though was realizing that she'd shared her body with a man that didn't even realize she hid anything.

She fingered the mark on the bottom of her neck, remembering how he'd suckled her there before he climaxed that first time. What was she going to do? If they were having an affair it wouldn't matter. But he wanted marriage—to make his ailing mother happy.

She raked her hands through her hair. What was she going to do? Bracing her hands on the counter she leaned in close to the mirror. But no answers came to her. Frustrated by her thoughts, she stepped into the shower.

She let the hot water steam the room before she opened the glass door and got inside. The water washed over her, sluicing away the doubts and the fears racing around in her mind.

One fact kept resurfacing, Tad was the kind of man she'd been secretly searching for. Which made him doubly dangerous to her. She liked that he worked hard to make his life a success. She liked that he was community focused. She liked that family was important to him. The only missing ingredient was that Tad saw her as the kind of woman she could never be.

That he thought she was open and fun-loving made her wonder if she really gave off that impression. Didn't he realize she'd never let anyone see the real her? That her work persona was one huge superficial layer that she used to make everyone believe she belonged there. In the office she was successful and energetic because that's what she needed to be to achieve her career goals. It was a role she played, an outer shell to protect the woman she was inside.

They'd had deeply soul-satisfying sex, she thought. She'd realized last night when she'd held him under her that there was more to Tad than any other man she'd taken to her bed. More than Marcus who'd taught her what pleasure could really be. She'd seen the man Tad really was and recognized layers still existed between them.

Frustrated with the world in general she wanted to scream but didn't. She took her loofah and angrily soaped it up. Scrubbing Tad from her body with rough strokes of the sponge. Except that even after she'd cleaned her entire body, she could still smell him on her. The shower door opened and a blast of cool air entered the stall with her.

Tad stood there naked and unsure. The way he watched her told her that he knew something was wrong between them. Understood that she wanted something more from him—but had no idea what it was.

She didn't know if she could do this. Maybe there was a reason why secret crushes usually weren't realized. Perhaps some people weren't meant to be more than a far-off fantasy. Her heart ached a little at the thought that this was probably the end for them.

"Ah, baby. Don't look at me like that," he said. He rubbed his hand on his chest through the patch of hair there. He smelled of sandalwood and sex. Primal instincts urged her to say to hell with forming a relationship, just grab him and make love to him again.

But her heart was weary. "Like what?"

Tilting his head to the side, he watched her carefully for a moment then said, "Like I've disappointed you."

She crossed her arms over her chest to protect herself. "Well you have."

"How?"

She'd forgotten how hard it was to talk to men. "If I have to tell you it won't mean anything."

He threw his head back, cursing savagely under his breath. Finally he looked at her again. "I can't read your mind."

She knew what he meant. But she didn't like letting anyone know she had any insecurity. It wasn't just Tad, it was any person. Even her sister Marnie who'd seen her at her lowest now believed that CJ was a fabulously successful ad executive. "I'm not expecting you to."

"Then tell me what the hell I did wrong?"

She just shook her head. How could she tell him that he didn't know her? That she wasn't the woman he remembered or the one he thought he knew. That she was an amalgam of them both and a silent third woman that lived deep inside her soul.

He sighed, stepping into the shower and closing the door behind him. He took the loofah from her hand and dropped it to the floor, then pulled her into his arms.

He tipped her head back and lowered his mouth to hers. The kiss he gave her was filled with masculine impatience and a tenderness she didn't know he was capable of.

After a few minutes, he lifted his head. "What's wrong?"

His gray-green eyes were so serious and patient. She had the feeling he'd hold her like this for an eternity until he received the answers he was seeking. Dropping her head, she mumbled softly, "You don't know me at all."

"You haven't let me."

Nine

After CJ got out of the shower. Tad grabbed her soap and washed himself. He wasn't going to keep chasing her. He'd done that with other women before and had been left with empty arms. CJ had changed a few images in his head last night. Marriage, though still important to him, might not be the right thing with her.

He turned off the water and dried off. He used CJ's razor to shave and nicked himself twice. Hell, this wasn't his morning. He wrapped the towel around his waist and entered her bedroom.

CJ stood in front of her mirror wearing a silk bathrobe. He watched her tame her wild curly hair into a neat looking ponytail. Then she applied her makeup and put in her contacts. She passed over the jeans and sweatshirts in the closet and chose instead a pair of camel colored wool trousers, an ivory cowl necked sweater and some fancy ankle boots.

Watching her dress was like watching a transformation. And he realized what she'd meant earlier. He hadn't realized how much of herself she hid from the world. But that didn't mean he didn't know the real woman.

She took a strand of pearls from a teak jewelry box and put them on. Then added matching earrings. Still he could only stare at her.

She was donning her armor, putting layers of clothing between them. He was tempted to say the hell with it but his gut said getting her out of his system wasn't going to be as easy as walking out the door.

"It's not going to work," he said at last.

She glanced over her shoulder at him. Lipstick pencil in one hand, eyebrow raised. A haughtier look he'd never seen on her face. It made him want to throw her on the bed and slowly peel each of those flimsy layers away until all that was left was the naked writhing woman who'd left his arms.

"You can't ignore me until I go away."

"Why not?" she asked. She'd turned back to the mirror and painted her bottom lip with a deep red hue. Only the fine trembling of her hand showed him there was a chink in her protective covering.

"Because we have unfinished business, Catherine Jane Terrence. It started that first day you moved in next door and fell off your bike. Remember that?"

"Yes," she said.

"I gave you my Band-Aid and told you I'd always be there for you."

She looked away from him. "But you weren't."

He crossed the room to her, put his hands on her shoulders and met her gaze in the mirror. She put the lipstick pencil down.

"I am now. Or at least I'm trying now. You have to meet me halfway."

"I know. You're right. I haven't let you close to me."

"Why not?"

She fiddled with the makeup brushes on her vanity. "I don't know."

He turned her to face him. She looked too sleek, too sophisticated for the woman he'd come to know. And yet he realized this side of her personality was as true as the stirring lover he'd held in his arms last night. "Don't know or don't want to tell?"

She squared her shoulders. "Don't want to tell."

"You can trust me." He opened his arms, inviting her into his embrace.

She turned away and paced a few feet from him. "No. I can't."

Tad couldn't play this game anymore. He wanted her. He was willing to try to work through the problems between them but he was a man. He needed to know what was wrong so he could fix it. And this guessing game wasn't doing anything but frustrating him. "This is getting us nowhere. I thought you said you'd meet me halfway."

"I'm trying."

"And I'm leaving. When you're ready to be reasonable, call me."

He donned his clothes quickly and CJ stood quietly, watching him.

He walked out of her bedroom and was aware of her following him down the hall. Her pants and shoes were on the tiled floor of the foyer. Her panties lay next to the couch. He remembered the shattering intimacy he'd felt when they'd mated and he didn't want to leave.

He wanted to take whatever she'd give him. But he wasn't some wimpy guy who'd hang around until she was ready to give him whatever crumbs of affection she was willing to throw his way. He couldn't deny her allure. He knew if he had the opportunity he'd sleep with her again. He also knew that wasn't the solution.

"Tad, don't go."

Instead of looking at her, he stared out the window. A light snow fell and the sky was cloudy and gray. Perfect weather for snuggling by a fireplace except the woman he'd chosen to get involved with wasn't interested in cuddling. "Give me something that will make me stay."

"I'm afraid," she said. Her words were faint, he went to her but didn't touch her. He knew himself. She'd said the words that conjured up all his latent protective instincts. The ones that made him want to slay dragons for her.

"Afraid of me?"

She shook her head. "Never of you."

"Who then?"

She twisted her fingers together and bit her lower lip. "Myself I think."

She stood in her living room. The Christmas tree behind her, homey pictures on the walls and instead of looking at ease in her sanctuary she looked frightened.

"I don't understand."

"You know how I said you don't know the real me? I don't either. I've been reinventing myself for so long that I'm not sure who I am."

"And that scares you."

"Partly. The other part that scares me is that you make me want to forget all about who I've always wanted to be and make myself into what you want in a woman."

"My wants are simple, Cathy Jane."

"They are?"

"Yes, I want you to marry me."

She shook her head. "No man has ever stayed."

He was humbled by her words. This woman was eons too soft for the world she lived in. This woman was waiting to see what he'd say, expecting him to brush her concerns aside and walk out the door. This woman he realized had been hurt in the past and badly.

Don't let me screw this up and wound her, just when she's coming to mean so much to me.

"Which men?" Tad asked.

CJ was sorry she'd opened her mouth. She wished she could go back in time and wake up again. She'd make love to Tad and then when he was in a weakened state, then she'd get out of bed and make him breakfast. Plying him with lots of food and sex until he was unable to think or ask her questions she didn't want to answer.

He held her with patience and she had the feeling he'd stand there all day until he got the answers he craved.

"Why don't we sit down?" she asked.

"Okay."

CJ awkwardly moved out of his embrace. He was so strong and comforting, she was tempted to stay there in his arms, hiding from herself and the past. But she couldn't. She had made a history of running when things went to hell, and she knew this time would be no different.

He was being too solicitous. It made her feel unreasonable and silly. She knew that wasn't his intent but it didn't change the way she felt. Glancing around the room, which still bore signs of last night's seduction, she shivered a little. They couldn't talk with her clothes everywhere.

Why couldn't there be some sort of magic that made embarrassing details like her panties disappear?

"Let me clean this up," she said.

"I'll help," he said.

"No."

CJ picked her clothes up off the living room and foyer floors. His stomach had growled twice.

"Want to go grab some breakfast?"

"I can cook something for us. We can talk while we work." She wasn't ready to face anyone else. And she was ready to trust Tad. To tell him a little of her past relationships with men, starting with her dad who'd left them long before the Terrence women had moved to Auburndale. Left them for a teenaged Lolita and made it very clear that the last thing he'd wanted to be saddled with was a wife and two daughters.

Marcus had left her for another woman as well, but he'd done it in a much quieter way, suggesting she leave the ad agency where they'd both worked to avoid embarrassment. Now Tad was tempting her to risk a little of her heart and see if he'd reciprocate.

"Let's eat first."

In the kitchen she boiled water and put the grounds into her French press. The silence was deafening, probably because she knew that she needed to talk to him about her past. About Marcus and her dad and how she'd never really trusted any man when he said he'd stay. And they never had, proving her right.

She flipped through the CD wallet on the counter and selected one by Ella Fitzgerald. Soon the sultry jazzy sounds filled the air. She turned nervously to find Tad staring at her.

"I guess you want to talk."

His stomach growled.

"Or not. Hungry?"

"Yeah. I wake up that way. Where do you keep your frying pan?"

She pointed to the cabinet. "What are you going to do with it?"

"Make breakfast," he said. He retrieved the pan and then opened her fridge.

"You can cook?"

"Don't sound so incredulous. I'm a bachelor. I don't like eating takeout for every meal."

"Sorry. What are you going to make?" she asked. He seemed so offended she wondered if he'd had some chef training.

"Fried eggs and bacon. You can handle the toast."

She rolled her eyes. She couldn't believe she'd let him make her feel guilty when all he could cook was a camping breakfast. "I don't know that you can call that cooking."

"Don't get sassy, Cathy Jane, or I won't let you have any."

"My heart might thank you."

He threw his head back and laughed. CJ smiled to herself as she squeezed oranges for juice and made toast. The lingering tension in her stomach disappeared as they worked.

Tad served them eggs and they sat at the counter in her tiny kitchen eating quietly when Ella sang about love and heartache. Thoroughly mirroring the sentiment in CJ's heart. She wondered if she should have left the CD player off. This wasn't really helping.

"Not bad," she said. The eggs were perfect and the bacon nice and crisp.

"For a guy, right?"

"Well…"

"That's what I thought."

"You can't take a compliment."

"Were you giving me one?"

"Yes. I was."

They finished their breakfast in silence. Then CJ cleared the table and stared at Tad where he sat watching her. She knew he was ready to talk. That she'd delayed things as long as she could. She poured them both one more cup of coffee and led the way out into the living room.

Settling down in front of the fireplace, she waited for Tad. He sank down next to her on the loveseat. His hipbone, rubbing against hers.

He settled his arm behind her on the back of the couch and then turned toward her. "Where were we?"

"I'm not sure. You wanted to hear about my past."

"I'm not asking you to tell me any big secrets, CJ."

"I know. But I've kind of built it into a big confession."

"It doesn't have to be. I'm sorry that you think I don't know you at all. I am trying but you don't make it easy."

"It's hard for me to let anyone close to me."

"Why is that?"

She shrugged. "I guess it's all tied up with my self-image. I've never really been the right size or look."

"I can understand you feeling that way in high school but you shouldn't now."

"Sometimes I still do."

"Is that what this is all about—looks? I'm not that shallow."

"I know. It's just when you say things like you want to marry me. You bring all those doubts back. Because I know that I can't be the perfect woman for you."

"Why not?"

"There's something inside me that makes men leave."

"I'm not leaving," he said. "I'm planning to marry you."

"So you keep saying," she said.

"I think you made a good point about us not knowing each other."

"I did."

"Let's just date for a while, sound good."

"Sleepover dates?" she asked.

"Definitely."

CJ felt the first ray of hope that she and Tad were really going to have a relationship. He was willing to stay with her. He wanted to get to know the real her. He made her realize that life outside of the advertising world could be good, too.

They spent the afternoon on Michigan Avenue, browsing through shops. He wanted to go into Tiffany's but CJ refused teasingly. And he'd relented about going into the store. But deep inside he wondered if they were both playing a game of pretend.

After purchasing a vase from Crate and Barrel, they strolled toward State Street. Carson's and Field's had their Christmas window displays up. They dined in the Walnut Room in Marshall Fields. A light snow began to fall as they walked back to CJ's place.

The day would have been relaxing for Tad except that he couldn't get the image of CJ as she'd been this morning out of his head. This woman had been hurt badly and he knew he owed it to her to make sure he didn't add to the pain she'd experienced.

But at the same time he was worried about protecting himself. CJ had been dancing just out of his reach since he'd found her again. But he was confident that he could get her to agree to marriage.

His parents were coming up the day after Christmas and his plan was to present CJ as his future wife to them. But suddenly ten days didn't seem long enough. He wondered if ten years would be. Though she hadn't said it, CJ needed something from him that he hadn't yet been able to figure out.

"Penny for your thoughts?" she asked. He held her hand loosely in his and as they walked he shortened his pace to hers. She wore a long camel-colored wool coat, a cream-colored muffler and a pair of black leather gloves.

She fit perfectly in the city and watching her now,

he wondered how she'd ever survived those tumultuous adolescent years in Auburndale. She wasn't a
small-town girl. And he'd been a small-town boy
who'd never really stopped to notice how that small
town could make a person feel. "Just thinking about
my folks."

"Are they coming up for the holidays?" she asked,
tipping her head back to watch the snow. CJ seemed
lighter tonight. Easier to know. And he realized that
she'd been more than a little bit accurate about the
fact that he'd never really tried to get to know her.

"Yes. Mom grew up in New England and loves a
white Christmas."

"Me too. I used to wish for snow every Christmas
growing up."

"Every Florida kid does," he said, but there was
more to her words than just a child's wishful thinking.
There was incredible longing right alongside the
knowledge that fairy tales didn't come true in CJ's
voice.

"What did you wish for?" she asked.

"The typical things, bikes, cars, video games.
You?" He was an only child and though his parents
had instilled him with a strong work ethic, they'd also
spoiled him on holidays.

"I'm not very materialistic," she said in a tone he
was coming to realize meant that she was hiding something.

"You aren't going to tell me?" he asked. Stopping,
he pulled them out of the flow of the foot traffic. Un-

der a streetlamp, he pulled her into his arms and tilted
her face up towards his.

She looked at him, her heart in her eyes, and he
wanted to tell her not to trust him that deeply. He
didn't feel worthy of that kind of emotion. "I used to
wish that my dad would be there on Christmas morning."

"He never was," Tad said. He'd never met CJ's
dad. Her mom, Marnie and she had moved in one
summer. They'd pulled up in a battered station wagon
towing a U-Haul and the three of them had moved
everything in. Mrs. Terrence had never had any boy-
friends and had worked all the time.

When he and CJ were twelve they'd been friends.
That entire summer it didn't matter that she was a girl
and therefore the enemy. Finally he had someone his
own age to play with and they'd spent the long days
exploring the orange groves and playing pretend
games.

"No. He'd left long before and he wasn't ever coming back. But we didn't talk about that." She pulled
out of his arms and hugged herself.

"Why not?" he asked. He wanted to pull her back
into his arms but he respected that she needed some
space.

"Because it was just easier to pretend he was away
for business."

"Easier on who?"

"I don't know," she said at last. "Maybe Mom."
She shivered a little, tucking her muffler up higher

on her neck. "Sorry. Not what you were wanting to hear, was it?"

"I wouldn't have asked if I didn't want to know. Ready to head home?" he asked.

"Yes."

He wanted to spend the night with her, but didn't know how to ask. And he didn't want to make their time together too heavy. She was too emotional now, he wanted to lighten the mood.

"Didn't you say you studied Tae Kwon Do?"

"Yes."

"Wanna spar?"

"I don't trust the gleam in your eyes. What exactly do you have in mind?"

"Just a friendly game of strip fighting."

"Strip fighting? You've got to be kidding."

"No, I'm not. I'll let you use all your gear. You're not afraid are you?"

"Of you. Never. Where are we going to have this match?"

"My place. I converted my spare bedroom into a workout room."

"Okay, are we betting on this match?"

"Oh, yes."

"What's up for grabs?" she asked.

"Loser cooks breakfast."

She watched him carefully. "I'm going to need some sort of handicap. You look a bit stronger than me."

"Just a bit."

"Yeah, just a bit."

"You're all heart, girl."

"Don't you forget it."

They teased and bantered all the way back home but once he had her in his condo the last thing he wanted to do was spar, so he took her to bed and made love to her all night long until they both fell into an exhausted sleep. But he woke deep in the night and held her tightly in his arms. Held her with a desperation that he'd only admit when no one else could see it. Held her like he'd never let her go.

Ten

Five days later, CJ was on the top of her game. Rae-Anne seemed to finally understand how most of their office equipment worked and hadn't lost any important documents or disconnected any busy clients lately. Butch Baker had called five minutes ago and she was in the elevator on her way up to meet him.

And if the tingling in her gut was any indication she was getting the promotion she'd worked so hard for. She checked her lipstick in the mirrored elevator walls, straightened the lapels on her burgundy suit and tucked up a wisp of hair that had escaped her chignon.

She smiled at her reflection and repeated her mantra. ''I'm successful and everyone wants me to succeed.''

The elevator doors opened and she pivoted to exit

the car. She entered Butch's office and his secretary Molly told her to go right in. She squared her shoulders and opened the door.

"You wanted to see me?" She hoped she sounded cool and calm but the pounding of her heart echoed in her ears, so she had no idea how she sounded to Butch.

"Yes, CJ. Come in and have a seat."

She sank into one of the leather guest chairs in front of Butch's large mahogany desk. The walls of his office were lined with many of the most popular advertisements of the past ten years. Anyone who entered this office could easily see why Butch was a top executive at Taylor, Banks and Markim.

The credenza showed a different side to Butch though. Pictures of his wife and kids were there along with the Little League baseball team he'd coached for the past five years. They'd won their division championship this year.

"I'm not going to keep you in suspense, CJ. I asked you up here to let you know you're our newest director. Congratulations."

CJ smiled calmly and shook Butch's hand. "Thanks for your confidence in me. I'm going to work hard to make sure you don't have any regrets about your decision."

"I have no doubt that you will work hard. That's one of the things I wanted to mention to you."

"Working hard?"

"Yes. You almost didn't get the promotion because you have so few activities outside of the office."

"I think that would be a good thing," she said.

"Statistics show that executives that have a balanced life are actually more productive at work."

"What are you saying, Butch?"

"You've worked hard for this promotion and you deserve it. But now it's time to take care of the other aspects of your life. Take time to date, start a hobby, volunteer in the community. Take some time for yourself."

Her stomach knotted and she started to open her mouth. To tell Butch that she was engaged. Hell, it was what Tad wanted. But she couldn't do it. Her job had always been the most important thing to her. Suddenly it paled in comparison to her relationship with Tad. But being with Tad meant taking risks. Risks that she'd never admit to another soul she felt each time she was with him. Risks that were capable of making everything, even this exciting new promotion, seem dull gray.

"I'm not sure I understand, Butch. You want me to get married?"

"Your personal life is your concern. I just want you to do something outside of work. The board likes all their executives married though we can't make that a qualification for the job."

"I'm dating someone now," she said.

He nodded. "Your promotion is effective today and we'll be moving you to a new office on this floor in

January. You're invited to meet the partners tonight at seven for drinks. Why don't you bring your friend?''

''I will.'' She left his office and made her way back to her own. This wasn't happening. She'd gotten her promotion now and they wanted her to change her focus.

She entered her office and Rae-Anne glanced up from her computer. ''Well, are we celebrating?''

''Yes. You are looking at the new director of domestic affairs.''

''Congratulations.''

''Thanks, Rae-Anne,'' she said, entering her office.

She should get the staff together for an announcement and have a catered lunch to celebrate the promotion. She'd have to start interviewing to fill her position. There were so many things to be done, she should be making a list of work responsibilities but she couldn't.

Her mind wouldn't stop. The pressure she faced doubled with Butch's words about balance and... *marriage.* She'd known since she was a little girl, since she'd watched her mother staring at her father's picture every night before she went to bed, that she'd never marry. She'd taken a chance with Marcus and he had left her even though she'd tried to be what he'd wanted in a wife.

Rae-Anne buzzed in on the intercom. ''Tad's on line one.''

''Thanks, Rae-Anne. Call around and see if we can get someone to cater lunch for the staff today. Then get everyone together for an announcement in the conference room.''

"Will do."

She pressed the button on the phone. "Tad?"

"Hey, Cathy Jane, are you free for lunch?"

"Uh, actually, no. I got my promotion and I'm bringing in food for the staff."

"Congratulations, you've worked hard for this promotion."

"Thanks," she said.

"I'll take you to dinner tonight to celebrate."

"Okay. Are you free for drinks at seven?"

"I can be, why?"

"It's this thing with the board and I don't want to go alone."

"I'll be there."

He sounded so confident and sure of himself, but that didn't alleviate the pressure inside her. Trusting Tad was the easiest thing in the world because despite the fact he looked like some buff hunk his heart was deep and true. But CJ was afraid to trust Tad. Afraid to trust herself. She hung up the phone feeling like crying instead of celebrating.

The restaurant Tad had selected for their celebration dinner was Gejas in Lincoln Park. They were known for Old World elegance. Tad had heard of the restaurant but had never eaten there. But tonight the secluded booths seemed perfect for dinner with CJ. Their table was along the wall so they could close the curtain and celebrate in private.

He'd stopped by Tiffany's this afternoon to pick up the ring he wanted to give her when he asked her to marry him. But he sensed CJ wasn't ready to be asked again. And this time he wasn't just asking to make his parents happy. This time he needed her to say yes and he wasn't taking any chances. So he purchased an amber and gold bracelet that reminded him of the amber specks in her dark brown eyes instead. The jewelry box was in his pocket and he wasn't sure when to give it to her.

He ordered a bottle of champagne to celebrate her promotion. CJ had been flushed with success during the cocktail hour with the partners of her firm. Frankly he'd been awed and intimidated by her. He'd suspected she would have turned out smart and successful when he'd known her in high school, but never guessed how far she'd go in the business world.

Butch had been surprised that he was CJ's date but had been happy as well. And several of CJ's co-workers had seemed glad to see them together.

The waiter took their order. Gejas was renowned for their fondues. Tad ordered a three course meal for them. Once the waiter poured their champagne he left.

Tad closed the curtain and pulled CJ into his arms. Damn, she felt too right there. And he'd missed her all day. Seeing her for drinks with her co-workers had intensified his need to hold her. There hadn't been time for anything but a quick embrace before they'd had to mingle. But now they were alone and isolated from prying eyes.

"First a toast," he said. He'd ordered a plate of strawberries to go with the bubbly beverage.

"And second?" she asked.

Next was CJ warm and willing in his arms. He had the evening planned. Delicious, sensuous food, warm, sexy woman. What more could a man ask for?

"Second…you'll have to wait and see."

"What if I don't want to?" she asked, lifting one of the berries. Her pearly white teeth carefully held the fruit before she took a bite of it. She closed her eyes and he imagined the deluge of juice flooding her mouth. Unable to help himself, he leaned forward. He traced his tongue over her lips, tasting both the berry juice and CJ. Her mouth parted on a gasp and he thrust his tongue inside. He pulled her closer to him. His arm supporting her neck as he savored her mouth.

"Is this my punishment?" she asked.

"I haven't decided yet."

"Make your toast so we can get on with your discipline."

Tad lifted his glass and stared at the bubbly beverage. He didn't know if he had the right words to tell her how proud he was to be her man. He wished he had Pierce's gift of always knowing the right thing to say. But he didn't have it and he wouldn't want CJ to think he was someone he wasn't. Yet she made him want to be better than he was and he knew he'd changed since they'd been friends and lovers.

"Congratulations, CJ. I'm so proud of everything you've accomplished with your life."

He lifted his glass toward her. But she was only staring at him, a sheen of tears in her eyes. "Thank you, Tad."

"You're welcome, gorgeous. Now take a sip of your drink. I have more surprises for you."

"What? You know I don't like surprises."

"You'll like this one."

"Promise?"

"Just trust me," he said, wishing she'd trust him on more than this night. Wishing she'd trust him with her future. But knowing he'd settle for her present.

She cupped his jaw, rubbing her fingers over the five o'clock shadow dotting his cheeks. "I'm starting to trust you."

"Drink," he said. Her hands on him started a fire that he wanted to put out in only one way. And Gejas, although the booth set up gave couples some intimacy, wasn't the place for the kind of seduction his pounding body demanded.

She took a sip of her champagne and he did the same. Then he took a bite of one berry and fed her the remaining fruits. Sharing each berry brought a flush of desire to her skin. He was tingling from head to toe. His arousal pressed against the zipper of his trousers and he relished the anticipation. Seduction and anticipation had never felt as good with any other woman.

The waiter brought their first course. And once he

left and they were alone again, Tad said, "Tradition says you have to kiss whomever is seated to your left if anything falls off your fork."

"And you are conveniently seated to my left."

"Funny how that happened."

Their meal progressed with a slow steady stream of kisses and sumptuous food. As the second course was cleared away. Tad removed the box from his pocket and placed it on the table in front of CJ.

She stared at the distinctive Tiffany's box. It was long and narrow, so she had to know it wasn't a ring, but still she hesitated.

"Oh, Tad. You didn't have to get me a gift."

"I know. I want you to do me a favor before you open it up."

"What?" she asked.

"Take out your contacts."

"Why?"

"Because you use them to hide from the world. But you don't need to hide from me."

She took a small contact case from her purse and removed the contacts. He reached up and pulled the pins from her hair, letting the thick mass curl around her shoulders.

"Do I look better now?" she asked.

"Not yet," he said. Leaning over he kissed her hard and long. Pulling back only when he knew her lips would be wet and swollen from his kiss. "Perfect. Open your gift."

Her hands shook as she pulled the box toward her.

She opened it slowly as if afraid a snake might spring out of it. But he recognized this vulnerable side of CJ. And it made him want to scold her for not trusting him.

Finally she pulled the bracelet from the box. Tears sparkled in her eyes again and this time fell. "I...oh, Tad. Thank you so much."

"You're very welcome," he said, taking her hand and fastening the bracelet on her. He dropped a soft kiss on her wrist. And saw trust in her eyes for the first time, and he knew that it was time to take her home and make love to her. Time to push harder at the barriers around her heart, which he sensed were already starting to crumble.

CJ unlocked the door to her condo and entered, turning on the hallway light. This day had been a roller-coaster ride of excitement, fear and joy and pressure and Tad's presence didn't exactly ease those things in her mind.

Her new bracelet glittered with the reflections of the soft lamp. She still couldn't believe Tad had given her such an expensive gift. Coupled with her boss's words earlier, the bracelet applied pressure to her already troubled mind.

Tad ran his hand down her back. Every nerve in her body had been sensitized by an evening of sumptuous food and lingering touches. Her pulse beat low and heavy. The only thing she wanted to do was stop thinking and make love with Tad.

He closed the door. "Let me take your coat."

She shrugged out of her wool coat and felt his warm breath on the back of her neck. He brushed her hair out of the way and dropped an openmouthed kiss there. He took his time stringing together that nibbling contact until she shivered with sensation rushing down her spine and pooling in her center.

"Are you cold?" he asked.

She couldn't answer. He smiled indulgently down at her, and pulled her into his arms, whispering in her ear the things he'd do to make her warm. His hands roamed up and down her back, lingering to cup her butt and pull her more fully into his embrace.

His mouth on her ear made her breasts feel full and heavy. Her nipples tightened against the satin fabric of her bra. She needed more. Leaning fully into the hard planes of his chest, she stood on tiptoe and pulled his mouth to hers. Their kiss was a series of long drugging touches that only intensified the struggle inside her. How could she live with or without Tad? She was flushed with desire when he moved away.

She stood awkwardly in the foyer while he flicked on the lights of the Christmas tree and lit a fire in the hearth. He'd hung his suit jacket up earlier and now stood facing her, back-lit from the fire. He tugged his tie loose and left the ends dangling down his chest.

"Come over here," he said.

She hesitated. She didn't know what to do. Tad had become more important to her than she'd ever thought he would. And tonight she'd seen the way Butch's eyes had followed them. It would be so easy to appease her boss.

"Cathy Jane, why do I get the feeling you're running again?" he asked, softly.

Damn. Why had she complained that he didn't know the real her? She didn't want to talk. So instead she started walking toward him unbuttoning her suit jacket. "Does this look like running?" ·

She shrugged out of her jacket and came to a stop in front of him wearing only her black satin bra and skirt.

"I stand corrected."

"Indeed you do," she said, trailing her fingers down his torso and rubbing his erection. He drew his breath in sharply but stood still for her caresses.

"One of us is overdressed."

"I'd say we both are."

"Let's do something about it." She unbuttoned his shirt and pushed it off his shoulders. She'd never tire of looking at his thick corded muscles and washboard abs.

Tad unhooked her bra and slowly peeled away the satin. He cupped both of her breasts with his large hands. Rotating his palms against her, he brought her nipples to throbbing attention. She tried to think but could only want.

"Tad…"

"You wanted something?" He bent toward her, tracing the rim of her ear with his tongue before drawing that wet caress down her neck.

He used his fingernail to delicately trace around her nipple until she almost couldn't stand his touch anymore. She was incapable of speaking or thinking. Finally his mouth covered her turgid flesh and she sighed. Holding tightly to his head while he suckled her.

He continued to undress her, pushing her skirt down her hips and she felt his surprise when he encountered the bare flesh of her buttocks. He stepped back and she stood in front of him wearing only a brief thong, thigh-high hose and black pumps. He growled and lifted her in his arms.

Settling her on the sofa, he followed her down. His hands and mouth were everywhere. Leaving no inch of her body untouched, he caressed her curves and whispered endearments against her skin. He pushed his fingers inside her panties and touched her deeply and intimately until she was hanging on the edge of climax.

She pulled his hand away.

"Why?" he asked.

"I want us to come together," she said.

He stood and quickly got rid of his remaining clothing. He pulled a condom from his pocket and handed it to her. "I had other plans for this evening."

"What plans?" she asked.

"Something a bit slower but you turned me inside out with those hose."

She waggled her eyebrows at him. "I wish I'd

known it was this easy to rattle you. I'd have tried it sooner.''

''You don't have to try,'' he said.

He pulled her thong down her legs and tossed it on top of his clothes. She reached for him caressing his thighs and penis. He moaned and she put her hands on his butt bringing him closer to her. She leaned up and tasted him. He moaned again, his hands burrowing into her hair and holding her close. She took the tip of him into her mouth. He tasted spicy and masculine.

''Enough,'' he said gruffly pushing her back. He took the condom from her and sheathed himself. Then spread her legs and came down over her. He guided himself to her entrance with his hand and then plunged into her with one deep sure stroke.

Even though they'd made love several times, it still took her body a few moments to adjust to the too tight feeling of being filled with him. As soon as she clenched her lower body muscles, Tad began to move between her legs.

His hands left her hips, gliding up her body to her breasts, where he lingered, then to her shoulders. Finally he cupped her jaw. Their eyes met and in his she saw her past, present and future. A shimmering of sensation started at her center and spread slowly throughout her body. Leaving her quaking in his arms. His climax followed hers and he groaned her name before collapsing in her arms.

She stroked her fingers up and down his back and held him with her arms and legs. They were both sweaty and she knew she should be exhausted, but all she could think of was that she couldn't risk staying with Tad. Couldn't risk losing anymore of herself than she already had to this man who easily dominated her entire world.

Eleven

Tad sent a car for CJ on Christmas Eve. His parents were arriving the next day and tonight he planned a small intimate dinner for the two of them. He'd gone back to Tiffany's and purchased an engagement ring. There was a bouquet of long-stemmed roses in the back of the limousine. He'd called his mother to find out which kind of candles to burn at dinner—unscented ones. He'd purchased some at Crate and Barrel.

He'd also spent some time in Barnes & Noble purchasing a half-dozen different books of love poems. Though he didn't want to risk his heart and actually say the words—he felt them deeply. CJ had pushed past his resolve too far to keep his emotions uninvolved. He loved her and somehow tonight he planned to find a way to tell her.

The food had been prepared by a friend who was a chef at one of the city's most exclusive restaurants. The limo driver called after he had picked CJ up and was on his way. Tad had every thing precisely how he wanted it when CJ knocked on his door.

He opened the door and took her coat. She wore a black velvet dress that ended at her midthigh. Her long legs were bare and on her feet she wore the sexiest pair of spiky heels he'd ever seen. He put his hand on the small of her back to escort her to the dining room and encountered bare flesh.

He slipped his finger between the warm satin of woman and the cool velvet of her dress. She undulated against his touch and he smiled to himself. They communicated so much better physically than verbally.

He had been so nervous about tonight, but suddenly his nerves had disappeared. A surge of lust pierced through him and he thought to hell with this romantic crap which he wasn't all that good at. Bending he dropped a kiss on her bare back. She shuddered under his mouth and he grinned. She was so easy to turn on.

Sliding his hands around to cup her breasts he continued to nibble his way down her back. He tongued the crevice where pale feminine skin met dark velvet. Taking the tab of the zipper in his teeth, he pulled it lower.

He continued kissing his way down her back, lingering at the small indentation right above her buttocks. Finding her naked under the dress made him moan. She shuddered and he tasted her lower. He wanted to take her like this, from behind up against the wall.

He stood and pressed his straining erection against her. She swiveled her hips against him. He reached between their bodies to free his throbbing length. Rubbing his penis against the curves of her naked buttocks. She moaned. "Tad."

He cupped her breasts through the cloth of her dress. She was caged by him. His mouth on the back of her neck, his hands on her breasts and soon he thought when she was a mass of quivering nerves, he'd penetrate her and make her his completely. Take her so deeply and so thoroughly that when he finally asked her to marry him, she'd have no choice but to say yes.

He pulled her more firmly against his chest. He slid the straps of her dress down her arm just far enough so that the bodice gapped and her pink nipples were framed in velvet. He turned her in his arms, and backed her up against the wall.

Taking her wrists in his hands he pinned them to the wall behind her. And though he knew it was illusion, at this moment she seemed to be totally his. The hard berries of her nipples beckoned him and he bent to tease her first with his warm breath, then with his wet tongue.

She tasted incredibly sweet. The scent of her perfume was stronger in her cleavage. He let go of her wrists for a moment to plump her breasts together and bury his face between them.

He turned his head from side to side trailing wet kiss over the full globes. She trembled in his arms, her hands falling to his shoulders, her nails biting into his flesh. She was close to the flash point. It was only fair since he felt in that state constantly around her.

She moaned his name and shifted her thighs, pressing them together. He thrust one of his legs between hers. Grasping her wrist with one of his hands, he used his other to urge her hips forward.

He pushed her skirt to her waist and thrust his hips forward until he settled her feminine notch over his penis. He resented every time he'd worn a condom because he'd never been able to savor her humid warmth against his skin. He hardened painfully and could count his pulse in his erect penis.

He switched his attention to her other nipple, pulling at it in search of some sustenance that he only found with CJ. He'd never tell her but when she was in his arms, she soothed a deep troubled part of his soul.

He stroked between her thighs, not entering her body, just teasing them both with the promise of what was to come. He lifted her completely off the ground.

"Put your legs around my waist."

"Yes."

Wrapped in her strong slender thighs, nails raking down his back and her mouth under his. He shifted his position and entered her.

A sigh of satisfaction escaped him. This was where she belonged—writhing in his arms. The urge to mate with her and claim her was so strong that he ceased thinking and just indulged his senses.

He thrust hard and deep into her. She nipped at his lower lip, pulling it between her teeth and suckling it. She ripped at the buttons of his shirt and she scraped her nail over his nipples. The added sensation made the base of his spine tingle. He felt so full, so hard and so heavy. He was going to come any moment. But not without CJ. He reached between their bodies and stroked her until he felt her body clench around him. He thrust into her once more and then joined her climax. His body emptying in jetting pulses.

He twisted so his back was against the wall and sank to the floor cradling her in his arms until their pulses slowed. CJ slid off his lap to sit next to him on the floor. They both leaned against the wall head turned to face each other. Her hair was in disarray around her face and he looked into her deep brown eyes.

"I'm sitting on something."

"What?" he asked.

"This," she said, pulling the Tiffany's box that had been in his pants pocket out.

She stiffened but didn't say a word.

"I was going to surprise you with that after dinner."

She continued to watch him with eyes that were too wide and too serious.

"Will you marry me, Cathy Jane?"

* * *

CJ's heart beat so loudly she thought she might pass out. There was too much pressure involved with her saying yes to Tad. At once it was a dream come true and a nightmare. Not just because of the way she felt about Tad but because of the way she knew she was when it came to men.

"I'm not letting you off the hook again. I know you, dammit. I know that you put your hair up and put in contacts when you go to work so that everyone sees a smart, sophisticated woman. I know you wear jeans and T-shirts at home because they are comfortable and suit your quiet lifestyle. I know you bake when you're upset and that you'd rather read books than go to a bar."

He pulled her back into his arms and she couldn't help herself. She snuggled against his broad chest. "I know you, baby."

She knew him, too. Knew that Tad needed more from her than she could give. More than she'd ever really be willing to give because the risk to her heart was too high. Though she wanted his love, craved his body and lived for the times they were together, she couldn't marry him.

And she knew this time she'd have to tell him more than she was afraid.

"I can't."

"Is it because of your job? I respect what you've achieved. Hell, you know I'm proud of you."

"No, it's not that. In fact, Butch urged me to find

a spouse and marry. He's concerned I don't have enough balance in my life.''

"He's right. You don't.''

"There's a reason for that. Tad, I don't juggle well.''

He ran his fingers through his hair. "So if it's not work then what is it? The emotional thing again?''

He grabbed his pants and stood up. Pulling them on he put his hands on his hips and canted them toward her. He was tough and angry-looking, a man anyone would be afraid to face alone but she'd never felt safer.

She straightened her dress and got to her feet. She struggled with the zipper until Tad brushed her hands away and pulled it up. He put his hands on her shoulders and turned her to face him.

What she saw in his eyes made her shiver with longing and an unnamed fear. Actually the fear had a name and she had a healthy respect for it. Because she knew that once she started depending on Tad he'd leave. Fate had made it plain that CJ Terrence wasn't supposed to have a continuous male influence in her life.

"I love you, Cathy Jane. I've never said those words to another woman.'' He watched her steadily. She felt the force of his will surrounding her. She wanted to reach out and take. Reach out and touch him. To go back to a few minutes earlier before she'd sat on that damned ring box, but she couldn't.

"That's not enough for you, is it?''

"Please don't do this. Can't we go on as we have?'' she asked.

"Damn you, CJ, no we can't. You're not the only one who's been hurt. Look at Pierce, his wife almost destroyed him when she left but he's happy now with Tawny."

"I don't care about Tawny and Pierce. I mean I'm glad they're happy but how can you understand what I'm going through when you've never been hurt," she said.

"The hell I haven't. I was engaged before this. Kylie decided she wanted a man who could give her the money she needed to be happy while not working long hours. She left me, Cathy Jane. Don't tell me about being hurt."

"I'm sorry," she said.

"My mind says don't confess your emotions to this woman but my heart knows not saying the words won't make the hurt lessen."

Tears burned the back of her eyes and a trembling started deep inside her. She was so cold. So damned cold. She wrapped her arms around her body trying to hold herself together but it wasn't working. She was splintering and shattering apart and nothing, no one—not even Tad—could make this right. "I can't stay."

"Why not?"

"Because I'm afraid."

"We've been over this before. I won't hurt you."

She didn't know how to explain to him that she knew he wouldn't intentionally hurt her. But he would all the same. She was an expert at playing the odds when it came to relationships. About understanding how much she could take before fate stepped in and shut her down. He didn't know that for her living with him would be the beginning of the countdown clock.

"Yes, you will. No man has ever stayed once he lived with me. I'm not like other women."

"How many men?"

"Just my dad. And of course there was Marcus."

"Who's Marcus?"

"He was my boss and my fiancé. He left me for a woman more suitable to be the boss's wife."

"I'm not like other men," he said.

No he was like the other half of her soul. And losing him was the one thing she wouldn't risk. "I know."

Tad cursed under his breath. The strength of his words and the anger behind them made her heart break. She glanced around the room. Saw the candles burning in the dining room. Heard the soft romantic music playing on the CD. That he should have gone to so much trouble to prepare this evening for her… "Tad, it's not that I don't care."

"Then what is it, CJ? Because you told me Butch wants you married. I offered you a business arrangement and that wasn't what you wanted. I've offered you love and still that's not good enough. Is it me? Is this some sort of payback for the insensitive boy I was?"

"No. Never. I love you, Tad, in a way I thought never to love another man. But I can't marry you."

"Why not?" he asked again, frustration in every line of his body.

"Because fate won't let me have it all when it comes to men."

"What men?"

"My dad. Marcus. You. Every man I've ever cared for has left me."

"Are you sure?" he asked.

"What do you mean?"

"Maybe you drove them away with your attitude," he said, then pivoted on his heel and crossed the room to the bar.

"I need a drink."

CJ couldn't move. Perhaps he was right and her attitude was responsible for this entire mess. From the time Tad had walked back into her life, she been searching for a way to escape from him. Be it through her contacts and hair color, or her career. Whatever the reason she needed more time than he'd given her. More time than Butch had allotted her and more time than her weary heart had been given. "Maybe you're right and I drove them away."

Tad opened a bottle of Dewar's and poured it into a shot glass. He knocked back two shots before he even glanced her way. "Screw it. I don't care if you love me or not. Marry me."

"Why?" she asked. Why would he still want to marry her unless everything he'd said had been a joke? Oh, God, don't let him be fooling me once again into believing he's better than he has to be.

He poured himself another shot but this time only

sipped it. "I told my parents they'd be meeting my future wife tomorrow."

"How could you do that? I told you how I felt."

"Obviously, I thought I knew how to change your mind," he said, throwing back another shot. He lifted the bottle again and she knew she had to do something. She couldn't stand by and let him drink anymore.

She couldn't stand to see him like this. This was her handiwork. No matter her intentions of protecting them both from heartache. She'd driven Tad to a bottle of Dewar's. The strong man whose only mistake was loving her. She crossed the room and tried to hug him but he shrugged her off.

"Tad, don't do this. I told you I only wanted an affair," she said. She'd known her track record. Understood herself better than Tad ever could. Her fears stemmed from a childhood spent moving from place to place following the trail of a man who didn't want to be found. Love and approval always seemed just out of her reach. She and Marnie had done their best for each other, but the sisters had known that nothing lasted forever and love was very fragile.

"I should have listened to you," he said with a mocking smile that cut her.

She needed to get out of here. Now. "Yes, you should have."

He threw back another shot.

"Drinking's not going to help."

"It might."

"Please, stop. I can't stand to see you this way."

He shrugged his massive shoulders. She knew he could take on many burdens but she'd never been willing to share hers. Even with this man.

"Apparently that's a common feeling for you," he said.

"It isn't." But there he was clearly not listening to her anymore.

"Perhaps, you should go," he said, walking to the dining area and blowing out the candles. He turned off the music with a discreet flick of his wrist.

"Yes, I should."

She had no idea how to make this right but knew staying with Tad wasn't the solution. There was too much in life that wasn't certain. Too many things she couldn't control and the only way she could protect them both was to stop this now.

She walked back across the room, and picked up her purse, which had fallen to the floor. She owed him something, some sort of explanation. "There's something broken inside me, Tad. It's been that way for a long time."

He looked at her with his wizard green eyes sober. "It's going to stay that way until you trust someone—until you trust me."

She wrapped her arms around her waist. Trying to keep it together until she could get back to her place. Until she reached her sanctuary so she could finally let go of all the hurt and dreams she'd secretly been building in her soul. "I don't know that I ever can."

"Because you've been disappointed before? Hell, we all have. Pierce's wife left him when he lost the use of his legs. Does that seem fair to you, CJ?"

"No, it doesn't. But you aren't Pierce and you aren't me. I've lived my life knowing I wasn't good enough for my father. Knowing that I wasn't woman enough to keep my fiancé. Knowing that sooner or later you'd ask me for something I couldn't give you. And I'm afraid I won't do it again."

"I can make you marry me," he said at last. They stood only a few inches apart but she'd put a rift bigger than Lake Michigan between them.

"How?" She had the feeling his words were motivated by ego and a thirst for revenge.

"I could talk to Butch and make marrying me a stipulation of your promotion," he said, a cruel sneer on his lips.

Her stomach knotted. She read the sincerity in him and knew that if he wanted to punish her for rejecting his proposal then he could do it. This wasn't her childhood friend who'd bandaged her scraped knee. This was the boy who'd cruelly told his popular friends that she'd paid him to talk to her. And this Tad was one she hardly knew.

"You wouldn't, would you?"

"That you even have to ask tells me everything I needed to know." He bent down to pull on his shoes and then stood and went to the coat closet. "I've dismissed the car for the evening. So I'll give you a ride home."

"I can take a cab."

"No you can't."

He took her coat and held it out to her. The bouquet of roses he'd sent in the car for her lay scattered on the floor. The Tiffany's box nestled in the middle of the petals. She felt like crying when she saw it. She shivered a little.

She crossed to him and slid her arms in her coat, but still she was chilled. She followed Tad out the door and down the hall. Each step she took was heavy and her heart beat slowly. He drove her to her condo and saw her to her door in a frosty silence that seemed too loud.

"This is it, then," he said. "I'm not coming back again."

"It doesn't have to be this way."

"How can it be, CJ?"

"We could still have an affair."

"No, we couldn't. I require trust from my lovers and you've proven the only person you trust is yourself. Enjoy your lonely life," he said and walked away. She watched until he disappeared around the corner and then sank to the floor and buried her head against her knees. She'd never felt more isolated from the world than she had at that moment.

Twelve

CJ woke Christmas morning feeling more alone than ever. She'd slept fitfully the previous night, plagued by dreams of Tad. Only the knowledge that Rae-Anne was coming over for brunch motivated her to get out of bed.

She entered her kitchen and made coffee first. Opening the refrigerator was a mistake. She'd purchased extra food anticipating the days that Tad would stay with her. For a minute she wanted to say the hell with her fears and go back to his place and beg him to forgive her. But she knew that she'd sabotage their relationship because in her heart she didn't believe it would last.

She didn't want to cook. Instead she climbed up on

the counter and pulled out that box of HoHos. There was only one cure for what ailed her. And that was the sugar-induced euphoria that chocolate cream-filled cakes could bring.

She took them to the living room and sat in front of her Christmas tree with the box. She opened the first cake and took a huge bite. But the cake didn't taste right in her mouth. She opened another package and tried that one. Again something wasn't right with the cake.

She threw the box on the coffee table disgusted with herself. Even her old comfort had been taken. She wanted to cry.

The doorbell rang. She was still in her pajamas. Her hair wasn't combed and she had coffee breath. Oh, God. Rae-Anne was here.

CJ had invited her secretary when she realized Rae-Anne had no family. As she had thought of her aging lonely secretary, CJ realized that could be the life she'd chosen for herself. Maybe she should get a cat.

"Just a minute," she called out.

She grabbed the HoHos and ran for the kitchen. She'd make omelettes or something. She grabbed a hair scrunchy from the basket in the kitchen and twisted her hair into a ponytail. Her flannel pjs weren't really company appropriate but she didn't want to leave Rae-Anne standing in the hall. She opened the door and tried to smile.

Rae-Anne took in her appearance. "What the hell happened to you?"

"Merry Christmas, to you too."

"*Buon Natale*. Is Tad here? Should I have stayed home?"

"No, come in. I'm all alone." The word echoed in her mind.

Rae-Anne placed a present on the hall table and CJ hung her coat up. "Let me run down the hall and change. Make yourself at home. There's coffee in the kitchen."

CJ hurriedly dressed in a pair of black leggings and a long black tunic sweater. She brushed out her hair and twisted it up in a knot. She put in her contacts and applied makeup and when she entered the living room and saw the tree she'd decorated with Tad, she paused for a moment, registering the pain deep inside of her and moved on.

Why couldn't Tad have been content with what they had?

Rae-Anne had made a breakfast of scones, clotted cream and fresh fruit. "Did you bring this food with you?"

"Uh...yeah. Where's Tad this morning?"

"At his home I imagine."

"You don't know?"

"Uh, things kind of didn't work out."

"What? Why not?"

"We just...I'm not...oh, hell. I don't want to talk about it."

"Did he treat you poorly?"

CJ was swamped with memories of how well Tad

had treated her. In bed he was her dream lover. Out of bed he was a surprising mix of macho determination and romantic notions. She'd never forget their dinner at Gejas or walking along State Street and looking at the Christmas windows.

But more than memories lingered. He'd made her feel special and accepted her for who she was. As if he didn't expect anymore or less from her than she was willing to give.

"No."

"Did you have a fight?"

"Yeah, a real doozy. Listen, it just wasn't meant to be. I learned that lesson a long time ago and there's nothing left to say on the matter."

"Why not?"

"I'm just not what Tad needs."

"He told you that?"

"No. He didn't have to. I don't want to talk about him anymore." It was hard enough dealing with all her doubts, fears and recriminations. She didn't want to discuss it with her secretary.

Rae-Anne took a sip of her coffee and then she stood up. "Will Tad take you back?"

"What? Are you listening to me, Rae-Anne? I'm not talking about this anymore."

"*Madon'*, that's what I was afraid of."

"Why do you care?"

Rae-Anne stood up and walked to stand in front of her. "I'm a matchmaker sent from Heaven."

"Give me a break."

"I'm trying to."

"I don't believe this. Have you been drinking?"

"No and neither have you," Rae-Anne said. She took CJ's hand, pulling her to her feet. "Come with me."

"Where are we going?"

"To your future." Rae-Anne snapped her fingers and the walls around them shifted. CJ knew she was having some kind of freaky nightmare as they flew through time.

"I think I'm freaking out," CJ said to herself. She closed her eyes tightly and muttered a prayer under her breath.

"Trust me, you're not."

"Where are we?"

"I don't know. This is the place you brought us to."

CJ pinched her thigh hard and gasped when the pain was real. This wasn't a dream. She stood in front of her childhood home in Auburndale. The yard had one of those tacky chain-link fences around it. The battered Buick Century she and Marnie had shared sat in the driveway. But Rae-Anne didn't lead her up the walk to her house.

"Why did you bring me here?" CJ asked. "I've spent my adult life never looking back at this time."

"Yet this is where your subconscious brought you. Why is that?"

CJ saw her teenaged self—wearing a pair of baggie

jeans and a long T-shirt. Rae-Anne took her hand and they followed that teenaged girl next door. And CJ stopped, refusing to take another step. She knew where they were and what day it was.

"Rae-Anne, let's leave now."

"Can't do it. What's going on here?"

Four days before prom and she'd been making her way over to Tad's place to ask him to go with her. Oh, God. This was her worst memory. No way had she chosen this place to come. No way.

"I don't think this is going to help unless your mission is to make me depressed."

Rae-Anne pulled CJ close in her arms and hugged her. "Of course it isn't. But you need to see this through adult eyes and not from a clouded teenage perspective."

They went around the back of the Randolphs' sprawling ranch house and CJ saw the pool and two boys who were drinking sodas at the table next to it. Tad was skinnier than she remembered him being. She didn't see her teenage self but knew that she'd been hiding behind the hedges out of sight of the boys and listening.

"I called last night and your mom said you were on a date. Did you get back with Patti?" asked Bart Johnson. He'd been the quarterback of their football team and had dated only cheerleaders.

"No. I was out with Cathy Jane Terrence."

CJ remembered that night. They'd gone to see the *Batman* movie and he'd teased her about being like

Michelle Pfeiffer—he'd called her Cat Girl. They'd had a lot of fun that night. She'd forgotten about her hair and weight. For once she'd felt like…a woman worthy of a man's attention.

"Who?" Bart asked. She wasn't surprised to realize he didn't even know her name.

"You know my neighbor." Tad gestured to her house with his Pepsi can.

"That fat girl? Why?"

"Why do you care?" Tad asked.

"I don't. It just makes no sense. You could go out with any girl at school."

"I don't want any girl," Tad said.

"Man, I don't get it."

Tad took a swallow of his drink then said, "She pays me to hang with her."

Bart started laughing and CJ saw her teenage self run by. Back to her house and the box of HoHos waiting there. This she remembered.

"Let's go. I didn't see anything that made a difference."

"We're not done yet," Rae-Anne said.

"How much is she paying you?" Bart asked.

"Man, she doesn't pay me. Did you hit your head on the diving board earlier?"

Bart shook his head and grabbed a handful of chips from the bowl on the table. He picked up his sunglasses and put them on. "I don't understand you. Why do you hang with her?"

Tad rubbed his stomach and glanced toward her

house. She couldn't see him clearly and wished she were closer to him. "She's sweet and I like her smile."

CJ's heart broke all over again. In all the time they'd been together he'd never mentioned this to her. Not that she'd have ever let him talk about it.

"You know what they say about fat girls?" Bart asked.

"What?"

"They're like mopeds—fun to ride until you're around your friends."

Tad punched Bart hard in the arm and Bart fell off balance into the pool. "Hey, man. What was that about?"

"Nothing you'd understand."

Rae-Anne gripped CJ's arm and snapped her fingers. CJ was sitting back at her kitchen table. The food was gone and her coffee cup was in front of her. Still warm. Rae-Anne was nowhere to be found and CJ wondered if she'd dreamed the entire episode.

She sat back in her chair. It didn't matter if it happened or not, she was coming to realize something. Fate was influenced by her perception of reality. She'd always thought she wasn't good enough for the men in her life. When all the time maybe she was projecting those feelings on them.

She stood up and paced her kitchen. She realized she had a choice to make—play it safe and live her life on the sidelines or take a leap. She closed her eyes and realized there really was only one choice.

But was it too late? Could she convince Tad that they could both find the happiness they deserved?

Tad's parents had been delayed in Florida because of bad weather and had decided to delay their visit until after the holidays. Originally, he'd planned to take them to CJ's for dinner. She'd promised to cook a meal he'd never forget. And he'd planned to make the holiday special for her. Well it looked like they both succeeded in making it unforgettable.

He'd spent most of last night in his weight room working out and wondering if he'd ever really understand women. He had a history of pursuing the ones who were most out of reach. And this time it had proved disastrous.

Traditionally, he and Pierce went for a run on Christmas morning. They'd started it the year Karen had divorced Pierce. Wracked with depression Pierce had almost overdosed on prescription medication on Christmas Eve that year. Pierce had dreaded facing the morning alone so Tad had suggested they meet early in the morning and exercise. That was more than eight years ago and they still continued the tradition.

It didn't matter if one or both of them were in relationships. If it was raining or snowing or twenty below—they still met. Some years they simply sat in a hotel lobby, drinking coffee. Other years they ran. Pierce was faster in his wheelchair than Tad, but that didn't matter.

This year, Tad knew he needed exercise. He needed

to run as far as he could until CJ was a distant memory and the pain of her rejection started to heal.

"Merry Christmas, buddy," Pierce said when he joined him in front of the Navy Pier. They started at the Pier and ran north.

"You too," Tad said.

"Tawny's picking me up in an hour. Want to call CJ and we can all go get brunch at the Hilton?"

"Uh, no."

"Why not?"

"CJ and I aren't together anymore. Let's go."

Pierce said nothing, letting Tad set the pace. His feet pounding on the pavement providing the rhythm of his thoughts, but the exercise wasn't helping. Nevertheless he kept going and finally they arrived back at the pier. Tawny was waiting out front with a couple of cups of hot tea. Tad slowed and then stopped.

He watched his friend pick up his woman and put her on his lap. Pierce bent close to Tawny and she laughed. And Tad felt a longing deep in his soul. He finally admitted to himself that he'd wanted marriage not because his mom and dad were getting older and wanted grandkids. He was getting older and needed the grounding that only a soul mate and a family could provide.

Tad also admitted that he hadn't really trusted CJ enough to let her all the way into his life. He'd been protecting part of himself from her. So that in case she left he'd still have a part that was untouched by her.

He waved goodbye to Pierce and Tawny and returned to his condo. He took the stairs instead of the elevator because he was too restless to wait for the lift. His mind was going fifty miles an hour and he wondered if he could convince CJ to start again.

He realized he'd pushed too hard and fast for something that neither of them were ready to admit they wanted.

He slowed his pace when he entered his floor. Someone was waiting on his doorstep. "CJ?"

"Can I talk to you?" She seemed hesitant and he didn't blame her. Her hair was twisted up and she had those damned blue contacts in again. He was disappointed deep inside.

He wished she'd give up the costumes and playacting and come to him as herself. He unlocked his door and stepped inside. The jewelry box still sat on the hall table. He glanced at her and saw that she was staring at it.

He tossed his keys on the table and went into the kitchen to put some coffee on. She followed him into the room. Even though he didn't face her, he knew exactly where she was.

"What do you want?"

"Um…I wanted to…" She walked over to him. He heard her footsteps on his ceramic tile floor. Her touch on his shoulder was light and tentative. He didn't turn. She took his shoulder and forced him to face her. He leaned back against the counter and crossed his arms over his chest. He hadn't expected his arms to feel empty when he saw her again. He hadn't expected the longing to hold her would be so strong. He hadn't expected her to brand his soul as thoroughly as she had.

"Please. This is hard enough for me."

"I haven't exactly had an easy time of it."

"I know. Listen I'm sorry about last night."

"You came over to apologize."

"Not exactly."

He arched one eyebrow at her and waited.

This was more difficult than she'd thought it would be and she realized that was because she was still afraid to really risk her heart. She took a deep breath.

"I want you, Tad."

"Not too badly."

"Why do you say that?"

"You're wearing your contacts, CJ."

"What?"

"You think I don't know that you use that upswept hairdo and those colored contacts to hide from the world. I showed you my soul. I bared myself to you last night—confessed things to you that I've never said to another person and still you're not willing to meet me as an equal."

"Is that what you think?" she asked.

He had nothing left to lose with her. "I know it."

"Fine," she said. Reaching up she pulled the pins from her hair and then took out her contacts. Then she surprised him by removing every stitch of her clothing.

"This is it, Tad. The real me standing before you without any shields, without any barriers."

He ached for her. "Why?"

"Because I'm not really living life and I can't stand the thought that I'll miss out on sharing my days with you."

"Why this sudden change of heart?"

She crossed her arms over her chest and he knew how vulnerable she must feel standing naked in front of him. He wanted to pull her into his arms and protect her but first he had to be sure she wanted him to protect her.

"I was running from my feelings and the uncertainty that comes with love. But not anymore. The only thing I fear is not ever waking up with you again."

He was humbled by her sincerity and the risk she took with her heart.

"Please say something."

"Come here," he said, opening his arms. She walked into them and he hugged her tight.

"I love you," she said, standing on tiptoe and whispering into his ear. "I want to spend the rest of my life with you."

Tad scooped her up in his arms and bent to kiss her. He walked down the hall to his bedroom. He placed her in the center of his bed. "Wait here."

He went back to the foyer and grabbed the engagement ring. He returned to find the woman he loved waiting for him. And realized deep in his soul that he'd found the kind of happiness he'd never really believed existed before this.

He felt like he'd been sucker punched by his emotions. "God, I love you, Cathy Jane."

"Come to bed and prove it," she said with a saucy grin.

"Not yet." He climbed onto the bed and sat next to her hips. He ran his hand down her body from neck to belly button and back again.

Her breathing grew heavier and her skin was flushed. He saw the signs of arousal on her breasts and bent to drop short kisses on each of her nipples.

"Ah, I need you," she said.

But he pulled back, he wanted her to be wearing his ring the next time he made her his. He pulled the ring from the box.

"Will you marry me?"

She smiled up at him, tears glistening in her eyes. "I will."

He put the ring on her finger and kissed her deeply. He made love to her with an intensity that left them both trembling. Afterwards tucked under the covers of his bed, he held her in his arms and they made plans for the future. And Tad knew that he'd found a treasure greater than gold in the woman in his arms.

Epilogue

──────

"Not bad, Mandetti," Didi said appearing beside me.

I was standing outside Tad's condo congratulating myself on getting another couple together. I'd had my doubts for a while that they would do it. But in the end a little angel magic had done the trick. "Hey, babe, what'd you expect from the King of Hearts."

The angel broad moved around to stand next to me. She wore another one of her ugly dresses but this one was in a yellow color that didn't look too bad. *Madon'* I must be getting soft.

"You're not a capo anymore, Pasquale."

I hated when she called me by my given name. "Maybe not like I used to be."

"You like matchmaking," she said.

"It beats the alternative." Which was me going to hell. God knows I'd have deserved it if they'd sent me there.

She smiled at me. What was she up to? "Yes, it does."

"This time wasn't too bad except for you making me a dame. I ain't doing that again."

"Who says you get a choice?" Didi asked.

"Babe, you are some piece of work."

She laughed. "Mandetti, what have I told you about calling me babe?"

"If I stop can I be a guy next time?"

"Maybe," she said and disappeared.

That one was always trying to drive me crazy. I'd never tell her but I liked doing good deeds. CJ had needed me as a friend and I'd never really been there for anyone before. I wished I'd done it for Tess when she'd been in my life. I was sounding like a *babbeo*.

But then there was something crazy about this love business. And though I'd never admit it to Didi I liked my new gig.

* * * * *

Look out for the next title in Katherine Garbera's
KING OF HEARTS mini-series:
Let It Ride *in February 2005.*

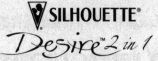

SILHOUETTE®

Desire 2 in 1

AVAILABLE FROM 17TH DECEMBER 2004

THE CINDERELLA SCANDAL Barbara McCauley

Dynasties: The Danforths

Tina Alexander kept being distracted by her wealthy, playboy neighbour Reid Danforth, who was enjoying showing Tina all the ways a man could please a woman, but if their families found out, there would be hell to pay...

MAN BENEATH THE UNIFORM Maureen Child

Dynasties: The Danforths

Zack Sheridan was a seasoned warrior and spending thirty days and thirty nights baby-sitting a sharp-tongued, wealthy young woman like Kimberly Danforth wasn't the piece of cake it should have been. Duty fought desire and desire was winning!

DRIVEN TO DISTRACTION Dixie Browning

Small town journalist Maggie Riley went on a trip to expose the man who'd swindled a friend of hers, but at every turn she found herself under the watchful, sultry gaze of lawman Ben Hunter. *He* wasn't the man she'd gone after, but *he was* the man she wanted to take home!

CHEROKEE STRANGER Sheri WhiteFeather

They were strangers in a bar, seduced by the music, their emotions and a truly physical and powerful attraction. In the morning they would part, unless this chance encounter could be turned into a future worth fighting for...

A TEMPTING ENGAGEMENT Bronwyn Jameson

The last time he'd seen Emily Warner, she was crawling out of his bed and out of his life. Now, six months later, Mitch Goodwin was determined to find out what had happened that night; why she had left him and his little boy?

REDWOLF'S WOMAN Laura Wright

Jared Redwolf was not a man to forgive and forget. And Ava Thompson had had his little girl and kept her a secret from him for nearly four years. Well, the secret was out now and Jared was determined that Ava stay and recognise that she was meant to be Redwolf's Woman!

AVAILABLE FROM 17TH DECEMBER 2004

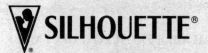

Sensation™

Passionate and thrilling romantic adventures

SURE BET Maggie Price
CROSSFIRE Jenna Mills
SHADOWS OF THE PAST Frances Housden
SWEET SUSPICION Nina Bruhns
DARKNESS CALLS Caridad Pineiro
IN THE ARMS OF A STRANGER Kristen Robinette

Special Edition™

Life, love and family

EXPECTING! Susan Mallery
ISN'T IT RICH? Sherryl Woods
THEIR BABY BOND Karen Rose Smith
PRINCE OF THE CITY Nikki Benjamin
HIS PRETEND WIFE Lisette Belisle
THE BEST OF BOTH WORLDS Elissa Ambrose

Superromance™

*Enjoy the drama, explore the emotions,
experience the relationship*

A FAMILY OF HER OWN Brenda Novak
THE SECRET FATHER Anna Adams
THE UNKNOWN TWIN Katherine Shay
THE HUSBAND SHE NEVER KNEW Cynthia Thomason

Intrigue™

Breathtaking romantic suspense

DAY OF RECKONING BJ Daniels
OUT OF NOWHERE Rebecca York
CONCEALED WEAPON Susan Peterson
UNSANCTIONED MEMORIES Julie Miller

1204/51b

0205/55/SH91

▼ SILHOUETTE®

Love Is
In The Air...

Stuck
On You

Cait London
Carolyn Zane
Wendy Rosnau

Available from 21st January 2005

Available at most branches of WHSmith, Tesco, ASDA, Martins, Borders, Eason, Sainsbury's and most good paperback bookshops.

New York Times *bestselling author*

DIANA PALMER

After Midnight

"No one beats this author for sensual anticipation."
– *Rave Reviews*

Published 21st January 2005